D0951532

**St. Martin's Paperbacks Titles
by Alexandra Hawkins**

All Night with a Rogue

Till Dawn with the Devil

TILL DAWN
WITH THE DEVIL

ALEXANDRA HAWKINS

St. Martin's Paperbacks

This is a work of fiction. All of the characters, organizations, and events portrayed in this novel are either products of the author's imagination or are used fictitiously.

TILL DAWN WITH THE DEVIL

Copyright © 2010 by Alexandra Hawkins.
Excerpt from *After Dark with a Scoundrel* copyright © 2010 by Alexandra Hawkins.

All rights reserved.

For information address St. Martin's Press, 175 Fifth Avenue, New York, NY 10010.

ISBN: 978-0-312-38125-7

Printed in the United States of America

St. Martin's Paperbacks edition / August 2010

St. Martin's Paperbacks are published by St. Martin's Press, 175 Fifth Avenue, New York, NY 10010.

10 9 8 7 6 5 4 3

I dedicate this book to my extraordinary literary agent, Lynn Seligman. Your encouragement and friendship have meant the world to me.

Love looks not with the eyes, but with the mind;
And therefore is winged Cupid painted blind.

William Shakespeare, *A Midsummer Night's Dream*, Act 1, Sc. 1

TILL DAWN
WITH THE DEVIL

October 20, 1812

"I curse the day that I married you, Rainecourt!"

"Aye, for once, we are in agreement, my lady."

From the bottom of the grand staircase in the great hall, Gabriel Addison Housely, the fifth Earl of Rainecourt, who was simply known as Reign by the *ton*, watched dispassionately as his wife of six months hobbled up the stairs at a reckless pace, her belly already swollen with the son or daughter whom she would deliver in two months because he had suffered the misfortune of impregnating the lady during their first coupling.

He glared at the servants who had appeared in several doorways seconds after Beatrice had vented her displeasure by knocking over the eighteenth-century ormolu-mounted Chinese porcelain vase that once belonged to his grandmother. A maid was already on her knees gingerly plucking up the sharp pieces of gleaming dark blue porcelain.

Reign dismissed them from his mind and focused on the decanter of brandy his butler had placed on a silver tray along with two glasses.

"The glasses will be unnecessary, Winkler," Reign said, snatching the crystal decanter from the serving tray. "Lady Rainecourt has broken enough glassware this evening."

"Very good, milord." The butler stepped back, his expression carefully blank.

Winkler had been around when Reign's parents had been alive, and had witnessed the former Lord Rainecourt's rage and impatience with his countess.

Like father, like son.

Both had made disastrous choices when picking their brides.

For the nineteen-year-old Reign, marriage had seemed the next logical step, though he had not offered out of obligation. Truth be told, he had fallen in love with the beautiful Miss Roberts at their first meeting, and for a time he had believed Beatrice returned the sloppy sentiment.

To Reign's everlasting regret, Beatrice had consented to marry him.

It had taken less than a month for him to realize that their blessed union was an unmitigated disaster. He should have listened to his friends. They had tried to talk him out of marrying Beatrice, but he had ignored their warnings. He had also turned a blind eye to his family's dark, tragic history.

None of this would be happening if I'd kept my bloody hands off Beatrice.

With the neck of the crystal decanter clasped tightly in his hand, Reign pivoted on his heel as a door slammed overhead, signaling that his countess had made it to her bedchamber unscathed. Beatrice had likely lulled herself into believing the locked door would keep him from pursuing the argument that had started before the first course of their supper had been served.

His wife had underestimated his determination.

Reign had grown weary of her mercurial moods and tantrums.

Of her hate.

If not for the child within her womb, he would have taken up residence in London weeks after he had taken her as his bride.

How odd, Reign mused grimly as he pressed his fingers into his brow. He had spent his entire life believing that he and his father were opposites in temperament. This evening, he could not help commiserating with the ruthless bastard.

"Return to your quarters," Reign ordered the butler, taking his hand away from his face so he could glare at the uninvited spectators to the humiliating demise of his marriage. "There is nothing left to see."

Winkler cleared his throat. "Milord, if I may—"

Reign closed his eyes to shut out the sympathy he glimpsed in the older man's expression. "No, you may not. Just go."

Without a backward glance, he marched up the staircase to confront his wife. Out of respect for her delicate condition, he had refrained from upsetting Beatrice further by pressing her for the answers he craved. Whether it was the wine Reign had imbibed at supper or his countess's icy discourse during the meal, he no longer cared about Beatrice's nerves.

In fact, Reign was certain that when he was finished, his wife would need the brandy more than he did.

"Beatrice!" He pounded a fist on her door when he discovered that it was indeed locked. "We have not finished our little chat about your harsh treatment of the servants."

"Go away," she said frostily from the other side of the door. "You are too drunk to be reasonable."

Drunk or sober, Reign sensed his wife would never accept him or their marriage. He removed the glass stopper from the decanter and took a hearty swallow of brandy. The alcohol burned as it coursed down his throat. So did his heart.

He shoved the stopper back into place and placed the decanter on a narrow side table near his wife's door. Without hesitating he threw his shoulder against the painted six-paneled oak door. Reign clenched his teeth together as the impact jarred his body. *Damn, that bloody well hurt!* From the other side of the door, he heard Beatrice shriek in outrage.

Reign took three steps backward and threw his body against the door again, and again. On the fourth attempt he heard the wood crack, and the door opened. He stumbled into the bedchamber, his heated gaze immediately seeking his wife.

Beatrice was standing near the bed he had never shared with her, trembling with fury and defiance.

"Leave this room at once! You are not welcome here, Rainecourt."

Reign shut the door. "Nor have I ever been. I have grown tired waiting for an invitation."

Absently rubbing his bruised shoulder, Reign moved to the center of the bedchamber, his gaze drifting from the charming Chinese wallpaper that had been hung before his birth to the unruffled bedding and finally to the barren surface of Beatrice's dressing table. He would have been the first to admit that he knew next to nothing about his wife's private rituals, but something seemed odd about the room. It lacked the personal touches one would expect to see in a lady's chamber.

Unless . . .

Reign's dark blue eyes glittered dangerously as he turned toward Beatrice. "When did you have your belongings packed: before or after supper?"

Beatrice clasped the carved bedpost for support. "Rainecourt, please do not make this any more difficult than it has to be," she pleaded, sounding tired.

Furious to have his accusation confirmed, Reign strode up to his wife and seized her by the shoulders. "Difficult? My God, woman, your actions have given new meaning to the word since I placed my ring on your finger!"

Her eyes bright and eloquent in their resolve, Beatrice shook her head. "Can you not see? All of this is a mistake—"

It mattered little to Reign that he had come to a similar conclusion months ago. Unlike his adulterous father, he intended to honor his vows. His countess, however, had other plans, and the notion that she was leaving him set the seething cauldron of pain and brandy in his gut ablaze.

"What were you planning? To sneak out of the house while I slept?" He tugged her closer, no longer caring if his touch distressed her. "Need I remind you, Lady Rainecourt, that you carry *my* child in your womb? Possibly my heir."

Her mouth thinned as her eyes took on a mutinous cast. "I have rights."

Beatrice pushed on his arms until he released her. Reign cursed under his breath and whirled away from her. The urge to strike her was so pronounced, he had to put some distance between them. He had never struck a woman in his life, and he had no intention of beginning with his wife.

Reign scrubbed his face with his hand as he sought for sobriety and composure. "When you married me, you ceded all your rights to me. I am your lord and husband, and my dictates are law."

Beatrice's laughter filled the room. "You sound more like a drunken bully than the man I married. If I had recognized this regrettable flaw in your character sooner, I would have never consented to marry you."

She squeaked as Reign closed the distance between them and backed her up against the wall. "I wish I had glimpsed the shrew hidden behind that pretty face. If I had, dear wife, I never would have been tempted to lift your skirts and tie myself to you for all eternity."

"Rubbish!" Beatrice said, her audacity startling him so much that he released her. She slipped under his arm and walked to the window. "You will not be tied for me to all eternity, Rainecourt. I will see to it, even if you do not have the courage to do so."

No Rainecourt had ever sought a divorce. It simply was not done.

"Divorce? Truly?" Reign mocked. "My dear lady, you have no grounds to divorce me."

Beatrice bit her lower lip as she studied him through a veil of dark eyelashes. "Perhaps not." She gave him a sly glance. "However, you do."

There was something in her expression that caused the walls of the bedchamber to close in on him. Reign tugged on the knot of his cravat.

"What are you babbling about?"

"Though it pains me to tell you this, my lord"—for a brief instant there was genuine regret in Beatrice's gaze—"you leave me no choice. The child I carry is not yours."

Reign froze. He was certain she saw the disbelief on his stark expression before his protest formed in his throat. "Come now, wife, is that the best you can do? I was your first lover . . . your only lover."

His wife shook her head. Her eyes were bright with unshed tears. "This is the reason why you must let me go. I have wronged you, my lord. My mother and father knew I—"

Reign picked up the small side table and sent it flying into the rectangular mirror hanging on the wall. He pointed a finger at her. "Not another word. I do not believe you."

Beatrice had been untouched when he had bedded her. A man knew such things about his lover.

"I speak the truth, my lord. I never wanted to marry you. I only did it to please my family."

He raised his hand. The gesture was enough to silence her. Reign stabbed his finger in her direction. "You are not leaving this house. No arguments. No outlandish lies in a futile attempt to force my hand. You have made it clear that you cannot abide my presence, so I am willing to grant you your freedom once you have delivered my son. Afterward, you are free to return to the protection of your family."

He walked over to the door and gave the room a final derisive glance. "I hope you enjoy the beauty of this bedchamber. You will not be leaving it without an escort."

Beatrice's hands curled into impotent fists as she comprehended that her bedchamber was her prison. "Rainecourt, you arrogant bastard, you have no right—" she screeched at him.

"I have every right, madam," he roared back, "until my child has been born."

Reign scowled at the door. He belatedly realized he had broken the lock. "Let me be clear. If you attempt to leave this evening, I will not be accountable for my actions and you will suffer dearly for your defiance."

His high-handedness provoked Beatrice's temper. She plucked a Chinese figurine from its narrow mount and flung it at him. The figurine shattered against the wall.

"A pity. That figurine was one of my mother's favorites," Reign said casually as he brushed a shard of porcelain from his shoulder. "I am optimistic that your aim will improve in the upcoming months."

He closed the door.

"Rainecourt!" Beatrice screamed like a wild, wounded animal caught in a trap. "You devil! You can keep me prisoner, but I will never love you! Never. *He* is the only one I will ever love! Do you hear me?"

Reign picked up the decanter he had abandoned and headed for the stairs. He was confident that Beatrice was too frightened to defy him this evening. All he wanted to do was lock himself in his library and wash away his wife's ugly words.

It was going to take a sea of brandy, but he was up for the task.

* * *

The next morning, Reign awoke to find himself on the floor of his bedchamber. Winkler was crouched over him with a concerned expression on his lined face, while several other servants crowded in the doorway.

"What is it?" Reign rasped as he tried to sit up. He placed a hand to his head and groaned. The world tilted with each movement. He froze, praying he was not going to disgrace himself by losing his stomach in front of the servants.

"Milord, there has been an accident," the butler said gently.

Reign squinted at Winkler. "What the devil are you talking about? What accident?"

"Lady Rainecourt . . . Milord, your wife is dead."

CHAPTER ONE

Spring 1821, London

"I predict this evening will end in ruin."

Lady Frances Lloyd, or simply Fanny to her friends, stifled a giggle. "What an utterly outrageous thing to say," she murmured under her breath.

Perhaps she was being a trifle dramatic, Sophia privately reflected. However, during her brief stay in London, she had come to dread Town balls. And she absolutely loathed being announced. In that moment, there were too many gazes judging her choice of evening dress and watching every gesture. There were too many opportunities for her to humiliate herself.

"Chin up, my girl," Griffin said, patting her gloved hand that gripped his forearm. "We are almost through."

"I detest this," Sophia hissed softly.

"Hush." Fanny held on to Sophia's right arm as if she expected her friend to flee. "It is time."

"Presenting the Lady Sophia Northam . . . the Lady Frances Lloyd . . . Mr. Derrick Griffin."

Head held high, Sophia stared at the confusing landscape of shadow and color that usually made little sense to her brain. Had the din in the ballroom diminished as they were announced? Were people staring? The unspoken questions only heightened her apprehension.

"Stairs," Fanny murmured, reminding Sophia to pay attention. "Six steps."

Earlier, Fanny and Griffin had described the layout of the ballroom in detail. With her friends' assistance and the stylish white-and-gold walking stick that matched her dress to steady her, Sophia prayed she would not disgrace herself by tripping down the remaining three steps.

"Smile, Lady Sophia," Griffin coaxed; his warm, steady arm was a source of great comfort. "You are stiff enough to crack into pieces. Do not tell me that you are afraid to face the *ton*?"

Crowds frustrated her more than frightened her.

"I fear no one," Sophia said fiercely.

"An intelligent response," Griffin said, sounding amused. "What say you, Fanny?"

Her friend sighed. "Sophia, your brothers were boorish to abandon you on your first evening in Town. If they dare show their faces this evening, I intend to let them feel the sting of my displeasure."

Her connection to Fanny and Griffin could be traced back to childhood. Both families had been close friends of the Northams, and they had remained steadfast even after her parents had died in what had appeared to be a tragic murder-suicide.

Sophia's smile was genuine as she cocked her head in Fanny's direction. Above the shadows and annoying mist of her faulty eyes, she glimpsed that her friend had pinned up her dark hair for the ball. Sophia peered closer. "Did you curl your hair?"

"Yes." Fanny heavily exhaled. "You will not dissuade me from speaking my mind to your wastrel brothers, Sophia. They would have happily left you to rot in the country again if they had not been persuaded by Griffin's parents and my own."

It was true. Her brothers, Stephan and Henry, had not been pleased that Sophia had joined them in London this season. She had overheard her brothers cursing Fanny's father and debating which one of them would be saddled with the burden of escorting her about Town. Henry, in particular, lamented the expense of a sister who would never attract a husband. As far as her brother was concerned, Sophia was doomed to spend the rest of her days as a spinster.

"Most brothers look upon their younger sisters as an inconvenience," Sophia said lightly. "Stephan was just annoyed that my presence would keep him out of the card rooms."

"Ravenshaw is an arse," Griffin muttered in her ear. "Henry, doubly so. If they do anything to upset you, let me know and I will beat them bloody on your behalf."

Sophia affectionately leaned into Griffin. "It is one of the many reasons why I adore you." She felt Griffin stiffen as she straightened. "Something amiss?"

"Miss Roberts has arrived with her parents," he said breathlessly.

Ah, yes, the mysterious Miss Roberts. The lady was Viscount Burrard's daughter. Griffin had been introduced to the eighteen-year-old young woman several days ago, and according to her friend he was smitten. At seven-and-twenty and the second son of a viscount, Griffin's family had high hopes that he would secure the affections of an heiress this season. Sophia did not know if Miss Roberts was an heiress, but she had certainly captivated Griffin's interest.

"You should go and pay your respects."

His hand tightened briefly over hers. "You do not mind?"

Sophia wrinkled her nose and waved away his concerns. "I do not expect you and Fanny to watch over me all evening. I am not a helpless child."

She focused on his face and gave him a reassuring smile.

"Very well." Griffin slipped from her grasp. He lifted her hand to his lips and kissed her delicately on the knuckles before moving on to Fanny. "Wish me luck, Fanny?"

Fanny snatched her hand out of his grasp. "With your roguish charm, I should be wishing Miss Roberts luck," she said wryly.

Griffin took several steps in Miss Roberts's direction before he stopped, pivoted, and returned. "Sophia, if Ravenshaw and Henry do not make an appearance—"

Sophia's face softened at his concern. "Fanny's parents should arrive later this evening. They will see to it that I have a way home."

"Ladies."

With an abrupt bow, Griffin disappeared into the crowd.

Fanny was quiet for several minutes, making Sophia wonder if her friend was watching Griffin's exchange with Miss Roberts. "Does he know?"

"I beg your pardon?" Fanny absently replied.

"Is Griffin aware that you have feelings for him?" Sophia clarified.

Her friend laughed. "I doubt it. Most gentlemen are blind when it comes to love." Fanny sounded resigned and a little sad.

"If you would prefer, we could find a quiet room—"

"Oh, no," Fanny said, cutting Sophia off in midsentence. "You are not going to hide away the entire evening. You are going to meet people, and perhaps even dance."

"Dance? Here?" Sophia said, trying to hide her anxiety at the notion of dancing in front of strangers. She and Fanny had taken dance lessons together, but she had only practiced with their instructor and once with Griffin. "If I humiliated myself by falling, I would never hear the end of it from Stephan and Henry."

"I do not give a farthing about your brothers' feelings. Like most gentlemen, they both can be insensitive twits!" Fanny said heatedly; she was always ready to battle Stephan and Henry on Sophia's behalf.

"You are a good friend, Fanny."

The compliment seemed to drain her friend's anger. "I love you, too." Fanny sighed. "Oh, come along. I see Lord and Lady Howland up ahead. We should go pay our respects. It will not be as amusing as yelling at your brothers, but it will have to do."

With a discerning eye, Reign surveyed the crowded ballroom and found it lacking. "Tell me, my friend, why are we not at Nox? At the club, we have the opportunity of increasing the weight of our purses, imbibing decent brandy, and—"

"Flirting with immodest wenches," Vane added, his blue-green eyes twinkling with humor.

Reign could always count on the Earl of Vanewright to focus on the essential needs of the merry group the *ton* had dubbed the Lords of Vice. "Precisely! Instead we have agreed to join Sin and his marchioness at Lord and Lady Harper's rather staid gathering this evening."

Nicolas Towers, Duke of Huntsley, or Hunter as he was called, overheard Reign's remark as he joined the two gentlemen. Side by side, Hunter and Vane could have passed for cousins. Similar in height and build, they both had straight, dark hair, though Vane preferred to wear his short, while Hunter wore his long enough to cover the nape of his neck. There was enough resemblance between the two men that Reign would not have been surprised if his friends shared a distant ancestor.

Hunter grinned at his friends. "Come now, gents, you both are made of sterner stuff. An evening of dance and conversation will not cause any permanent damage. Besides, Sin is merely indulging his marchioness. Lady Sinclair's mother, Lady Duncombe, is good friends with Lady Harper. It would be rude to slip out too early."

Vane's gaze warmed with sensual heat as a fetching blonde in green strolled by the trio. The lady glanced back at them, but her elderly companion swiftly urged her charge in the opposite direction. "I can stomach the insult."

"As can I. You are only amendable to this tedious evening, Hunter, because Sin bribed you with Lord Harper's fine brandy," Reign grumbled, annoyed that his friend had the audacity to flaunt his prize in front of them.

Smug bastard.

"True," Hunter said, smiling as he brought the

glass of brandy to his lips. "If you behave, perhaps Sin can persuade Harper into unlocking his cabinet for you as well."

"I doubt Harper's excellent stock is worth more than an hour," Reign said, feeling that he was being generous.

More than eight years had passed since his wife's tragic accident. Since that fateful morning when the servants had found Beatrice's cold, unresponsive body at the foot of her bed, Reign had been subjected to endless speculation about his part in his wife's demise. It mattered little to the *ton* that the magistrate had declared Beatrice's death an unfortunate accident. His selfish wife had apparently tripped and broken her neck when her head had struck one of the bedposts. Polite society, on the other hand, thrived on rumors and scandal, and his brief marriage to his countess had provided plenty of fodder. It was one of the reasons why he avoided such gatherings. After his disastrous marriage to Beatrice, he had no desire to seek out another bride.

"I concur," Vane said, clapping Reign on the shoulder. "If Sin had any sense, he should—" The earl paused as something or someone caught his attention. His fingers bit into Reign's shoulder as the man cursed.

"What is wrong with you?" Hunter asked, leaning back as he tried to guess the source of Vane's agitation. "Did one of your irate mistresses enter the room, or perhaps the lady's husband?"

"Burrard," Vane said tersely.

Reign flinched as he recognized the name. Viscount Burrard was Beatrice's father. He assumed Lady Burrard was attending the Harpers' ball as well. "This is another reason why I abhor these quaint gatherings. There is always the chance that I will encounter my former in-laws."

Hunter grimaced in sympathy. "It has been eight years, Reign. How long are you supposed to pay for what the magistrate deduced was an accident?"

Reign met Hunter's somber gaze. "The Burrards believe that I murdered their daughter. I highly doubt an eternity will satisfy them."

From across the room, Lord Burrard greeted a male companion. Together they disappeared through the open doorway that led into the card room. Reign had been so focused on the viscount's departure that he had not noticed Lady Burrard. She stood only twenty yards from Reign and his friends.

Out of respect for their loss, Reign had taken great care to avoid Beatrice's family. He had been aware of the Burrards' low opinion of him, and assumed the couple was the source of the speculation that whirled about him. However, any hope of slipping unnoticed from the Harpers' ballroom evaporated as Lady Burrard's horrified gaze remained on his face.

The viscountess shook her head as if she had glimpsed a terrifying apparition. Several ladies circled around her in a futile attempt to calm their distressed friend.

"Forget Harper's brandy," Vane said, nudging Reign toward the closest door. "Sin will understand."

"Perhaps. It depends on the mischief," said Alexius Braverton, Marquess of Sinclair, as he and his wife approached.

CHAPTER TWO

"Good evening, gentlemen," Juliana Braverton, Marchioness of Sinclair, warmly greeted each man in turn. Reign was the last to receive her extended hand. "Reign, this is an unexpected surprise." She sent her husband a puzzled glance. "I was told that you were unable to attend."

Reign bowed, and nodded to Sin. "I am merely delaying my plans for the evening. After all, how could I ignore such a pleasant affair when I was told that Lady Harper is one of your mother's dearest friends?"

Lady Sinclair's green eyes gleamed with undisguised appreciation. "It was incredibly sweet of you to sacrifice your evening, Reign."

"Think nothing of it," Reign said, following Lady Burrard's movements from the corner of his eye. The lady had not dashed off to warn her husband of Reign's presence. Perhaps there was a measure of hope that his evening would not end with a challenge. Burrard could be rather protective when it came to his viscountess and daughter.

From a distance, a cheerful light blue bow caught Reign's attention as the shifting crowd parted momentarily, giving him a teasing glimpse of the graceful curve of the owner's neck and shoulder. Every muscle in his body tensed as his view was blocked by several guests.

Without thought, Reign took a step toward the mysterious lady only to realize that Lady Sinclair was observing him too closely and knew exactly what he had been about to do.

Annoyed by his wife's interest in Reign, Sin cleared his throat. Sin took his wife's hand and tugged her gently away from Reign. "Earlier, you called me sweet." He playfully flicked the diamond-and-emerald earring dangling from her ear with his finger.

"Did I?" The marchioness tapped the folds of Sin's cravat with her finger.

Sin grinned down at his wife, his expression a potent mix of playful outrage and lust. "Yes," he said gruffly.

Reign silently enjoyed the couple's teasing discourse.

Lady Sinclair was truly a diamond of the first water. Reign could understand why his friend had lost his wits and married the charming green-eyed blonde. "You are so *sweet* when you are jealous, my dear husband," Sin's wife purred.

Almost a year ago, Sin had shocked his fellow Lords of Vice when he had taken Lady Juliana Northam as his bride. Reign had not been optimistic about Sin's happiness in his love match, but he had kept his opinion to himself. Their friend Frost had been less circumspect about Sin's keen interest in Lady Juliana, and their opposing opinions had for a time created a small rift in the two men's friendship. However, once the couple had married, Frost had learned to hold his tongue, which was rather smart of the earl since Sin would have ruthlessly severed the waggling flesh from Frost's big mouth if he had persisted.

Vane was growing impatient. "Yes, Reign is sweet . . . Sin is sweet. It's enough to make my teeth ache."

Sin's hazel eyes abruptly faded from indulgence to vague annoyance. "I can think of another way to make your teeth ache, and I can guarantee that I will enjoy it if you continue behaving like an arse."

Hunter, the selfish bastard, was still not sharing his brandy. Nevertheless, he was watching the crowded ballroom just in case Burrard returned. "Vane may not be the only gent you will be forced to punch if we do not get Reign out of here."

Sin's hazel eyes narrowed on Hunter. "Explain."

Hunter gave a respectful nod toward Lady Sinclair. "Perhaps your lady should check on her mother. Lady Duncombe slipped into the card room the moment you approached us."

"Good grief!" Juliana instinctively reached out to Sin for reassurance as she searched the ballroom for her mother. "Why did you not mention this sooner?"

Hunter shrugged and took a sip of his brandy.

The marchioness gave the gentlemen an exasperated look. She was aware that something was afoot and the Lords of Vice considered it private business. "Fortunately for you all, you have picked the one person that I cannot ignore." To Sin, she said, "I may need you. Do not stray too far, my love."

With a determined look in her green eyes, Juliana marched off to ruin her mother's evening.

Sin watched his wife's hasty departure for a few seconds. Once their conversation could not be overheard, the marquess squared his shoulders and asked Hunter, "Why does Reign have to leave?"

Before Hunter could explain about the Burrards, Reign gripped his friend's arm to silence him. "I am not going anywhere," he said as he once again caught sight of the lady who had adorned her shoulders with jaunty light blue bows.

"Devil . . ."

Sophia's eyes opened as the ominous word distracted her from her private thoughts. Weary from the countless introductions Fanny had made on her behalf, Sophia had pleaded a headache, which was not far from the truth. When a mutual friend of theirs, Mr. Tulloch, or Kit as he insisted on being called, had approached them to ask Fanny to dance, Sophia seized her chance to escape the curious scrutiny of Lady Harper's guests. Fanny and Kit had escorted her to a quiet alcove that had been created in one corner of the ballroom by huge potted plants filling in the space between the colonnades. Fanny promised to return to her shortly, but Sophia waved her away, telling her friend to enjoy Kit's harmless flirtations. The cream-colored sofa was comfortable, and the orchestra was pleasing to the ear. It had been a peaceful way to spend the evening until she realized someone was on the other side of the wall of greenery.

"He must have bullied his way in," one woman suggested, the slight rasp in her voice hinting that she was recovering from an illness. "Lady Harper has more sense than to invite a murderer into her house."

Sophia warily glanced about her as she silently agreed with the unknown woman's assessment of their hostess's intelligence. According to Frances and Griffin, the *ton* was filled with liars, adulterers, opportunists, bullies, and, yes, she conceded, murderers. Although her brothers were reluctant to speak of the ugliness in the world when she was in the room, she assumed that when two gentlemen dueled, a few of them actually intended to kill their foe.

"His title and wealth open doors," the woman who had called the mysterious man a "devil" explained. "I have heard that each year he secures a voucher to Almack's—"

"I do not believe it!"

"It's true!" her friend retorted. "Of course, he never attends. Lord Burrard would never stand for it. Nor would—"

Sophia scowled. The rest of the comment was muffled by the laughter of several guests as they strolled past the two unknown women. Who was this devilish murderer they were discussing?

Sophia worried her lip as she mulled over the question. Indeed, there was a gentleman who many claimed fit the women's description. And while she had never been introduced to him, his name was as familiar as her own. Gabriel Housely, Earl of Rainecourt. Was he truly here? If her brothers were to learn of her plans to seek out this unsavory gentleman, they would not hesitate to bundle her into the nearest stage-coach headed out of London.

Nor, for that matter, would Fanny and her family approve. Her parents, Lord and Lady Notley, had been the ones who convinced Stephan and Henry that it was time for Sophia to enjoy the delights of Town. The earl and countess would never forgive themselves if something happened to Sophia.

Especially if it involved a Rainecourt.

Suddenly a shadow dimmed her limited vision, causing her to gasp.

"Good eve—forgive me, I did not mean to startle you," the gentleman said, his voice laced with sincere regret.

"No, no . . . the fault is mine," Sophia said, hastily rising from the sofa. "I was woolgathering."

The two women on the other side of the wall of greenery were now silent. Perhaps they had walked away when they realized someone had overheard their conversation.

Sophia cocked her head to the right in an attempt to get a better impression of her visitor. He was older, more seasoned, and well dressed. If she were to guess, she would place the gentleman in his early thirties. His hair was dark and straight, but the cut was short and in fashion. The scent surrounding him was fresh, as if he had recently bathed, and reminiscent of orange and rosemary.

From where he stood, he could see the most of the ballroom. "I must concede Lady Harper's gathering is a trifle boring," he said dismissively.

"No, not at all," Sophia protested, leaning heavily on her walking stick because of her increasing anxiety. It would be bad form to declare to all and sundry that Lady Harper's lovely ball was dull. She had been introduced to Lord and Lady Harper when she, Fanny, and Griffin had entered the couple's front hall. "I am just not in a position to fully appreciate the ball as others might."

The gentleman cursed under his breath. "You are injured," he said bluntly. "And my unexpected arrival has forced you to stand. Pray forgive me, Miss—"

Sophia held out her hand. "Lady Sophia Northam. Perhaps you are acquainted with one of my brothers, Lord Ravenshaw or Henry?"

"Lady Sophia . . . a pleasure," the gentleman

said, bowing over her hand. "I have encountered your brothers a time or two, but I confess, I do not know them well. My name is Enright. Mr. Theodore Enright. I am a distant relation to Lady Shawe."

Sophia withdrew her hand. "It is an honor to meet you, Mr. Enright," she said, wishing the gentleman would step closer so she could study his face. She was unfamiliar with Lady Shawe, but assumed his relationship with her was his entrance into polite society.

"Now that we have been properly introduced, I must insist that we forgo propriety and sit as if we were old acquaintances." He gestured toward the sofa. "Think of your injured leg."

Sophia settled on one side of the sofa, giving her companion enough room to claim the other side of the cushion. "Oh, my leg is not injured, Mr. Enright. It is my eyes. I must confess that I have very poor vision."

"Perhaps a pair of spectacles would improve your outlook?" he teased, and she laughed softly at his play on words since it was expected. "Or is it vanity that keeps you blind?"

Sophia shook her head. "No, I would wear my spectacles proudly if it would solve my problem. Unfortunately, I lost a considerable portion of my eyesight in an accident."

"Forgive me. My question was incredibly rude."

"No apology is needed."

Sophia tried not to smile as Mr. Enright peered

into her eyes as if he could see the damage. Most people she encountered reacted in a similar fashion. It also gave her a chance to study him. It was a marvelous discovery to learn that his face matched the gentleman's voice. It was flawless, solid, and kind. As for his eyes, the color was either gray or a light blue.

"I was a small child when it happened," she said, unwilling to discuss the particulars with a complete stranger. "I have learned to compensate."

"That is why you use the walking stick," Mr. Enright said, sounding pleased with himself for solving some unspoken mystery. "I thought you might have injured your leg."

"Or that I was eccentric," Sophia added, fluttering her lashes. Mr. Enright laughed, and it was a heartwarming sound. "Now you know all of my secrets."

Naturally, she was lying.

Anyone familiar with the Ravenshaw family would know of the tragic tale of betrayal and murder.

"If I may be bold, I would like to sit and learn more about you, Lady Sophia."

Flattered by the gentleman's attention, Sophia lowered her gaze and nodded. "You may."

"I am not leaving," Reign said, his tone implacable.

If he told his friends that an unknown lady

and her pretty light blue bows were partially responsible for his change of heart, they would laugh until their sides ached. Reign did not quite understand it himself.

Sin turned to Vane for an explanation since he had decided that Reign was in no mood to be reasonable. "If there is trouble, I want to know about it."

Hunter drawled, "Well, we had the forethought to prevent Frost from showing up unannounced. Saint and Dare are distracting him until we can join them later at the club."

"However, no one bothered to warn Lady Harper against adding Lord and Lady Burrard to her guest list," Vane added.

Sin immediately comprehended the problem. "Bloody hell." The marquess's expression was apologetic when he stared at Reign. "It's an old scandal, Reign. I doubt Lady Harper was even aware of your unfortunate connection to the Burrards."

The muscle in Reign's jaw flexed under his skin as he ground his molars. "No one owes me an explanation or an apology, Sin. As you said, Beatrice's death is old news."

Reign noticed that Lady Burrard's circle of friends had increased, and several women could not resist glancing in their direction. The Lords of Vice had an innate talent for drawing attention and trouble. He suspected most of the trouble this evening was focused on him. It felt like a persistent itch under his skin that he was forbidden to scratch.

"You have nothing to prove by staying," Vane said.

"Actually, I do," Reign said, taking the glass of brandy from a startled Hunter and draining its contents. It burned as it warmed his stomach. He handed the empty glass back to his friend. "I have grown weary of tiptoeing around the Burrards. I married their lying bitch of a daughter—"

"Uh, Reign," Sin began.

Reign did not care if his voice carried all the way to France. "And I have suffered for my stupidity. It was not my fault Beatrice broke her foolish neck in her haste to leave me."

"I'll find the coach," Hunter said, his broad shoulders disappearing into the crowd.

Vane squeezed Reign's shoulder. "I will make certain Burrard remains in the card room."

Reign scowled at Vane's back. "There is no need—" His hands parted in surrender when his defiant gaze settled on Sin. "And what are you going to do? Toss Lady Burrard out the nearest window?"

The marquess chuckled. "If need be. Reign, this is an old wound. I understand—where are you going?" he demanded, sounding exasperated.

"Living up to my reputation," Reign said, over his shoulder. "There must be some young innocent who could use a thorough ravishing."

Reign stalked away from his friends, his steady gaze searching the crowded ballroom for another glimpse of the intriguing lady and her light blue bows.

CHAPTER THREE

Reign was only half serious about ravishing an innocent miss. Or the mysterious lady adorned in bows that begged to be untied. With his luck, the lady was happily married to a gent with no sense of humor when it came to other gentlemen lusting after his wife. No, a soiled dove suited his nasty mood. Mayhap one of Madame Venna's girls, or any of his former mistresses. He craved a lady greedy enough to grant his every wicked whim without question. Reign openly prowled the ballroom, searching for a familiar face or a new one that tempted him.

His expression must have hinted at his dangerous mood.

Gentlemen and ladies separated, giving him a clear path. Several mothers seized their daughters by the arms and dragged them away for fear his mere presence might tarnish the girls' reputations. Others shyly glanced away as he passed. Reign heard the gasps and whispers in his wake. Scandals never truly died. They were akin to dust on old floorboards that choked the air whenever anyone dared to tread over them.

And then he saw her.

Miss Light Blue Bows.

With Theodore Enright.

Well, well . . . this was most unexpected. Lady Harper's little ball was riddled with surprises.

Standing near a wall of potted plants, the blond-haired angel dressed in a charming white satin frock with light blue Claremont braces, and matching bows and ribbons at the bottom of her skirt, appeared to be hanging on every prosaic word Enright was uttering. Reign shook his head in disgust. Snatching the beautiful blonde away from the preening dilettante would be a pleasure. In truth, he was doing the chit a great favor, though he doubted she would thank him for it.

"Enright."

Reign watched with a bland interest as the gentleman turned a sickly pale green.

"Y-you!" he sputtered.

Concern furrowed the blonde's brow as she peered intently at her companion. "Mr. Enright, are you ill?"

Reign scowled at the woman. Her concern for the sniveling bastard irritated him. "There is nothing wrong with him that a little fresh air will not cure. Is that not correct, Enright?"

"Yes." Enright retrieved a handkerchief from the pocket of his waistcoat and wiped his forehead. "With your permission, Lady Sophia, I will escort you to your friends."

Reign's dark blue eyes narrowed on Enright's pinched face. "Do not trouble yourself. I have come to claim a dance from Lady Sophia." He extended a gloved hand, but the lady rudely ignored it.

"Dance?" The lady wrinkled her nose. "I must regretfully decline, my lord . . . ?"

"Reign," Reign politely supplied to the bewildered chit. "And I really must insist."

Lady Sophia squeaked as Reign shackled her wrist and pulled her into his arms. Not expecting his high-handed maneuver, the lady stumbled and her walking stick went skidding across the polished marble floor. Without the stick as support, she was forced to embrace him to keep from falling on her lovely backside.

The blonde straightened, but his iron grip on her wrist prevented her from stepping away. "Oh, I do beg your pardon, my lord."

"See here, Reign," Enright said, working toward righteous indignation. "Lady Sophia is *not*—"

"Your concern, Enright," Reign said, displaying plenty of sharp teeth. "Leave, at once, or I just may decide to spare Lady Sophia and play with you. The choice is yours."

"Mr. Enright?" Lady Sophia queried hesitantly.

"Forgive me, Lady Sophia," Enright said, backing away. As Reign had assumed, the coward was more than happy to leave the lady to meet her fate alone. "The devil take you, Rainecourt!"

"He already has, Enright," Reign drawled. "And he is looking forward to meeting you."

* * *

Rainecourt.

Sophia tugged, attempting to free herself from the earl's unyielding hold. The silky menace in the man's voice as he spoke to her companion was enough to convince Sophia that Rainecourt was intimately acquainted with the devil. And curse Mr. Enright for abandoning her.

This is the son.

For a long time, Sophia had forgotten that the Earl of Rainecourt had had a son. How old had Reign been when his father had cold-bloodedly murdered her parents and then taken his own life?

Reign started to drag her toward the other dancers. "I have promised you a dance."

"That is hardly necessary," Sophia protested, barely keeping up with him. This was not how she had imagined their first meeting. "If you could help me find my walking stick, I will leave you to pick a fight with someone else who has offended you."

Reign abruptly halted. He caught Sophia before she went sprawling forward onto the floor. "You are the clumsiest creature I have ever encountered."

Sophia gasped, appalled by his casually uttered insult. "My eyesight is ruined, you horrid man!" Sophia seethed, resisting the urge to hit him with her reticule. "You are walking too fast and everything is scrambled. I want my walking stick!"

Reign hesitated. Instead of apologizing as Sophia had expected, he waved his hand over her eyes.

Exasperated, she said, "I said, 'ruined,' not 'blind,' you twit!" Utterly provoked, Sophia slapped his arm with her reticule. Where was Fanny or Griffin? Why was the earl just staring at her? Good grief, had she just made a complete fool out of herself in front of Lady Harper's guests?

"Do not move," Reign ordered tersely.

Sophia dutifully stood there trembling and imagining the worst. Blinking furiously to battle the tears that threatened to add to her humiliation, she listened as Reign exchanged a few pleasantries with a helpful gentleman who had collected her walking stick from the floor.

Reign held up the white-and-gold stick. "I have it."

Not feeling gracious, Sophia snatched it from his hand. The smooth firmness of the painted wood clasped within her palm calmed her. It helped banish the vulnerability she was feeling, and gave her the strength to find her way back to her friends without the assistance of the Earl of Rainecourt.

"Good evening, Lord Rainecourt," Sophia said, grinding the tip of the walking stick into the floor as she stepped away from the infuriating gentleman.

The earl caught her elbow. "And what of our dance?"

Sophia was getting weary of wrestling Reign for her freedom. "I do not dance."

"Nonsense. Your vision is impaired, not your feet, Lady Sophia," Reign said, leading her away from the edge of the ballroom toward the other dancers.

A waltz was playing. The flashes of movement and color made her head spin. No, she could not do this. Not with so many people looking at her. Sophia locked her ankles together, refusing to move.

"No."

Reign did not seem to comprehend the meaning of the word. With a soft sigh of impatience, he captured both of her hands. He guided the hand holding the walking stick to his shoulder so her stick dangled down his back. To keep her from pulling out of his brazen embrace, he placed his free hand on her waist.

"What are you doing?"

"The waltz," he said, immune to her outrage. "This is not the time to fuss. People are watching us."

She ceased struggling at his announcement.

"How many?"

Reign grinned. "Enough. Everyone is curious. They will think I chased Enright off because I wanted to claim your first dance."

"That was not the reason why you ran Mr. Enright off."

As they stirred the air with their movements, Sophia noted that Reign's scent differed from

Mr. Enright's. It was heavier, a heady mix of musk, wood, and smoke. She tried not to inhale too deeply.

"No, I ran him off because I despise the sniveling bastard." They slowly circled about with the other couples. "Of course, only you and I know the truth."

"You honor me," Sophia said, her voice laced with sarcasm.

Reign tossed his head back and laughed. "More than you know, my lady. Lord and Lady Harper's guests are watching you with interest. Who is Lady Sophia, the mysterious lady who lured the Earl of Rainecourt out onto the ballroom floor to dance the waltz? I wager half the *ton* will be knocking on your door tomorrow afternoon."

Gracious, her brothers would be furious with her if the earl was correct. "I do not want to be mysterious or interesting, my lord!"

"Liar," the earl countered, his smile taking the sting out of the insult. "All ladies crave attention."

"Perhaps I am a different sort of lady, Lord Rainecourt," she said, mildly annoyed with the earl's opinion.

"Reign," he pleaded, infusing enough charm into the request that Sophia could not think of a reason to refuse him. "Mayhap you are correct, dear lady. After all, you have managed to do the impossible."

"Now you are teasing me."

"A little," he conceded. "However, I cannot

resist. Your cheeks turn a delightful pink hue and your blue-green eyes sparkle like a chest of priceless gems. It flatters a gent to think all that beauty shines for him alone."

Sophia glanced down and would have stumbled if Reign had not pulled her closer.

"Now you truly flatter me," Reign said, smoothly setting her apart without missing a single step. "The secret is to keep your gaze on my face. I am tolerably good-looking, would you not agree?"

Sophia bit back a smile. She did find him more than tolerable in looks. Not that she would dare admit it. "You want compliments? I thought you told me that it was only the ladies who craved attention?"

"Only a foolish man would not desire a beautiful lady's interest," he said lightly.

Was Reign actually flirting with her? The deadly intent that had driven the man to separate her from Mr. Enright had vanished, and now she was uncertain how to proceed. After all, once the earl learned of their connection, their friendly alliance would come to a sudden end.

"Ah, now you are frowning. What are you thinking about?"

Sophia gave Reign what she hoped was a scolding look. "It is rude of you to inquire."

The annoying shadows and blurring that obscured her vision ebbed and flowed as they circled the ballroom with the other dancing couples.

Focusing on Reign's face helped to quell her frustration. It was no hardship to study such masculine beauty. Dark brown hair that was as rich and thick as molasses. Strong cheekbones, a fine blade of a nose, but it was his eyes that drew her gaze, ensnared her. Framed by dark, thick brows and long lashes, his dark blue eyes were an unfathomable sea of restraint, confidence, and intelligence. During their brief encounter, Sophia had glimpsed in those beautiful eyes cold mute fury, calculation, humor, and—even though it rankled to silently admit it, since it had been directed at her—pity. What she now saw in his gaze wasn't pity. It was frank appreciation for the lady in his arms. Sophia's stomach fluttered like restless butterflies in a cage at the thought that Reign's interest was more than gallant flattery to bedazzle his dancing partner.

Reign ruined her speculative thoughts with his next words. "Squinting like that should give you a megrim."

Sophia's lips parted in surprise at his rude observation. Perhaps she had been wrong about the appreciation. "Forgive me. It is the reason why I never dance. My eyes . . ." She let her explanation trail off into silence.

His hand flexed and then tightened over hers. "So you were telling the truth. I thought you might have exaggerated your claims in an attempt to refuse my invitation."

Invitation? The man had literally dragged her

across the ballroom floor to join the other dancers. "Why would I decline such a polite invitation, Lord Rainecourt?" she asked a tad too sweetly.

The earl had the grace to wince. "If you wish to berate me for my boorish behavior, let us adjourn to a less public setting," he muttered, taking charge of the situation in his usual high-handed manner. He took Sophia by the elbow and escorted her away from the dancers.

"My lord—Reign, I cannot just leave the ballroom with you!" Sophia protested.

"No one will object, Lady Sophia," Reign said, guiding her toward the open doors that led to the terrace. "My reputation does provide certain benefits, and I am selfish enough to savor them."

CHAPTER FOUR

"And what of *my* reputation, Lord Rainecourt?" Lady Sophia demanded, punctuating her concern by driving the end of her elegant walking stick into paved stone that was laid out on lead.

Reign glanced out, noting that Lord and Lady Harper's sunken gardens had four tiers, each darker than the last. If he had been the total scoundrel Lady Sophia assumed he was, he would have dragged her down to the final tier where couples dallied with the forbidden.

"So tell me, my lady, why have we never met until this night?" Reign asked, curious about the lady he had practically abducted from the ballroom. "Do I know your family?"

"My family," Lady Sophia said, stumbling over the words. "My brothers—are protective. I usually do not join them when they come to Town."

"Because of your eyesight?"

"Not quite," Lady Sophia hedged, clearly reluctant to discuss her family or the reasons why she had been tucked away in the country.

The lady's brothers were almost certainly attempting to protect their beautiful sister from being ravished by lusty rakes like him and his friends.

"Perhaps we should return to the ballroom before we are missed?"

Instead, Reign gestured toward an empty stone bench that was positioned beneath a cozy arbor covered in a tangle of grapevines. When Lady Sophia did not move, he belatedly realized that the night probably hindered her limited vision.

He lightly placed his hand on the small of her back and nudged her toward the bench. "There is no sin in taking fresh air into your lungs. With the light of the ballroom in sight, you are quite safe from my baser instincts. Ravishing innocents is best done on the lower levels."

Lady Sophia gave him an odd glance as she sat down on the bench. Her walking stick was clutched firmly in her hand. Reign suspected she was capable of cracking his thick skull if he misbehaved.

"Is that how you usually spend your evenings . . . ravishing young innocents in the lower bowels of your host's gardens?"

"Only on Thursdays," Reign said in a matter-of-fact manner as he settled down next to her on the bench.

"How could you? Why Thurs—?"

Reign chuckled at her horrified expression. "I confess, though teasing you is a delightful amusement, I would not wish to blacken my character beyond what I deserve. In truth, I stay away from innocents and their enterprising mothers."

Lady Sophia stared off in the distance as she mulled over his confession. "But you are here with me," she said, turning her head and giving him a curious side glance.

"Should I worry about your mother?"

Lady Sophia hastily turned her face away. "No, my lord. You are quite safe. My mother died when I was a small girl."

The lady's dear mother in all probability had died in childbed. It was a common enough tale of female mortality. Still, it had left its mark on Lady Sophia.

"Forgive me . . . I am being rude."

Again.

Without looking at him, she raised her right hand to silence his apology and nodded.

She had not spoken a single chastising word, and yet Lady Sophia made him feel like a damn bounder.

"I understand your loss. I—my mother died when I was a boy," Reign said, wondering why he had mentioned his mother to a stranger, especially when she seemed unwilling to discuss her own family. Even under the best of circumstances, he never spoke of his mother.

Lady Sophia seemed equally startled. Reign's stomach clenched in response to the empathy he saw in her eyes.

"I am sorry for your loss, my lord."

Frost and Vane would have laughed if they

had been eavesdropping on his and Lady Sophia's conversation. Dead mothers hardly inspired passion in a young lady.

This evening had gone from mildly annoying to an utter farce.

If he had any sense, he should apologize to Lady Sophia for his abominable manners and leave.

And yet, he remained.

Reign did not want to dwell too much on his reasons for straying from his own rules. Lord and Lady Burrard's presence at the Harpers' ball might have spurred him on his wicked quest to scandalize the *ton,* and Enright had led him to Lady Sophia; nevertheless, he remained at the lady's side because he desired her company.

Lady Sophia was unlike his first wife or the conquests that came after her. At first glance, she seemed so delicate, though she had proven to have a streak of stubbornness bred into her spine. Her pale blond hair, refined slender bones, flawless skin, and large blue-green eyes gave her the appearance that she was touched by the fae as she tried to discern the world around her.

"What do you see?" Reign asked quietly, knowing that it was extremely rude of him to ask.

Lady Sophia did not seem offended by the question, which told him that it was a subject she had addressed often. She lightly bit her lower lip as she stared off into the distance at the light shimmering from the ballroom.

"Think of a bottle filled with oil, water, and

warm pitch that shifts and churns as I go about my day," she said, her eyelids narrowing as she concentrated on the light. "The pitch is black and impenetrable, the oil distorts and blurs, while the water is what anchors me and permits a certain amount of independence."

To Reign, it sounded like hell. His admiration for Lady Sophia increased as he thought about the chaos in the ballroom, and how she had dealt with his outrageous behavior when he pulled her into his arms and insisted that they dance the waltz. Had he described her as delicate? A weak-spirited creature would have fainted or screamed at his touch. Lady Sophia had the courage of Boudica. Or perhaps she was a poetic incarnation of Atë, the Greek goddess of infatuation and mad impulses. The comparison seemed apt. Lingering at Lady Sophia's side certainly bordered on recklessness since the longer he remained at the ball, the greater the risk of a confrontation with Burrard and his friends.

Instead of leaving, Reign asked, "Were you born with this affliction?"

Lady Sophia shook her head. "No. There was an incident when I was a child. I took a blow to the head that should have killed me."

"Christ! What man would strike a child?"

She gave a dainty shrug, seemingly unwilling to satisfy his curiosity. "I was incoherent and feverish for days. When I awoke, I found myself in a world of shadows."

An unexpected wave of protectiveness rose

within him. Where were Lady Sophia's family and friends? How could they abandon her for their own selfish pleasures and leave her at the mercy of strangers? "How do you bear it?" he asked, silently regretting the thoughtless question.

"How could I not?" Lady Sophia countered; her smile was friendly and guileless.

Reign felt the impact of it like a punch to his temple. Later, when he reflected upon the evening, he would decide that a type of madness had seeped into his brain. Born of instinct, he leaned forward and lightly kissed her. Lady Sophia stiffened as his lips brushed over hers. He swallowed her breathy surprise, and savored the tantalizing sweetness of her soft, yielding lips.

Her walking stick hit the paved stone with a clatter.

"So this is what innocence tastes like," Reign murmured against her lips, in undisguised wonderment.

"Get your bloody hands off my sister!"

Lady Sophia groaned, clearly recognizing the voice of the angry gentleman.

Reign nipped her lower lip in a playful farewell. "A pity, sweet Lady Sophia," he whispered into her ear. His fingers lightly caressed the light blue bows on her shoulders, the ones that had caught his eye from across the crowded ballroom. "Your mouth is a tempting treat, one I could have taken pleasure in for hours."

"Hours?" Lady Sophia soundlessly echoed.

Reign had known that someone was bound to

rescue the lady from the Devil of Rainecourt. Ever since he had taken Lady Sophia onto the terrace, he had expected one of his friends to charge through the open doorway and tear him away from the obvious madness that had struck him this evening.

Rough hands seized him by the upper arm and attempted to separate him from Lady Sophia. Reign was pulled to his feet, only because he allowed it. At six feet in height, he had a five-inch advantage over the lady's brother.

"Stephan . . . no!"

"Sophia, stay out of this," her brother snapped, barely sparing her a glance. "What are you doing outdoors without a chaperone and with *him*?"

Reign glared at Lady Sophia. Her guilty expression only fired his temper. He could not believe it. Stephan Northam, Earl of Ravenshaw, was her brother. "Lady Sophia . . . Northam. How wicked of you not to mention your family connections. For you see, I had forgotten the name of the little girl who had managed to survive my father's brutal attack when her parents had not."

Lady Sophia glanced warily at her brother before she faced Reign. "When I realized who you were, I did not know how to tell you."

"Once you realized who Rainecourt was, you should have sought out your friends," her brother shouted at her. "Have you taken leave of your senses? Why did you leave the ballroom?"

With a snarl curling his upper lip, Reign said, "Do you really want to hear Sophia's answer,

Stephan?" Reign was deliberately provoking the gentleman by using their given names.

Lady Sophia crouched down and retrieved her walking stick. She foolishly walked toward them, positioning herself between the two men who were staring at each other with mutual loathing.

"Leave him alone, Stephan. If you must blame someone, blame me. Lord Rainecourt was unaware of my connection to you or the Northam family. Besides, there is no sin in taking some fresh air after dancing," she said, restating his earlier words.

"Fresh air?" Ravenshaw sneered. "He was close enough to—"

"To do what exactly?" Lady Sophia glared at her brother and dared him to speak his accusation aloud. She waved a delicate handkerchief like a flag in front of Ravenshaw's face. "Lord Rainecourt was kind enough to remove an irritant from my eye."

Despite his annoyance, Reign could not help but admire the lady's inventiveness. She must have pulled the handkerchief from her reticule when she bent down to collect her walking stick.

Regrettably, Ravenshaw remained unconvinced. "Rainecourt? A gentleman? Not bloody like—"

Lady Sophia was no longer listening. She was distracted by the appearance of another gentleman. "Henry, is that you? Thank goodness! Pray talk some sense into Stephan before he does something foolish."

Reign raised his brows in a mocking fashion. "It would not be the first time, eh, Stephan?"

The earl's mouth flattened. "That is Lord Ravenshaw to you, sir!"

He and Lord Ravenshaw had clashed several times over the years. Their most recent encounter occurred when the young earl had solicited membership to Nox. Reign had taken great pleasure in rejecting Ravenshaw's petition.

His only mistake was that he had forgotten about the younger sister.

"There was an incident when I was a child. I took a blow to the head that should have killed me."

Reign shut his eyes against the painful realization that his father had struck down the six-year-old Lady Sophia after he had murdered her parents.

"Stephan, be reasonable," Lady Sophia begged, striving to soothe her brother's anger. "Nothing untoward has happened."

Ravenshaw grabbed his sister by the arm and shoved her at his younger brother. "I knew it was a mistake to bring you to London. Take Sophia home, Henry."

Unlike Ravenshaw, Henry Northam shared his sister's fair coloring. "Why do I have to be the one?" he whined, unhappy with his role as his sister's chaperone. "Let her friends return her home."

"Thank you so much," Lady Sophia said, shaking off her brother's hold. "I feel so wanted."

Reign shifted his stance, half tempted to tell the troublesome lady that if they had dallied longer over their kiss, he would have been able to give her proof that she was truly wanted. The disheartening fact that she was Ravenshaw's sister kept him silent.

"Do not argue with me," Ravenshaw said, his voice heavily laced with fury. "Leave us before someone sees you with *him.*"

"Reign," Lady Sophia said, struggling against her brother's hold. "Stephan seeks only to protect me. Please do not hurt him."

Ravenshaw was so aghast by his sister's plea that he dropped his guard and turned his back on Reign. It was the earl's first mistake. The second occurred when he uttered, "Silly chit, since when do I need your protection?" The earl dismissed her and pivoted toward the true source of his ire.

Reign was still angry at Lady Sophia for not revealing their unpleasant connection. Nevertheless, he liked Ravenshaw's vitriolic tone toward the lady even less.

"Which one bothers you more, Stephan: the notion that we are sharing the same air or the knowledge that Lady Sophia was handling me just fine without your interference?" Reign crossed his arms. "In fact, if you had tarried longer in the ballroom, I would have returned the favor."

Even someone as thickheaded as Stephan could not miss Reign's insinuation.

Ravenshaw's eyes flared before he slammed his fist into Reign's jaw. Lady Sophia cried out as Reign staggered back a step. He rubbed his injured jaw as he stared at the young earl. There was murderous intent in Ravenshaw's dark gaze. Earlier, Reign had been looking for an outlet for his frustration with the Burrards. Since Lady Sophia was beyond his reach, her irate brother would suffice.

"Get her out of here," Reign barked at Henry from over his shoulder. There had been bad blood between him and Ravenshaw since the tragic death of their parents. Reign was not squeamish about shedding a little of it.

"No!" Lady Sophia vigorously fought her brother. "Reign!"

It was a losing battle. The two men were beginning to draw Lord and Lady Harper's guests. No one seemed to notice her and Henry as the guests pushed by them and formed a small crowd on the terrace.

No one seemed to care who or what had started the argument.

The spectators just wanted to see blood spilled.

Sophia fought the hands that dragged her away from Reign and Stephan. Everyone was talking at once. The noise and pressing bodies were making her light-headed. She was scared for her brother. There was no doubt in her mind who would be the victor if the two men fought. Tears burned beneath her eyelids. This was all her fault. She should have had the courage to reveal her full name, and her notorious connection to his family.

"Sophia!"

Sophia felt Fanny's gloved fingers on her face. The familiar scent that her friend favored assailed her nose. The two women embraced. It was then that she sensed Griffin quietly standing off to the side.

"Forgive me, Sophia," Fanny said, drawing back so she could see for herself that her friend was unharmed. "I did not intend to leave you so long. When I finally returned to the alcove to tell you that your brothers had arrived, you were gone. I almost fainted when someone announced that Lord Rainecourt had carried you off into the gardens."

Sophia wiped the corner of her right eye with her finger. "A ridiculous exaggeration. We stepped out onto the terrace for some fresh air," she said, determined that no one would learn of the kiss Reign had stolen.

Not even Fanny.

"If Stephan gets trounced by Rainecourt, he's going to be in a devilish mood," Henry muttered under his breath. He had always been a little fearful of his older brother, and past beatings had forged his loyalty.

"Then perhaps he should not pick fights with opponents who can soundly trounce him!" she snapped.

Her brother did not know how to respond to

her angry retort. "Well, it is best if we get ourselves home."

Sophia held her chin up as she allowed Henry to escort her through the crowd that had gathered around the doorway and across the ballroom. Reign had been looking for trouble when he pulled her into his arms and danced the waltz. He had found it in spades. By breakfast, everyone would be eagerly chatting about the brawl between Rainecourt and Ravenshaw. It was as if a twisted version of the past was being played out, and there was nothing that Sophia could do to stop it.

CHAPTER FIVE

"You must have been distracted for someone like Ravenshaw to have planted a good one," Simon Wyndham Jefferes, Marquess of Sainthill, observed from the threshold of one of Nox's private rooms.

"Your excuse sounds better than mine, Saint." Reign accepted the damp cloth Nox's steward, Berus, had prepared the poultice to help bring down the swelling on his left cheek. Suspicious, he sniffed the cloth. "It stinks of oil of elder and beeswax."

"Among other things," Berus said, unruffled by the complaint. His lofty position as the Lords of Vice's steward had afforded him many privileges and given him a unique perspective about his employers. These days, there was little that astounded the servant. "Since you have your friends to coddle you, I will return to my duties downstairs."

Reign winced as he pressed the cloth to his sore cheek. "Thank you, Berus. You are too good to us."

The steward sniffed. "Indeed, milord. Best you remember that fact when I demand higher wages." He shut the door, leaving the gentlemen to their evening.

"So what is your excuse, Reign?" Dare asked, looking up from his cards. He had been born Hugh Wells Mordare, the second son of the Duke of Rhode. Anyone foolish enough to call him "Lord Hugh" never repeated the mistake.

Reign glanced over his shoulder at Dare as he played cards with Frost. "Sentimentality?"

Saint and several others chuckled at the absurd notion.

"It doesn't wash," Vincent Bishop, Earl of Chillingsworth, or Frost as he was called, blurted out as he discarded a card. "In situations like this, a pretty wench is always involved."

Vane and Hunter snickered. A silent exchange passed between the two men as they raised their glasses of brandy and let the sides collide with a distinctive *clink*. Knowing the pair, they had probably placed a private wager on how swiftly Frost would deduce the details Reign had carefully omitted.

With the exception of Sin, who had promised to join them later after he had escorted his wife home from Lord and Lady Harper's ball, the Lords of Vice had all congregated at Nox. On the level below, their gambling hell thrived under Berus's watchful management. Fortunes were being won and lost at the turn of a card or the casual toss of the dice. Usually Reign and his friends were in the thick of it, but his mood had turned decidedly somber after his brief, violent brawl with Ravenshaw. The arrogant puppy never would have landed his lucky punch if some helpful arse hadn't hooked his arm around Reign's neck in a futile attempt to pull him away.

"So who is she?" Frost drawled.

Reign hesitated. Impulsive and always looking for a fight, Frost could not be trusted. His meddling in Sin's affairs when he was quietly courting Lady Juliana was proof enough. Nevertheless, by now half the *ton* knew about Reign's outrageous behavior with Lady Sophia and her brother. If he did not reveal the lady's name, Vane and Hunter were likely to surrender it.

"Lady Sophia Northam."

The cards slipped from Frost's fingers. "Northam? As in Ravenshaw's younger sister?"

"I had forgotten about the sister," Hunter said, his voice reflective as he privately contemplated the ramifications. "She must be of marriageable age by now. Is she pretty? I will wager her brothers are of the mindset of marrying her off this season."

"Yes. And if you wish to keep your teeth in your head, you will stay away from her," Reign said, inexplicably annoyed by Hunter's suggestion that Ravenshaw might have brought Lady Sophia to London in hopes of finding her a suitable husband. "As for her aspirations for marriage, the subject did not arise."

Frost was still recovering from Reign's revelation. "Are you mad?"

Reign could not blame his friend. No matter how tempting, Lady Sophia was forbidden territory. He would have never approached her if he had learned beforehand that she was related to Ravenshaw.

"The lady in question did not volunteer her full name," Reign said with a shrug.

Hunter placed his arm behind his head as he reclined on the sofa. "And why would she? After you threatened Enright and bullied the fair lady into dancing the waltz with you."

Frost ignored the part about Enright and concentrated on the part that shocked him the most. "You danced . . . with a woman?"

Now the gent was being simply nasty. "No, I danced with a baboon. Of course I danced with Lady Sophia. What did you expect? That I had asked that sniveling bastard Enright?"

"You never dance," Vane added helpfully.

Reign took his time adjusting the medicinal cloth Berus had provided. "It seemed like a good idea, though I might have reconsidered if I had known the lady was related to Ravenshaw."

"I do not recall dismissing you."

Defeated, Sophia pressed her forehead against the cool wood of the door. Since Stephan had entered their town house with a split swollen lower lip and several spectacular bruises around both eyes, he had been an absolute tyrant to her and Henry. She had wondered if Lord Rainecourt had also been terribly injured in the brawl with her

brother. However, she did not have the courage
to inquire after the gentleman's health since the
animosity between Stephan and the earl had been
palpable on the Harpers' terrace.

Stifling a sigh, Sophia whirled around and carefully crossed the library to join Stephan near the
fireplace. She could feel the weight of her brother's brooding stare, his beautiful blue-green eyes
so much like her own clouded with anger and disapproval.

"What do you want from me? I have apolo-
gized more than once for dancing the waltz with
our sworn enemy," she said, her voice laced with
exaggerated sarcasm.

Lord Rainecourt was not their enemy, even if
Stephan had decided to name the man a villain.
Like Sophia and her brothers, the earl had been
orphaned when his father had brutally murdered
Lord and Lady Ravenshaw before taking his own
life.

"You should not have attended the Harpers'
ball without me," her brother said mulishly.

"I would not have been alone if you had done
what you promised," Sophia said, refusing to
back down as Henry had. Her unhelpful brother
had abandoned her to her fate, and was currently nursing his wounds that Stephan's temper
had inflicted by raiding the larder.

"And what was that, dear sister?"

The ornate top of the walking stick cut into
Sophia's palm as she strived for patience. "You
promised to escort me to Lord and Lady Harper's

ball. Instead, you left me to rot in this house while you and Henry spent the evening drinking and gambling."

"You are becoming hysterical."

Sophia flipped the walking stick and slammed the end against the fireplace mantel to prevent Stephan from moving away from her. "And you are a rude, drunk, patronizing prig," she said, her slender body seething and vibrating with suppressed emotion. "If not for the generosity of Fanny and Griffin, I would have spent another evening alone in this house."

Stephan knocked her walking stick aside and sauntered to a side table where he had left his glass of port. "I told you that London would not suit you."

"London suits me fine," Sophia said stubbornly. "You and Henry are just worried that having poor, almost blind Sophia underfoot will ruin your grand plans of overindulgence."

Stephan finished his glass of port and poured another. "You place too much importance upon yourself, Sophia," he said, brushing by her as he sought out his favorite chair.

His careless cruelty stung. "On occasion, you can be cold, Stephan, but you are not heartless," Sophia said, following him. "Why did you agree that I could spend the season in London if your intention was to keep me locked up in this house? I might as well have remained in the country!"

"My point exactly!" her brother said, setting the delicate stem of his glass down on the small square table beside him with enough force to make Sophia wince. "I told you weeks ago that there was no justification for the additional expense of bringing you to London. The expense of your gowns and frills would beggar a lesser man."

Guilt burned like acid in Sophia's throat. Stephan had a real talent for making her feel shameful for the simple luxuries that he afforded her. "You and Henry do not fret about expenses when you desire a new coat or pair of boots."

Stephan pretended not to hear her. "And what do Henry and I get for our investment?" His hands came together to form a steeple as he stared at her. "I will concede that your looks are fair enough for most men to stomach."

Sophia bit the inside of her cheek to prevent herself from screaming at him. "You are too kind, brother."

Her brother gestured vaguely with his hand. She frowned, absently wondering why Stephan was not wearing the heavy gold signet ring that was passed down to each Ravenshaw heir.

"If I thought we could make a profitable arrangement with another family, I would have brought you to London years ago and married you off to the first gentleman who offered."

Stephan spoke as if she were akin to one of his horses or, worse, a bad investment that he could not dump on some unwary investor. "What prevented you from trying?" she asked, her temper increasing with each passing minute.

"It's those damnable eyes of yours," Stephan

said bluntly. "They're practically useless. No respectable man desires a flawed wife. How can you run a house and see to your husband's interests if you have to be led about like a child?"

"Your opinion is unjust." Sophia had heard enough about her flaws. "I am no man's burden," she said tightly, unable to quell her defensive tone. "With the assistance of Lucy and the rest of the staff, I have managed to keep the household at Northam Peak running without too much fuss. You would know this to be true if you visited more often."

Stephan sighed. He rose from the chair and placed his hands on her shoulders. "Oh, Sophia, I do not say these things to hurt you. Nevertheless, I speak of gentlemen's needs and your limitations. I blame myself for not schooling you properly; however, you have a forthright manner that is disconcerting to most men. Both Henry and I have resigned ourselves to the notion that you will live out your life under our protection."

She backed away, using the walking stick to steady her slow escape. "Do not mince words, brother. The term is *spinster*. In my humble opinion, it is not such a dire fate if it means that I will have one less gentleman in my life who takes pleasure in telling me that I am unworthy to be loved."

The catch in her voice was going to be her undoing. Sophia pivoted and headed for the door. She refused to cry in front of Stephan. It was unkind for her to think ill of her own flesh and blood, but she suspected he took perverse delight in hurting her.

"Sophia, come back here," Stephan cajoled, sounding exasperated and annoyed at her retreat.

"Forgive me, Stephan," Sophia said, reaching for the door latch. "I have grown too weary to continue this discussion. Blame it on my flawed disposition."

Stephan slapped his hand on the wood surface, preventing her from opening the door. "One more thing before you take your leave."

"You have said enough."

"Not in this," he said, his tone as unyielding as his stance. "Stay away from Rainecourt."

Sophia glanced at him in disbelief. "I doubt Lord Rainecourt will bother with me now that he knows I am connected to *you*."

Stephan appeared oblivious to her insult. "I am serious, Sophia. You cannot comprehend how dangerous this man is. If the rumors are true, he murdered his own wife and unborn child in a drunken tirade."

Sophia trembled as a chill wafted down her spine. She thought of Reign's strong hands that had held her while they had danced the waltz. His touch had been slightly rough and commanding. Were those same hands capable of murder? "You speak of rumors, brother. Lord Rainecourt was never accused of any crime."

"He carries the violence in his blood. His father drove his wife into taking her own life. Then he went on to claim the lives of our own parents before the madness burning in his brain forced him to turn a pistol on himself," Stephan said, his body vibrating with the old pain of what Reign's father had cost their family.

Sensitive to Stephan's distress, she instinctively reached out and caressed his cheek, even though she was still irked with him. "You worry too much. Rainecourt has as good a cause to avoid us as we do him."

It was hours later that Reign shed his clothes and crawled into the bed Berus had prepared for him. Bedchambers were available to all club members, but he rarely took advantage of the convenience, preferring to reside at his town house. This evening, however, he was too drunk and sore to bother. Thanks to Berus, Reign had everything he needed. If he had asked, the steward could have even procured a willing wench to warm his sheets. The tempting suggestion had been offered by Vane, but Reign had declined. His head was too full and his heart was empty.

He did not have the patience to handle a woman, even if it was for one night.

Ravenshaw.

His thoughts kept circling back to the earl. The hotheaded young nobleman was likely cursing Reign's name and vowing revenge. Reign had been too easy on Ravenshaw. His father had believed that fear and respect were entwined, and violence was the hammer that forged the two. It was a lesson his sire had repeatedly beaten into Reign as a child. If his father had not decided to shoot half his face off with a dueling pistol, Reign would have enjoyed returning the favor.

Like he should have done with Ravenshaw.

Christ, what a muddle!

Reign tugged the corner of the sheet and covered the lower half of his body. First, the Burrards, then Enright, and finally Ravenshaw. There was nothing more entertaining than a room filled with a man's enemies. He had not expected Enright to provoke a confrontation. The man was too cowardly, preferring to ambush his unsuspecting quarry. The Burrards were another matter entirely. The couple simply loathed him because Beatrice and their grandchild were dead. Even if he was not guilty of murder, Reign acknowledged that he had failed his wife and unborn child. He deserved their hatred. All the same, he was not going to linger in the shadows just because his visage offended the couple. He had lost that day, too, a fact the Burrards conveniently liked to forget.

As Reign absently scratched his abdomen, he willed himself to dwell on more pleasant thoughts. Lady Sophia's face flickered like smoke in his mind. He was not surprised. After all, the lady had an irrefutable connection to Ravenshaw. Thanks to his father, he, too, shared a regrettable and unflattering connection to the lady.

Not that Lady Sophia had seemed troubled by the Rainecourt name, Reign mused. Although she had not formally introduced herself, she had been more upset about dancing the waltz in front of Lord and Lady Harper's guests than the notion that she was in the Devil of Rainecourt's arms.

Reign's hand slid lower. He was half aroused, which was a minor revelation. Anyone branded with the Northam surname should have shriveled his flesh like bathing in a spring-fed lake. Lady Sophia seemed to be the exception. His turgid cock expanded beneath his fingers, the silken flesh smoothing and becoming rigid. The blunted length bobbed as lust took hold of Reign. Unashamed of his body's needs, he leisurely stroked himself and thought of Lady Sophia. If she viewed dancing as scandalous, the poor lady would likely have a fit of apoplexy if she learned that by proxy she was satisfying the needs of a Rainecourt. Her brothers—no, this was not the time to think of Ravenshaw and Henry.

Instead, Reign conjured an image of Lady Sophia's face, the feel of her in his arms. He had been too angry encountering Enright to fully appreciate the delicate bones beneath his grasp. Lady Sophia was taller than most of the ladies of the *ton*. Still, he towered over her by five inches. In hindsight, he decided that the lady had fit rather nicely. He had been too distracted arguing with her one minute and soothing her fears the next to savor the closeness of that sleek body.

He thought of those long, slender limbs wrapped around him.

Yes-s-s . . . , he thought, lifting his hips as his testicles were pulled tight. Using his other hand, he cupped the firm sack and massaged the ache. Pleasure spread like warm honey in his abdomen as electric tingles pulsed up and down the length of his cock.

Reign mentally stripped Lady Sophia of her clothes and imagined the opinionated lady astride his hips as he plunged into her welcoming sultry sheath. He pinched the tip of his cock to delay his ejaculation, unwilling to surrender to his passion to the Greek goddess Aphrodite, nor the mortal lady who had fired his lust.

His hips pumped into the air as Reign's hand frantically stroked the hot length of flesh in his hand. His other hand moved over the head of his cock, squeezing and coaxing the unspoken relief he craved to the point of madness.

Wetness seeped from the tip, signaling that he was close. Reign conjured in his mind the brief kiss that he and Lady Sophia had shared on the Harpers' terrace. Her lips had been soft and moist from her nervous habit of nipping her lower lip. He had longed to bite the soft swell of her lip, and taste the hidden sweetness of her tart mouth. Reign had sensed her initial surprise when he had actually kissed her, which had gradually eased into a wary curiosity. If he had not been interrupted, he might have deepened the kiss, using his tongue and teeth to ease her toward the slow slide into seduction.

Circle . . . stroke . . . squeeze . . .

If Lady Sophia had given him any encouragement, he would have carried her down the stairs to the farthest regions of the Harpers' sunken gardens. There, in the darkness, he would have tugged down her bodice and tasted her breasts. Small and firm, Reign could almost feel her hard nipples against his worshiping tongue. Some ladies had very sensitive breasts. He could imagine Lady Sophia as one such lady, twisting against him and moaning in delight as he pleasured her.

His mind clouded with lust and a kind of desperation, Reign could see himself unbuttoning the flap on his trousers, pushing up Lady Sophia's skirt and petticoat, and plunging his cock through the hidden slit in her drawers and into her tight core.

Christ!

Reign's hoarse exclamation was abruptly silenced as his lips peeled back into a grimace. His seed exploded from his cock, pumping onto his stomach in potent spurts. He curled his toes as his fingers stroked wave after wave of blinding pleasure.

His lust was sated.

Minutes later, Reign's vision cleared and his humor resurfaced as he wiped away his seed. If just thinking about Lady Sophia could engender such powerful response from his body, making love to the real lady was likely to kill him.

The fact that he was idly contemplating seducing Ravenshaw's sister sobered Reign. It took several hours before his body relaxed enough for sleep to claim him.

CHAPTER SIX

"You must tell me everything!" Fanny whispered as she and Sophia walked the length of her family's conservatory. Two days had passed since Lord and Lady Harper's ball, and her friend had been anxious to learn all about Sophia's encounter with Lord Rainecourt.

"Hush, your mother will hear," Sophia said, glancing back to catch a glimpse of the older woman seated in front of an easel before the shadows in Sophia's vision eclipsed the woman. Lady Notley had decided to include her daughter and Sophia in her latest watercolor painting of the conservatory, and Fanny's protests had fallen on deaf ears.

Sophia did not really mind. She enjoyed the scents of orange leaves, myrtle, camellias, and several varieties of pelargonium that mixed with herbs and fertile earth.

The slate roof and glazed glass walls were part of the old orangery, which had been constructed in 1724. Fanny's mother, the Countess of Notley, had been arguing with her husband for years that the old building needed to be torn down. She desired a lighter structure to take its place, one that allowed the sunlight to warm every inch of the interior. Lord Notley had refused. In an attempt to offer his lady a compromise, the earl had added to the older building, which was made up of wrought iron and glass. The countess was unhappy with the results, and the conservatory had become a ridiculous source of contention between husband and wife. The lady vowed to all who would listen to her grievances that someday she would have her glass house.

"Tarry at your task, my girls," Fanny's mother said, moving her easel to the left so it did not obscure her view of the two ladies. "Fanny, darling, could you give your skirt a good shake. The lines are all wrong."

"Yes, *Maman*," Fanny said, dutifully adjusting her skirt. She touched Sophia on the elbow and said, "So what did you and Lord Rainecourt discuss?"

Sophia frowned as she pondered the question. "Nothing inspiring to a lady's heart. He called me a clumsy creature."

"Oh, how dreadfully rude!" Fanny exclaimed, outraged on her friend's behalf.

Sophia knelt down and snapped off a sprig of blooming myrtle. She inhaled the pleasing fragrance that reminded her of camphor. "He did not like Mr. Enright very much. In fact, the earl did everything he could to frighten the gentleman."

"Perhaps Lord Rainecourt was jealous?"

"Ridiculous. I had nothing to do with Mr. Enright's and Lord Rainecourt's animosity. The air was literally charged with it. And before you weave romantic intentions into the earl's actions, let me clear up any misunderstanding. Lord Rainecourt's desire to dance with me was merely an excuse to deny Mr. Enright my company. Any interest in me was secondary."

"Are you certain?" Fanny said, sounding unconvinced. "Griffin thought differently."

"Since Griffin was not there, his opinion is irrelevant," Sophia said carelessly.

Still, if Griffin had heard rumors, then Lord Rainecourt had been correct when he had told her that their dance would be fodder for the inquisitive *ton*.

Lady Notley muttered something under her breath, drawing Sophia's and Fanny's attention. "No, this will not do at all!" the countess said, her gaze searching for the perfect setting. "Mayhap the fountain. Girls, if you please, go over there and position yourselves on either side."

The countess smiled as her reluctant models complied. "Yes, much better. The symmetry creates an unspoken harmony. Do you not agree, Sophia?"

Fanny grinned at Sophia, silently daring her friend to disagree.

"Yes, my lady," was her meek reply, but the countess's attention had already shifted back to the sketch in front of her.

Both women were familiar with Lady Notley's

artistic temperament. "Did you reveal your connection to Ravenshaw?"

Sophia laughed. "Are you mad? It seemed prudent to keep that knowledge to myself. The earl might have never learned my family name if Stephan had not stumbled upon us."

Fanny hesitated, almost reluctant to ask her next question. "What exactly did your brother stumble upon when he discovered you and Lord Rainecourt outdoors?"

A wistful smile tugged the corners of Sophia's mouth as she thought of the earl's kiss. No man had ever touched her in such a manner—both tender and demanding. "I was dizzy from the waltz. Lord Rainecourt thought the night air would help," Sophia lied to her dearest friend.

She did not know what prompted her to behave so dishonorably. Fanny would have kept Sophia's secret. Nevertheless, Sophia had been stunned by her brazen response to the earl's kiss, and she wanted more time to dwell on what had occurred between them before she confided to Fanny.

"Nothing more?"

Fanny was obviously very disappointed in the earl. She had expected more from one of the Lords of Vice. Sophia brought the spray of myrtle up to her nose to conceal her smile.

She slipped her other hand behind her back and crossed her fingers. "No, I am afraid not."

"Rumor has it that your appearance at the Harpers' ball upset Lord and Lady Burrard."

Reign had suspected there had been more to Dare and Frost's invitation to spar in one of Jackson's training rooms at No. 13 Bond Street, but he had agreed because the temptation to pummel Frost was irresistible.

However, Frost always proved to be a challenging opponent—strong, agile, and possessing skills that complemented Reign's. Their sparring matches were a test of endurance rather than brute strength. After the third contest, the muscles in Reign's arms were thrumming and his body was drenched in sweat. He bowed out of a fourth match and allowed one of the naive spectators to tangle with Frost.

Even winded, his friend could trounce any arrogant puppy.

Reign presented both wrists to the waiting attendant so the man could free his hands from the padded gloves. He shot his friend an exasperated look. "Nothing new there. My very existence upsets Burrard and his wife, Dare."

Impatient with the man's clumsy fumbling, Reign brought his right wrist to his mouth and used his teeth on the bindings. He spat out the leather thong. "Enright was there, too. Though personally, I did not care about upsetting the gent at all." He pulled off the remaining leather glove and handed it to the attendant.

"What was Enright lurking about for?" Dare's face darkened with anger. "I thought he was abroad."

Both Reign and Dare glanced over at Frost

when several shouts distracted them. Frost had landed two solid punches to the young nobleman's face, causing the man to stagger backward into the arms of two spectators.

Reign winced in sympathy.

"Apparently, Enright's circumstances have improved since I last saw him." Reign shrugged, not really concerned about Enright's return to England. He had lost interest in the man, and if Enright had a modicum of sense, he would not do anything to change Reign's mind.

Dare snorted. "You are being generous."

"Not exactly," Reign countered. "There is no challenge in thrashing a coward."

The apparent victor of the latest contest, Frost strutted toward his two friends, accepting congratulations and praise from the lingering spectators.

"Who is a coward?" Frost asked, tilting his face so the attendant could wipe the sweat from his brow and chin.

"Congratulations on your victory," Reign drawled as he nodded toward the viscount's dazed and slightly bloodied opponent. "You do know that's one of Howland's younger sons?"

The Marquess of Howland was rather prickly when it came to slights aimed at his family, both real and imagined. He had once threatened to shoot a man just for sneezing on him. Another tale claimed that he had ordered his wife's favorite spaniel to be hanged from the nearest tree for pissing on his boots. Rumor had it that the gentleman had been wearing them at the time.

Frost glanced back at the young nobleman and chuckled. "Howland prefers to level his challenges at weaker quarry, and I doubt I qualify," he said without a trace of arrogance. "Though if he can find his shriveled cods, he is welcome to try." Once his padded leather gloves had been removed, he took the towel from the attendant and scrubbed his face and chest. "So who is the coward not worthy of thrashing?"

Dare gave him a measured look. "Enright."

Frost discarded the towel and sneered. "Oh, I do not know, Reign, you might want to reconsider. Breaking the bastard's nose sounds appealing."

Reign picked up his shirt and pulled his head through the opening. "Later, perhaps. Besides, Enright is expecting me to do something about him. At the Harpers' ball, it was rather amusing to watch him twitch and stammer as he made his disgraceful escape from the ballroom. If I am lucky, he will trip and break his damn neck."

Frost arched a brow. "Need some help?"

Reign's dark blue eyes hardened. "Enright is mine. Leave him to me."

"And what about Ravenshaw, and his dull-witted sister?"

Frost meant well. Still, Reign had to fight back the sudden urge to punch his friend in the jaw for insulting Lady Sophia. He stepped forward until he was inches from Frost's face. "The lady is far from dull-witted, and neither she nor Ravenshaw is your concern."

Reign glanced down at Dare, who gave him a pitying glance. His defense of the lady he barely knew was more telling than if he had shouted his feelings aloud.

CHAPTER SEVEN

Sophia had assumed that Lord Rainecourt would avoid her after their unfortunate encounter at Lord and Lady Harper's ball. While Stephan's threats might have annoyed the earl, she suspected that their tangled family history would encourage the man to keep his distance. No one knew for certain who had fired the first shot that awful night she was struck down and her parents were slain, but she was compassionate enough to accept that while many people concluded it was Reign's father who had murdered her mother and father, he, too, had lost a parent.

So when he stepped in front of her at Lady Wold's fete, Sophia could merely gape at him. Fanny had been delayed by one of her cousins, but she expected her friend to return at any minute.

Remembering her manners, Sophia slid into a graceful curtsy. "Good afternoon, Lord Rainecourt."

He bowed. "Lady Sophia." Without permission,

he placed her hand on his bent arm. "I thought we were beyond formalities. Reign will do."

Sophia blushed as she lowered her gaze to her hand on his arm. Vitality and strength coursed through his veins like blood. "My friend should be joining me soon."

"Already trying to rid yourself of me, eh?"

After the violent clash with her brother, the earl's teasing only served to fluster her. "Not at all. I just did not expect to see you again after Stephan—" She inhaled sharply and mentally chastised herself for mentioning her brother. "Oh, never mind."

"Did your brother cajole you into confessing about our kiss?"

"What kiss?" she asked, feigning puzzlement.

Reign chuckled. "Ah, so that is the way of things."

The earl was laughing at her, but Sophia was in no mood to be teased. "Lord Rainecourt, you know better than most that my brother does not require a reason to despise you. The Rainecourt name will suffice."

He guided her away from the house toward the lawn, where targets had been set up for the archery contests that were planned. Sophia cast a longing glance at a table that displayed numerous bows and quivers stuffed with arrows. When she had been younger, she had once asked her brother Henry to teach her how to handle a bow. He had laughed at her request. Although he had not meant to be cruel, Henry saw the endeavor as a waste of his time.

"Do you like archery?"

Lord Rainecourt's question brought her up short. Sophia had not realized that her gaze had remained fixed on the table. "Does not everyone?"

Sophia saw a flash of white teeth before her companion pulled her toward the table. "Then let us put your skills to the test."

"Uh, no"—she was getting awfully tired of being dragged about by this gentleman—"my lord . . . Reign, I cannot."

The earl snorted. "Like you cannot dance the waltz? Something tells me that you can do anything when you have your heart set on it."

He turned to a servant. "Let me see that one," he said, pointing to one of the shorter bows laid out on the table. Reign extended the bow out in front of him and tested the weight. He frowned. "What about that one?"

"You cannot make me do this," she hissed. "Have you forgotten that my poor eyesight will render it impossible for me to concentrate on yonder target?"

Where is Fanny?

"Yes, this one will do," he said with satisfaction. "Here, my lady. Hold it thusly." Reign demonstrated what he expected of her.

The yew bow was almost as long as she. From nock to nock, the length was just under five feet.

Sophia gasped in amazement. "It is heavier than I thought." She shook her head. "No, I cannot do this," she said, attempting to push the longbow into the earl's hands. "If your purpose is to mock me, my lord, I will not—"

"Hush, Sophia."

She fell silent at his quiet command.

"Move the target closer. Thirty yards will suffice," he ordered the servant, who rushed to do the earl's bidding. He left her clutching the bow with both hands while he selected an arrow from a quiver.

"Oh, no, you expect me to use a genuine arrow?" she asked, backing away. "Could we not start with a dull stick or something less deadly like the leg bone of a turkey?"

She could sense that Reign was struggling not to laugh.

"Sophia, a dull stick or a leg bone is likely to injure you more than an arrow." He came up from behind, positioning himself indecently close to her. "You can trust me. I will not let anything happen to you."

As if she were a doll that he could touch and pose her at whim, Reign slid his hand down her left arm, encouraging her to raise the bow. "Now turn and present your left side to the target. That's a good girl!"

"I feel as if everyone is watching us."

"We are alone," he said soothingly into her ear. "No one will bother us. Let me help you."

Reign adjusted her grip on the handle several

times until he was satisfied, then tilted the bow diagonally. With practiced movements, he slipped the arrow under the string and over the bow, using his thumb over hers to hold the arrow in place while, with his right hand, he fixed the arrow on the string.

"Relax your muscles. Stiffness will hinder your aim. Everything from your footing to the position of your head should be commanding and yet graceful," he explained.

"At the Harpers' ball, you called me a clumsy creature."

Reign used his body to slightly alter her stance. "You found your balance quick enough," he said drily. "Now pay attention. We will do this together."

Without warning he pulled the string back until their right hands were level with her cheek. "Keep your left arm straight. Elbow turned out. String taut. Focus on the target, not the arrow in front of you if you want your aim to be true."

"It is harder than you think," she muttered under her breath as she concentrated on the target in the distance. The target was partially obscured by her unstable eyesight. She blinked and willed her vision to clear. "It is akin to aiming through tendrils of fog."

"Hmm . . . reminds me of several dawn appointments in which I have participated," he murmured against her right ear. "Aim . . . and release!"

At Reign's command, Sophia's fingers released the string and sent the arrow flying. She was keenly aware that the earl had not stepped away. Instead he boldly placed his hand on her right hip to hold her in place as his gaze followed the arrow.

"Did I hit the target?" Sophia resisted the urge to jump up and down. She turned into Reign and stared up at his face.

His face was expressionless as their gazes met. "A solid hit. I promise you that the dirt did not suffer any pain."

The dirt. Sophia groaned and let the end of the bow touch the ground. "A total disgrace!" she said, disgusted by her efforts.

Reign gave her hip a playful squeeze. "It is rare for anyone to hit the target on their first attempt." He returned to the table and grabbed another arrow. "Try again."

As he had before, the earl fitted his body against hers and guided her through each step. He praised her for her natural abilities when the second arrow sprang from the bow.

It arced and landed six inches from the target.

"Better." Reign reached for another arrow. "Again."

For a ruthless taskmaster, the earl was a benevolent one. The third arrow landed to the right of the target. The fourth overshot it. The fifth went wild and almost hit the servant in the leg.

Sophia was ready to give up. Her arms were weary from her efforts, and her head was beginning to ache from the concentration. Reign insisted that she make one more attempt.

The sixth arrow struck the bottom of the target with an extremely gratifying *thud*.

"I did it!" Sophia whirled about and impulsively embraced him. Horrified by her brazen behavior, she released Reign and took several steps backward. "Good heavens, I actually hit the target!"

"Do not sound so amazed," Reign said, his eyes glittering with something more than indulgence. "I told you that you could do anything if you wanted it badly."

"Sophia!"

Fanny rushed up to her friend. The two ladies embraced.

"Oh, Fanny, did you see?" Sophia gestured toward the target. "Reign—uh, Lord Rainecourt has been teaching me the finer points of archery."

Fanny gave Reign an assessing glance. "Has he, indeed?" Her face softened with undisguised affection when her gaze shifted to Sophia. "Well done, Sophia. Do not fret, dear friend, I have not come to spoil your fun. When you have finished your archery lesson, I pray you will join me and my cousin in the music room."

"I will," Sophia said hastily. She felt Reign's hand on the small of her back, and she found the gesture soothing.

If Fanny noticed the silent exchange between Sophia and Reign, she was too polite to call attention to it. "Until we meet again, Lord Rainecourt," Fanny said as she curtsied.

"I am looking forward to it, Lady Frances," murmured Reign.

Sophia frowned at her friend's departing figure, wondering if there was an underlying meaning to Fanny's final words.

Reign bided his time, knowing he and Lady Frances had unfinished business. Sin and his wife had arrived at Lady Wold's fete, and if they were astounded by his presence, neither one mentioned it. He and Sin discussed neglected club business while the marquess's wife, Juliana, was distracted by her mother's arrival. Thirty minutes later, he discreetly observed Lady Wold as she introduced Juliana to Sophia after he had politely whispered the suggestion to their hostess. Lady Wold had been too flustered by his proximity to refuse or question his request.

Both ladies were attired in white muslin dresses, though Juliana had draped over her shoulders a sky-blue scarf that matched her gloves and kid sandals while Sophia's dress had been trimmed in Pomona green satin just under her breasts and half sleeves with matching shoes. At first glance, one might have even mistaken the pair for cousins. However, a discerning eye would have noted that Juliana had green eyes and blond tresses with a golden cast whereas Sophia's eyes were blue with a hint of green. Her hair was flaxen rather than gold, but there was no doubt that together they were striking beauties. Whenever a bold gent wandered too close to the ladies, Sin had warned the scoundrel off with a hard look. Although he had no claim on Sophia, Reign could commiserate with his friend because he discovered, much to his astonishment, that his fingers itched to punch something every time the lady shyly smiled at a gentleman.

When Vane arrived with his matchmaking mother at his side, Reign and Sin parted ways. While Sin wandered off to greet their friend, Reign strolled in the opposite direction. Juliana and Sophia had joined Lady Wold and her small circle of friends. Lady Frances, on the other hand, had yet to rejoin her friend. Reign suspected that the lady would not be able to resist approaching him, now that he was alone.

Lady Frances did not disappoint him.

"Lord Rainecourt?"

Lady Frances was standing near one of the doors that led into the library. Her brown eyes betrayed her, revealing that his frightening reputation had preceded him. The lady was terrified, but she stood her ground.

His respect for Sophia's friend increased.

"I was hoping that we would have another chance to talk."

"I thought you might," Reign said easily as he approached her. "Fortunately, I always have time to visit with a beautiful lady."

The words were meant to flatter and put Lady Frances at ease. He rarely devoured a lady without first gaining her permission.

Lady Frances glanced down at the ribbons she

had been fingering at her waist. "I wish to speak to you about Sophia. However, you should be aware that she would not appreciate my interference."

In the past, it might have amused him to prolong the lady's discomfort, but Reign was aware that Lady Frances was concerned about her friend. "What do you wish to say to me, my lady?"

"Why are you interested in Sophia?" she asked, sending him a quick look to judge if she had offended him.

"I suspect half the *ton* is aflutter with speculation," Reign conceded. "You, however, are the only soul brave enough to ask."

"Because of the waltz."

"Is that what Lady Sophia told you?"

Lady Frances nodded. "Sophia admitted that your first meeting was entirely by accident. You did not know that she was a Northam."

How interesting. It was obvious that Lady Sophia had not told her dearest friend about the brief kiss she had shared with Reign on the terrace. Had Lady Sophia been appalled that she had been kissed by a Rainecourt—or was she trying to protect him?

Reign would have paid handsomely for the answer to his unspoken question. "True. It was only when Ravenshaw appeared and started bellowing threats that I learned Lady Sophia was his sister." Reign crossed his arms and considered the dark-haired woman in front of him. "Come now, Lady Frances, do not mince words with me. What troubles you?"

"I have heard rumors about you, and I am aware of the bad blood between you and Lord Ravenshaw."

And yet, Sophia had kept their kiss a secret from her dearest friend.

Intrigued, he said, "Pray continue."

"Whatever your differences with her brother, I beg you to leave Sophia out of it. She is not like her brothers. Sophia has lived a sheltered life at Northam Peak. Even knowing that you are the son of the man who murdered her parents, she harbors no ill will toward you. In fact, I would not be surprised if Sophia views you as a kindred spirit of sorts since you lost your father that night, too."

"Kindred spirit," Reign mused. "I have not viewed Lady Sophia in such a light."

Lady Frances's brown eyes narrowed. "You force me to be frank, Lord Rainecourt. I do not trust you any more than I trust Sophia's brothers. None of you cares who gets hurt while you play your games, and I will not have it!"

"What do you plan to do, Lady Frances?" he asked silkily.

"I just wanted you to know that Sophia is not without friends," she said stiffly. "Hurt her, and I will find a way to make you pay for it a thousandfold."

Reign raised his brows. He had never been

threatened by a lady in such a fashion. It was a novel experience. "Lady Frances, do you honestly believe that you can keep me from Lady Sophia's side?"

Lady Frances's lips trembled. "No. Sophia likes you. The patience and kindness that you displayed this afternoon on her behalf would be touching if I did not suspect that you had less-than-noble reasons to seek her company." She gestured helplessly. "She probably views you as some sort of angel—"

"And you and I both are aware that my lineage has more to do with the devil," he finished for her.

Lady Frances sighed. "I just hope you are worthy of her esteem." She curtsied and disappeared into the library.

Reign stirred, letting his arms drop to his sides. "An angel?" he scoffed, finding the description naive and oddly disarming.

Was that how Lady Sophia truly felt?

Lady Frances had been right to worry about his interest in her friend. Courting Lady Sophia would be just the thing to needle Ravenshaw, and provoke him into doing something reckless. If Reign was as calculating as most of the *ton* believed him to be, his next move would be to return to the lady's side and begin his seduction.

Nevertheless, that was not what he was going to do.

His plans for the lady were slightly more complicated, he decided, as he strolled toward his waiting friends.

Lady Sophia had no notion of the man he was. Her friend was right about that.

After their brief exchange, Reign feared Lady Frances would not be pleased once she deduced his true intentions toward Lady Sophia.

By then, it would be too late.

No, Lady Frances would not be pleased at all.

CHAPTER EIGHT

Sophia grinned as she brought the card to her nose, adjusting the proximity until her vision cleared. In a bold, almost savage handwriting, Reign had written on the back of his calling card.

"'A steadfast arm and aim, has won this gentleman's heart,'" she read aloud for the tenth time.

Along with the card, Reign had sent a small box. Inside was an oval cameo brooch mounted in silver. The blue jasper was sprigged with an image of a lady allowing a young Cupid to sit on her lap as he took aim at an unsuspecting gentleman. Sophia had laughed in delight when she saw it.

His archery lesson at Lady Wold's had become a private joke between them. Each time she encountered Reign, and there had been four occasions so far, he always asked if she had been practicing her aim. She, in turn, vowed that she had, and then began to regale the earl with outrageous tales of firing her arrows into horses, dogs, and hapless servants who wandered into her path.

The brooch was a thoughtful gift.

Sophia would treasure it always, and think of Reign if she had the courage to wear it. Stephan would never approve. If her brother learned of Reign's gift, he would toss the brooch into the hearth.

She started at the sound of masculine voices arguing in the front hall. Had her brothers returned? Sophia wondered as she tucked Reign's gift and card into her bodice. She opened the door to the drawing room and walked to the stairs. Below were three gentlemen unknown to her. One was arguing with their butler as the other two removed one of her grandmother's paintings from the wall.

"Gedding, who are these men?" she inquired, her voice icy and unwelcoming.

"My apologies, milady," the butler said, managing to bow and glare at their unexpected visitors at the same time. "These *gentlemen* claim that they have come for their property."

Sophia watched in outrage as one of the men walked out the front door with one of the paintings. "You there. Halt!" The man simply ignored her. She placed her hand on the banister and hurried down the stairs.

When she reached the bottom, she headed for Gedding and the gentleman who seemed to be in charge. She gasped as another man carried off an

Etruscan vase. "See here, you cannot just wander into our house and steal our property!"

The gentleman standing beside the butler lifted his hat from his head and bowed. "Forgive our intrusion, my lady. You must be Lady Sophia. Perhaps you do not recall, but we met several summers back when I visited your brother at Northam Peak."

Two more gentlemen exited the library. The sculpture they carried horizontally between them was so heavy that both men were panting and sweating from their efforts. "Did we? I confess, I do not recall our meeting," she said, distressed at how many family treasures had left the house.

"There is no cause for alarm, my lady," the gentleman said, his voice friendly and patient. "I am Pearse, and that fair-haired gentleman over there is my partner, Ram. The rest of our companions have been employed by us."

Sophia clutched Gedding's arm for support. "I do not know who you are, but if you do not return our property at once, I will send for a constable."

"Oh, dear, I think there has been a misunderstanding." Pearse glanced upstairs. "Is Ravenshaw at home? Or perhaps your other brother, Mr. Northam?"

Were her brothers responsible for this?

Fighting back tears, Sophia replied, "No. I believe you might find them at one of their clubs."

Pearse sighed in an exaggerated manner. "A

pity. Clearly you were not informed of our arrangement."

More treasures were casually hauled away. Sophia turned her back to the door, unable to watch. "What arrangement?"

"Lord Ravenshaw was regrettably short of funds last evening," the gentleman explained, his steady gaze noting her agitated state. "Would you care to be seated? Forgive me for saying so, but you do not look well."

"No, I am fine," Sophia lied.

With his voice heavy with regret, he continued, "This is not the first time I have covered your brother's losses. The debt is . . . considerable." Pearse unfolded the paper in his hand and held it out to her. "As you can see, I have a list of valuables that your brother offered in trade to compensate me for my troubles. His signature is at the bottom. I swear it is authentic."

Sophia dutifully stared at the paper, but the words turned into pools of black ink that dripped from the paper like blood.

Pearse brightened as he looked beyond her shoulder. "Excellent! Ravenshaw, your timely arrival will ease your sister's mind. I was just telling her about our arrangement."

Without looking at her, Stephan said, "Sophia, go upstairs."

"How could you?" she said, glaring at her brother. "How long have you been selling off—"

"I do not have to explain myself to anyone." Stephan nodded to the butler. "Gedding, be so kind as to escort my sister to her bedchamber while I conclude my business with Mr. Pearse."

Sophia's hands clenched impotently at her sides. "I will not forgive you for this!"

"I think I can bear the strain of your disapproval," Stephan said drily. "Now be a good girl and go upstairs."

Sophia's lips parted as she prepared a scathing retort. There was nothing she could do to stop her brother from selling their family's treasures one by one.

Or was there?

Without a word, Sophia pivoted and walked away.

A business meeting had brought Reign to Lincoln's Inn Fields. He had never expected to glimpse a tearful Sophia exit one of the offices and head for a waiting coach. He called out her name, but she did not seem to hear him.

What had lured Sophia to this part of town where she only had the protection of her coachman?

Forgetting about his own appointment, Reign hurried after the reckless lady and caught up to her before the weather-hardened sixty-year-old coachman could close the door.

"Lady Sophia!"

Sophia yelped and clapped a hand over her mouth, her blue-green eyes wide from the terrible fright he had given her. She collapsed against the leather seat, crushing the plume of white ostrich feathers attached to her bonnet. "Lord Rainecourt, good heavens, I thought you were a footpad!"

"You deserve to be frightened, you little fool! What if a footpad or some young ruffian had decided to relieve you of your reticule or virtue?" Reign shouted at her. He gripped the top portion of the door to keep from throttling her. "What are you doing here? You took a hell of a chance, traveling alone. Why did you not call upon Lady Frances or one of those gallants that tend to hover around you when my back is turned?"

Fresh tears filled Sophia's eyes, causing his heart to skip several beats. "I had to be certain."

Later, Reign might regret involving himself in Lady Sophia's troubles. His instincts told him that her brother was the source of her misery, and the lady silently weeping in front of him was no match for Ravenshaw. Without asking for her permission, Reign leaned into the compartment of the coach and took Sophia into his arms.

"W-what are you doing?"

"You need a keeper." Reign nodded curtly to the coachman. "I will see your lady home." With Lady Sophia cradled against his chest, he gave the coachman a level stare. "If Lord Ravenshaw should happen to inquire after his sister, for your lady's sake and your own, it might be for the best if you were vague on the details of your drive."

"Aye, sage advice is that, milord." The coachman tipped his hat to the couple.

"Oh, for heaven's sake, Lord Rainecourt, put

me down!" Lady Sophia exclaimed. "People are staring."

"It upsets you when people stare?" Reign asked, recalling the other occasions when she seemed distressed by the notion that she was being observed.

"Yes."

The bitterness he detected in that one word caused him to halt. Reign weighed Lady Sophia's discomfort over the risk that she might be angry enough to run from him. He slowly lowered her legs until her feet touched the ground.

"Come along, my lady. My coach is not far."

They did not speak again until Reign had settled Lady Sophia into his coach and given his own coachman orders to drive. She seemed to find her tongue once the small trapdoor was shut.

"Where are you taking me?"

Reign removed his hat and placed it on the empty seat bench beside him. "You are safe with me, Sophia. I merely ordered my coachman to drive us about town until you tell me why you are walking about Lincoln's Inn Fields without a companion?"

She clutched her reticule to her abdomen, and seemed bemused by his casual use of her given name.

Reign was not above pressing his advantage. "Earlier, you told me that you had to be certain. What did you mean by those words?"

Sophia stared blankly out the window at the passing buildings and pedestrians. Reign had gleaned from previous conversations that movement send her limited eyesight into a confusing mix of color and shadows. At such times, she was literally blind.

Reign closed his eyes and tried to bank the fury he was feeling on Sophia's behalf.

"I know it seemed rather reckless, but I had to see our solicitor, Mr. Fawson, this afternoon," Sophia said, tracing the edge of the small window with her finger. "After what Stephan did—"

"What did Ravenshaw do?"

Sophia wrinkled her nose, putting Reign's question aside for a moment. "I had to talk to Mr. Fawson. To see if there was some legal recourse to prevent my brother from . . ." Sophia shuddered, reluctant to confess her brother's most recent sins.

"Tell me." Reign leaned forward and captured Sophia's wrists. His gloved hands dwarfed her smaller ones as he cupped her hands into his. "Your brother's sins are his alone. There is no shame in telling me."

Sophia's silence was damning, but Reign persisted.

"You can trust me with your secrets. Tell me; I might be able to help."

Sophia's shoulders slumped with resignation and defeat. "There is nothing anyone can do. According to our solicitor, what Stephan is doing is perfectly legal and within his rights as Earl of Ravenshaw."

Reign stared at the top of her silly bonnet,

which was a confection of white ostrich feathers, Brandenburg silk, and lace, silently willing her to explain what Ravenshaw was doing so Reign could think of a painful way to discourage the bastard from hurting his sister.

After several minutes, she said, "Stephan has been turning to moneylenders for credit. I can only assume that this has been going on for several years. Yesterday several gentlemen entered our town house to claim valuable paintings, statuary, and other *objets d'art* that have been in our family for several generations. The one man, Pearse was his name, showed me a paper that had my brother's signature."

"Did you read it?"

Sophia shook her head. "I was so upset; all the words seemed to run together."

Her soft-spoken confession shamed Reign. His father had done this to Sophia. What fury had driven his sire to strike down a six-year-old girl? To slay her parents and make her an orphan? For that alone, he owed Sophia what assistance he could give her. "Perhaps this Pearse was lying?"

"Oh, how I wish that were true." Sophia raised her tearstained face until their gazes locked. The depths of her misery touched something deep within Reign that he thought long dead. "My brother arrived and did nothing to contradict the gentleman's claims. To insult me further, I was sent to my bedchamber like some sort of simpleton for daring to question his authority."

"Sophia, I am sorry for your troubles," he said, meaning every word.

Sophia gently pulled her hand away and wiped one of the tears tickling her cheek. "No more than I."

CHAPTER NINE

Sophia started at the sound of the front door being slammed, heralding her brothers' return.

How long had she been asleep?

When Reign had taken her home, Sophia had entered the town house with a dreaded anticipation that her brothers would be waiting for her. She had braced herself for hurtful accusations and questions that she was unwilling to answer.

She had been spared both.

Stephan and Henry had already departed the house for the evening. Neither Gedding nor, her maid, Lucy could tell her anything more. Sophia had changed her gown and quietly rejoiced that no one would ever know about her visit to Mr. Fawson's office or that she had spent most of the afternoon with the one gentleman her brother seemed to despise above all others.

Stephan's voice could be heard as he called out for the butler. Sophia rubbed her eyes, surprised that she had fallen asleep in the chair, her needlepoint abandoned in her lap. Uncertain of the hour, she set the frame aside and stood. With her arms stretched above her head, she yawned as she strode over to the clock that adorned the mantel of her small sitting room and noted the time.

One o'clock.

By now, Lucy and the rest of staff had retired for the evening. For most of them, their duties started at dawn. However, such concerns would not matter to her brother.

With her left wrist braced against the edge of the mantel, Sophia's slender fingers curled into a fist as she silently debated whether or not she should intercede before her brothers woke up the whole house.

Or perhaps it was too late.

Sophia could hear the soothing baritone of the butler as he attempted to pacify his employer. Unwilling to leave the servant to handle Stephan alone, she returned to the chair and picked up her walking stick.

In truth, she did not need the stick to navigate the town house. Upon her arrival, she had spent the first few days learning the layout of the house so she could move around with confidence. However, when dealing with her disagreeable brothers, it did not hurt to be prepared.

Still attired in the printed muslin round dress bordered with flounces in black that she had worn since the afternoon, Sophia slowly made her way down the passageway to the stairs. Several footmen were scurrying about lighting the lamps under Henry's supervision.

The butler, his arms laden with greatcoats, walking sticks, and hats, was trailing after Stephan as he barked his orders.

"Where is my sister?"

Sophia's hand gripped the banister. Stephan was drunk, and most likely Henry was, too. She swallowed the bitter disappointment welling up within her.

"Above you," she said, causing both of her brothers to glance up.

"I thought you'd retired for the evening," Henry said, his gaze shifting from her to Stephan in a nervous fashion.

"A slight change of plans."

Not waiting for an invitation, Sophia slid her hand along the banister as she continued down the staircase. Neither brother rushed to assist her, nor would their help have been welcome. She prided herself on what independence she had managed to achieve, and she was apt to take her walking stick to anyone who tried to treat her like an invalid.

"You both are home early," she said lightly, praying that her brothers had not encountered Reign during the evening. "Did you have supper? I am certain we can find something in the larder that—"

"Sophia, I require your presence in the library," Stephan interrupted, and staggered away from his siblings toward the door that the butler hastily opened.

She looked askance at Henry. "What has happened?" she whispered.

Henry shook his head in warning while he brought a finger to his lips to silence her. "Come along, Sophia," he said, taking her firmly by the elbow. "You know it is best not to keep Stephan waiting."

This did not bode well.

Shaking off Henry's hand, Sophia marched into the library. She tilted her head, and the faint clink of glass alerted her that Stephan had found the brandy. The last time her brothers had summoned her to the library, Stephan had ordered her not to see Reign.

Keeping the end of the walking stick planted into the rug, Sophia gestured broadly with her unencumbered hand. "As you can see, Stephan, I have obeyed your command. Now that we have adjourned to the library, can you please tell me why you are behaving as if I have done something wrong?"

"You'd best sit down, Sophia," Henry said from behind.

She glanced back at her brother before stalking to the closest chair. "If this is about me paying a visit to the solicitor, I will have you know that I had every right to seek his advice."

Stephan stared at her over the glass of brandy. "Damn you, Sophia, what right did you have to meddle in my affairs? When did you pay him a visit?"

Belatedly, Sophia realized that her brothers had not been aware of her visit. She silently chastised herself for her slip. "Days ago," she said dismissively. "What does it matter? He did not tell me anything that I had not already deduced."

Her brother slammed down his glass. "I did not summon you because of the damn solicitor. We have more pressing concerns to discuss."

"Such as?"

Stephan brought his fingers to his brow. "Henry, will you be so kind as to shut the door. This concerns the family, and I will not have the servants whispering about us behind our backs."

Concerned, Sophia leaned forward in her chair. "Stephan, what is it?"

"I may lose the town house."

"What?" Sophia looked to Henry for confirmation, and her brother nodded. She turned back to address Stephan. "How? I thought you had sold enough to satisfy your creditors?"

She watched as Stephan traced the circumference of the glass with his finger. "A card game," he said finally.

"Several, actually," Henry added.

Stephan glared at his brother. "Henry, this will go better if you keep your bleating mouth shut!"

"Well, Sophia needs to know the whole of it," Henry muttered.

A cold foreboding coalesced in Sophia's stomach. "I do not understand."

"What is there not to understand, sister? I sat down at one of the tables with Angrove, Newton, and several others," he said, his voice almost devoid of emotion. "Strategy and skill are useless without luck, and that fickle bitch abandoned me when I needed her the most."

Restless, Sophia stood and moved closer to her brother. "How could you be so reckless? First the pictures, and some of mother's jewelry, and now this?"

"I had no intention of losing!" Stephan shouted at her, his control snapping. "Why are we discussing the bloody card game?"

"You were the one who brought it up, Stephan," Henry interjected as he swayed slightly to keep his balance.

"This card game—" Sophia began.

"Forget the card game, Sophia," Stephan said through clenched teeth. "Such losses can be recovered. Our family has bigger problems."

Sophia slowly glanced from brother to brother. Stephan's voice revealed more than her ruined eyesight. "Such as losing the town house?"

"It is merely a possibility, Sophia." Stephan threaded his hand through his already mussed hair. "Several investments that I was counting on have dried up. I have been selling what I could to compensate for my losses. Christ, what a muddled mess!"

"So what do we do now, brother?" Sophia asked. If her brother expected sympathy from her, she feared that he would be disappointed. Stephan should have told her about the mounting debts. "Pack up what you have not managed to sell, and return to the country?"

"Actually," Henry said, approaching his siblings, "if the town house must be sold, then the contents will be auctioned as well."

"How long have you both kept this from me?" Sophia demanded.

The town house had been purchased by their grandfather. Although she was too young to remember in great detail, her father and mother had entertained their friends in this house. They had left behind remnants of themselves. And now it might be auctioned off piece by piece?

In a fit of temper, she kicked one of the legs of the table that separated her and Stephan. The decanters and glassware wobbled and rattled. "How could you be so careless?" She whirled away, uncertain of her destination. "Our mother and father traversed these very rooms. I can go upstairs and sit on our mother's bed and if I concentrate, I can still smell her."

Sophia plucked one of the books from the shelf and marched back to brothers. "This book—" She heaved it at Stephan, and he fumbled to catch it before it hit him in the chest. "It belonged to our father. You and Henry are planning to just give it away to a stranger?"

"Not give away, sister," Stephan said, placing the book on the table. "If need be, it will be sold."

"What else are you planning to sell, Stephan? That fine horse you love? Or maybe Henry's snuff box collection? Lord knows, you would never sell anything that you actually cared about!"

"You are being unfair to Stephan," Henry said, touching her on the arm to get her attention. "Those bad investments were not his fault. Besides, we have a plan."

Sophia rubbed her forehead. She was so furious at both of her brothers that the limited vision she possessed had dimmed, giving her a headache. With the roar of her blood rushing in her ears, it took her a minute to sense the unnatural stillness that had struck both of her brothers, warning her that she had not heard the entire tale.

"What are you not telling me?" Since Henry was the closest one to intimidate, Sophia glared at him. "What plan?"

Henry silently appealed to his brother. When Stephan said nothing, Henry shrugged and said, "Marriage."

The word was so unexpected, Sophia laughed. "So you have found two heiresses that are willing to marry you and Stephan?"

Henry smiled weakly at her. "Not us, my lovely sister. You."

Sophia's hand fluttered to her throat. She took a step forward, and stumbled into the corner of the table. The pain was minor when compared with the ache in her heart.

"You cannot expect me to agree to such a thing."

Henry took a step toward her, perhaps with the thought to comfort her. His hand dropped limply to his side when he saw her expression. "Lord Mackney . . . do you recall meeting him?"

Sophia cast a wary look at Stephan. "Of course. He has visited Northam Peak on numerous occasions. I suppose he took part in the card game that transpired this evening," she said coolly.

Henry opened his mouth.

Stephan stirred. "Mackney offered for you this evening. I have accepted."

"Generous of you," Sophia muttered.

"Mackney is a decent and generous gentleman," Stephan said, selecting one of the decanters. He poured himself a drink, and sloshed the liquid into a second glass. "You could do far worse in choosing a husband."

Stephan picked up a glass. Instead of drinking, he surprised her by extending the glass to her. "Drink it. You've lost most of the color in your cheeks."

Sophia accepted the glass, but she refrained from imbibing. "Do I not have a say in this matter?"

"You forget that I do not need your consent," her brother said brusquely. He grabbed his glass and sipped. "Face it, little sister, there have not been many gents sniffing around you who want to relieve you of your virtue, let alone are willing to marry you for it."

Sophia dashed the contents of her glass into Stephan's face and tossed the glass at his head. He instinctively knocked it aside, and it shattered when it hit the floor. "Curse you; I am growing tired of your vulgarity and insults!"

Sophia brushed by Henry and marched toward

the door. She made it to the stairs before her drunken brother managed to catch up to her. His fingers dug into the flesh of her upper arm as he dragged her back a step.

"I gave Mackney my word. Do not make a liar out of me, little sister."

"Then you marry Mackney," Sophia said dismissively, tossing her long braid over her shoulder so it fell down her back.

It was the wrong thing to say.

Sophia cried out in pain as Stephan's fingers threatened to crush her bones. She fought against his unyielding grip, only ceasing her struggles when her gaze collided with his. Stephan looked positively capable of throttling her where she stood. His face had deepened to a reddish hue, and his blue-green eyes had darkened into a merciless black. The front portion of his hair still dripped with the brandy she had tossed into his face.

"Stephan, don't hurt her," Henry said from the threshold of the library. "She is merely frightened."

"Keep out of this!" Stephan hissed at his brother. He turned his attention back to Sophia.

His brandy-laced breath soured her stomach. Sophia did not like the way he was looking at her—as if she had ceased to be his sister. He had told her often enough that she was an inconvenience. Perhaps he viewed her simply as he did any other possession. Something to be used, bargained, or discarded depending on the whim.

"I shall not do it," she said, her body trembling with fury and fear. "You cannot make me."

"Shall we test that theory?"

With his hand manacled around her upper arm, he pushed and dragged her up what seemed an endless flight of stairs. Henry shouted something at Stephan, but Sophia was too busy concentrating on her balance to pay heed. As it was, she could barely keep up.

Stephan was clearly unhappy with her defiance, and for the first time in her life Sophia actually feared her brother. Would he beat her until she agreed to marry Lord Mackney?

"Stephan, please . . . listen to me."

He did not seem to hear her.

Stephan halted in front of the door to her bedchamber. Sophia was more than willing to go into her private quarters if her brother stayed on the other side of the door. She moved to enter the room, but he squeezed her upper arm, holding her in place.

"A promise was made to Mackney, and you will honor it. I will not be called a liar because you are a little squeamish about having a man put his hands on you."

She had encountered Lord Mackney over the years when he had joined them at Northam Peak. Like most of Stephan's friends, he seemed to tolerate her presence, but he had never openly expressed any interest in her. "You had no right—"

"I clothe you, see that you are fed, and provide shelter," Stephan yelled. "I have every right!"

Sophia despised begging, but all she had left was to throw herself at his feet and ask for mercy. "Please do not ask this of me."

"I must." Stephan shut his eyes and pressed his face into her hair. He swayed against her. "No, do not say anything. Just listen to me. Mackney is offering a generous dowry. I will be able to settle my debts and still have enough to invest in several new ventures that seem credible. The town house will stay in the family. I will even be able to buy back the items that I sold to Pearse." His voice softened, reminding her of the brother who had loved and protected her all these years. "It was inevitable that you would marry someday. It is what our parents would want for you."

"Wrong," Sophia said coldly. "Our mother and father would not want me to marry someone that I barely know so you can make your creditors happy. What happens the next time you find yourself full of brandy, and short of blunt and common sense? Are you going to marry off Henry?"

On a muffled oath, Stephan shoved her into bedchamber.

Sophia tripped over the small rug and landed on her side. She ignored the pain. "Where do you draw the line, Stephan? Are you willing to marry some hideous heiress for the sake of our family?" With her palms on the floor, she pulled herself up and straightened. "Or are you handing me over to Mackney because you are afraid that you might be saddled with a spinster sister for the rest of your life!"

"Stop pushing me, Sophia!" her brother said in a thundering tone.

In defiance, Sophia raised her chin. "I will not do it."

Stephan took a threatening step toward her, and she braced herself for his fist or worse. Something in her expression seemed to stop him in his tracks. His dark eyes narrowed as he leashed his temper.

"You have no choice." He backed out of the room. "Until Mackney and I can settle this business between us, you will remain in your bedchamber. No one, not even Henry or Lucy, may visit you."

How lovely! Stephan was denying her access to anyone who might be willing to help her. "Are you planning to starve me into complying?"

"One of the servants will bring a tray to your room." He removed the iron key from the keyhole. "Do not work yourself into hysterics, Sophia. You are marrying Mackney. You are behaving as if I had sentenced you to Newgate. By tomorrow night, all of this will be over and you will be Lady Mackney. Perhaps, in time, you will come to thank me for this night."

Sophia bowed her head and remained silent. She felt the weight of her brother's gaze before he sighed and closed the door. The clicking sound of the lock confirmed that Stephan intended to keep her imprisoned in her bedchamber until he could hand her over to Lord Mackney.

Sophia never thought she could feel this way, but Stephan had done the impossible: She despised her brother.

Drained, Sophia drew her legs to her chest and rested her forehead against her knees. Squeezing her eyes shut, she whispered a prayer to the heavens. Perhaps, when Stephan sobered, he would regret his harsh words and withdraw his consent to Lord Mackney.

Until then, Sophia was forced to wait.

CHAPTER TEN

Reign brought the bamboo-and-copper tube up to his mouth and blew. The sharp, two-inch steel spike shot out like a bullet and struck the small target mounted to the wall. Behind him, Hunter, Dare, and Vane jeered his efforts. Damn! He had missed the red center by half an inch. Again. None of his darts had hit the center circle.

"A lousy round," he grumbled, handing the long tube to Vane. "Was it not you who suggested that we spend our evening playing Puff and Darts?"

Vane's mother was trying her hand at matchmaking this season, much to her son's chagrin. The twenty-seven-year-old earl was having too much fun to settle for one lady, and he was doing his best to spoil his mother's efforts. Reign had contemplated joining Sin and his wife as they attended several balls this evening with the added benefit of possibly encountering Sophia. Instead Reign was sitting in the main room of Nox getting utterly trounced by his three friends at a game he was beginning to loathe.

Vane chuckled. "Drink a pot of ale. It might improve your aim."

"You wouldn't be so cheerful if my aim was better," Reign threatened, tempted to fire one of those darts into Vane's backside.

Hunter handed Reign a pint pot. "Best to watch your arse, my friend," the duke called out to Vane.

Vane raised the blowpipe without hesitation and blew. The bastard hit the center circle on his first attempt. "Why should I?" he asked, giving Hunter a cocky grin. "You seem up to the task."

Vane shifted his hips in an exaggerated fashion as he turned to accept the small dart Dare was offering.

Reign watched with amusement as Hunter lunged for Vane and put him in a headlock long enough to slam his fist into the earl's arm.

"Christ, Hunter!" Vane snarled. "The point went into my palm, you idiot."

The duke gave Vane a loud kiss on the ear and released him. "Serves you right. You're lucky I don't feed those darts to you one by one."

Sensing trouble, Berus started to make his way through a crowd made up of gamblers, merry-makers, drunken sailors, and a dozen of Madame Venna's girls. Reign waved the man away. The steward bowed and moved away to handle another pressing task. Despite appearances, the two men were not about to come to blows. Vane had a bad habit of provoking people to violence, but he usually walked away from these encounters unscathed.

"Good evening, gents!" Frost said, his arms open wide to encompass everyone, including a pretty blonde he had managed to steal from one of the gamblers. "What have I missed?"

Saint followed sedately behind him. Before he could approach their small group, another gentleman intercepted him and led the marquess away. He raised his hand in greeting, then signaled that he would be joining them later.

"Where have you been?" Hunter asked. Since he had changed his mind about feeding the two-inch darts to Vane, he had settled back into his chair. "Do not tell me that Sin talked you into attending Mrs. Burton's ball."

"Sin tends to get prickly whenever I am in close proximity to his marchioness." He paused to whisper something in his companion's ear. She nodded, and walked away to satisfy Frost's request. "While poking at Sin does provide me with a certain amount of amusement, Saint and I decided to patronize one of the less discriminating hells in town."

Reign sipped the ale one of the barmaids had placed in front of him. "Most of the *ton* would claim that Nox qualifies."

"True," Frost said, his intent gaze lingering on Reign. "However, I think we all would agree that the patrons at the Golden Stag are not picky on how they collect their winnings."

The Golden Stag catered to anyone with a purse, and attracted the enterprising criminal class. It was common for a man to get his purse cut—or his throat—in such an establishment. The danger appealed to brash young noblemen ready to cut their teeth on the forbidden or try to win a fortune in an evening. Years before the Lords of Vice had opened the doors to Nox, they had been faithful patrons of the perilous hell. Reign's interest in the Golden Stag had gradually waned, but it was apparent that Frost and Saint were still drawn to the darker sections of town.

The blonde returned with a pint pot for Frost. The earl rewarded her with a slow, thorough kiss on the mouth that promised the pretty wench he had other business with her as well.

"Now, where was I with my intriguing tale?"

Vane plucked the sharp darts from the target and tossed them on the table. He handed the blowpipe to Hunter so he could take his turn. "You and Saint were at the Golden Stag."

"Right."

Frost was staring at him again. Reign felt a tingling sensation go up his spine. Something had happened at the Golden Stag, and his friend seemed to believe that Reign, in particular, would be interested in his little tale.

"Are we playing a game, Frost?" Reign asked, keeping his voice casual.

"Not at all." He kicked an empty bench to alter its angle and sat down. The blonde whore tumbled into his lap. "While I was there, I noticed a certain young gent who was participating in some rather deep play over there."

So they were playing a game, after all.

"Anyone I know?"

Frost held the pot up to his companion's lips and allowed her to sip. "Ravenshaw and his cronies."

Damn.

"Why should I care about Ravenshaw?"

Frost shrugged. "I do not expect you to care about young Ravenshaw's heavy losses this evening. The Greek goddess Tyche makes fools of us all."

Reign's heart clenched as he thought of Sophia. Ravenshaw seemed determined to spend his way through his fortune. What would happen to Sophia if Ravenshaw could not settle his debts? Her wastrel brothers were worthless protectors for such a delicate beauty.

"A tragic tale, Frost," Reign drawled. He paused when he realized that Dare, Hunter, and Vane had abandoned their game of Puff and Dart. "I suppose there is a point?"

Frost's piercing turquoise eyes gleamed with unholy delight. "None, really. I am aware that you despise the young puppy, Reign. I thought you would be as amused as I by Ravenshaw's not-so-original means to spare himself from his embarrassing predicament."

Reign tensed. "Exactly how much did Ravenshaw lose at the tables this evening?"

Frost grinned at Reign like some dark angel

of death. "His losses are no longer a concern now that Lord Mackney has offered for the fair Lady Sophia."

Frost took a moment to kiss his neglected companion.

Reign felt as if ice water had replaced the blood in his veins.

He shot up from his chair. "I will tear Ravenshaw apart if he hands Sophia over to that man."

Hunter, Vane, and Dare appeared startled by the vehemence in Reign's voice. Frost, on the other hand, was not surprised at all. His friend had known all along how Reign would react to the news. Reign could not decide if he should punch Frost for toying with him or thank him for tipping him off to Sophia's disconcerting predicament.

Gratitude overrode Reign's desire for vengeance.

"Reign, where are you going at this late hour?" Frost asked as he took his watch out of the pocket of his waistcoat and peered at its face. "I highly doubt Ravenshaw will marry Lady Sophia off to Mackney this morning. Such a gentle, wounded dove as his sister will have to be properly prepared. Who knows, Ravenshaw may decide to draw out Mackney's anticipation by posting the banns. Besides, it is hardly your affair what Ravenshaw does with his sister."

Frost was not really expecting an answer from Reign. He had merely sought out his friend to deliver what he considered news that might be amusing.

Oh, Reign was interested in the news, but unlike Frost he was far from amused.

Now Reign had to decide if he was going to do something about it.

CHAPTER ELEVEN

Sophia awoke to a soft knock at the door.

She sat up in the bed, momentarily puzzled why she was still attired in her dress. Then the events of the night before flickered in her brain like a magnificent summer lightning storm.

Stephan had locked her in her bedchamber.

"Milady, I have your breakfast," a soft feminine voice said from the other side of the door.

Someone fumbled to fit the key into the keyhole, and there was a clank of metal as the mechanism tumbled into place. Sophia did not waste any time, hurrying toward the door that was opening before she reached it.

Her smile faded as she noticed that the young scullery maid was not alone. Arms crossed, Stephan was standing behind the servant.

"Planning to escape, dear sister?" He nodded to the maid. "Put the tray on the table and return to your kitchen duties."

The maid sent Sophia an apologetic look. "Aye, milord." With her arms burdened with the tray, she walked into the room and headed for the small table.

Her brother had chosen wisely. The young girl was terrified and would follow his orders without question. "Where is Lucy?"

"Your beloved maid and confidante? Unlike you, dear Sophia, Lucy knows her place in this house." Stephan did not enter her bedchamber. His body filled the doorway as if he expected her to fight her way past him. "She has been ordered to remain in her quarters. If she defies me, I will sack her without references."

"Excuse me, milady," the young maid said, slipping by her. Stephan stepped aside, and the servant disappeared down the hallway.

Sophia was disheartened, but she refused to show any weakness in front of her brother. Instead, she said, "You cannot keep me a prisoner forever, brother."

Her brother had the audacity to appear amused. "As tempting as that sounds, you shall be free once Mackney secures a special license." He reached for the latch.

"Wait!" Sophia said, seizing the edge of the door to prevent him from closing it. "Please, Stephan. There must be some other way."

Her brother stared down at her, his face carefully blank. "Forgive me, Sophia. I take no pleasure in this." He slowly closed the door, giving her a chance to release her hold.

The key turned, and she was alone again in her prison.

Sophia pressed her face against the door and cried.

Reign had only managed to sleep for a few hours when he knocked on Sin's front door. Hembry, the Sinclair butler, opened the door. His forbidding expression indicated that he had been prepared to lecture the person who dared to call on the household at such an early hour. The lines on his face relaxed with recognition.

"Lord Rainecourt, it is an unexpected pleasure."

"Forgive me for calling at such an ungodly hour, Hembry," Reign said, stepping into the front hall. "Is Sin awake?"

"Lord and Lady Sinclair are in the morning room, my lord."

The butler started up the stairs, assuming that whatever had brought Reign to the door so early was important enough to disturb his employer's breakfast. Reign did not stand on ceremony and wait to be announced. He simply followed the butler.

Sin and his wife were sitting side by side when Hembry opened the door. Reign walked through the door while the butler remained at the threshold. "Milord and lady, Lord Rainecourt is here to see you."

"Thank you, Hembry. I can see that for myself," Sin said drily. "Set another plate for our friend."

"Very good, milord."

"Sin . . . Juliana, my apologies for intruding."

"Nonsense, Reign," Juliana said, looking quite charming in a light blue morning dress and lace cap. "You are always welcome."

Sin stood and gestured for Reign to sit. "Good God, man, you look like hell. Has something happened?"

"Yes, and nothing good."

The marquess's mouth thinned at the enigmatic statement. "When is it ever?"

Reign wearily collapsed onto the chair next to Sin's. His appetite had abandoned him, but the enticing fragrance of coffee caused his stomach to growl. He ignored his discomfort.

Whether she wanted it or not, Sophia needed his help, and Reign was determined not to disappoint her.

"I have come to ask both of you for your help."

There was nothing better than a good cry and some warm food to clear a lady's head. Sophia knelt down in front of the door and inserted one of her small hat pins into the keyhole.

Originally, she had contemplated rending the sheet linens and tying the pieces together to form a makeshift rope. She realized almost immediately that her daring plan had several problems. First, she did not possess a knife to cut the strong cloth, and the sewing shears that she used for her needlepoint were too dull for the task.

Second, even if she had managed to fashion a

rope out of the sheets, she was uncertain if it would be long enough for her to safely reach the ground. Her eyesight was too poor for her to judge the distance properly, and what good was escaping if she broke her neck?

No, a rope was too risky.

She had also ruled out using the spoon the maid had given her for her breakfast to dig a hole through the thick plastered walls. Such a feat would take days. Besides, if Stephan was about, he would most likely notice the thumps and scratching sounds emanating from the wall. It would be too much to expect that he would believe that rats were suddenly infesting one particular wall in the town house.

A weak-spirited miss might have given up, but Sophia was determined to best Stephan. Even if she had to prostrate herself at Lord Mackney's feet and beg for his mercy. Sophia had no intention of marrying the earl. When faced with possible financial ruin, her brothers had decided to sacrifice their little sister rather than place their own necks through a marriage noose. All things considering, their high-handedness seemed quite unfair.

No, Sophia would save herself from Stephan's tyranny.

The hat pin bent as she jabbed at the hidden mechanism inside the keyhole.

"Blast it all!" Sophia muttered, tugging the pin out of the hole. It slipped from her fingers and vanished, swallowed by the keyhole.

"Hmph!" she said, disgusted with the useless hat pin and her limited skills. "There has to be another way."

She pulled herself to her feet and marched over to the forgotten tray that held the remains of her breakfast. She snatched up the spoon and returned to the door. The handle of the spoon was too wide for the keyhole.

"No. This is not fair!" she complained aloud. She jammed the handle against the lock in frustration before she discarded it with a flip of her wrist. "What else?"

The sewing shears.

Sophia strode over to the chair she had been dozing in when her brothers had returned. Kneeling down, she shifted items in the basket until her fingers closed around the shears. Armed with a new tool, she went back to the door and dropped to her knees.

"Please work."

Biting her lower lip, Sophia slipped one of the short blades into the keyhole. Her eyelids lowered as she concentrated on her task. She had never studied the internal workings of a lock. Nevertheless, how complicated could the shifting bits of metal within be? Something clicked within the keyhole, causing Sophia to smile.

Perhaps this would not be so difficult, after all?

The blade snapped off.

"No!" Sophia squinted at the dark keyhole in disbelief. She began to stab the remaining blade into the hole when the recognizable sounds of a key being inserted on the other side of the door froze her in place.

Had her brother returned?

Panic caused her heart to race as she scrambled backward. She quickly got to her feet and realized she still had the broken sewing shears clutched in her hand. Sophia hid them behind her back just as the door cracked open.

"Milady?"

Sophia almost fainted as she recognized her maid's voice. "Lucy!" she whispered, placing her hand over her heart. "Good heavens, I thought you were my brother."

The two ladies embraced.

"Stephan told me that he had ordered you to remain in your quarters."

"Now, now . . . ," Lucy went on. "We have so little time. Most of the staff is terrified of your brothers, and everyone has been warned that they will be sacked without references if any of us interfere with Lord Ravenshaw's business."

"Where is my brother?"

"He left the house fifteen minutes ago. Mr. Northam has orders to watch over you, but he is currently in the kitchen flirting with one of the maids."

Sophia could not quite trust her good fortune.

"Lucy, I have to get out of this house before Stephan returns," she said urgently. "I am not sure what you have heard—"

"Enough." Lucy pressed a small leather pouch into Sophia's hand. "It isn't much, I'm afraid."

Sophia walked over to her dressing table and collected her reticule and bonnet covered in straw-colored diaphanous satin. "I gathered what jewelry I have. Stephan has sold most of the larger pieces."

"It will have to do." Lucy plucked the bonnet from her mistress's boneless fingers and placed it on her head. With brisk movements, she tied the ribbons under Sophia's chin. "Use the back stairs. The door to the gardens is unlocked. From there, go to the stables. I have one of the grooms preparing a horse—"

"I am not properly dressed!" Sophia protested.

"This is about haste, not propriety, milady." Lucy strode purposefully over to one of the chairs and retrieved Sophia's walking stick. "If you leave by carriage, Lord Ravenshaw will know that the staff helped you. Here." She pressed the top of the walking stick into Sophia's hand. "Toss it away when you get to the horse. It will be a distraction, and might frighten the beast if he catches sight of it."

Sophia clutched the other woman's hands. Her riding skills were adequate, but navigating London with her limited vision would be difficult. The horse's movements usually unsettled her stomach. "I am terrified, Lucy. I cannot do this. Perhaps I could hail a hackney coach—?"

"There is no time for this nonsense," Lucy

snapped, pushing Sophia toward the door. "Lord Ravenshaw could return at any moment, and Mr. Northam will only be distracted for so long."

With a firm hand on Sophia's upper arm, Lucy escorted her mistress down the hallway toward the servants' hidden stairs. "I can go no farther. The rest is up to you."

Sophia embraced the maid she also considered her friend. "I thought I would ride to—"

Lucy covered Sophia's mouth. "It is best if you do not tell me or anyone else where you will be heading. When Lord Ravenshaw discovers that you have escaped, he will question the servants. Wherever you go, I suggest that you choose a place your brother will not expect. He has a frightful temper when provoked, nor will he be reasonable if he discovers your whereabouts."

"I owe you more than I can ever repay. Now go." Sophia gestured with a nod of her head. "You have risked much for me, and I do not want you to come to regret it."

Sophia's eyes adjusted quickly to the dim staircase as she hurried down as swiftly as she dared. It was strange, but fear seemed to have sharpened her eyesight. Within minutes, she reached the unlocked door to the outer gardens. She opened the door, and fresh air bathed her face.

Sophia peered up at the gray, cloudy sky. The air held a hint of rain, but there was a chance that the light wind would blow the storm clouds away.

With the help of the walking stick, she crossed the back garden and headed for the stables.

She almost stumbled as she realized that Lucy had not told her the name of the groom. Was it important? Indecision slowed her pace. Had Stephan thought to warn the stable not to prepare a carriage for her? Mayhap not. Her brother had a bad habit of underestimating his younger sister. With Henry guarding her, Stephan would not have considered that Sophia might leave her bedchamber, let alone slip out of the house.

Her heart was pounding in her throat as she observed from a distance two grooms stroll into the stable. Lucy was right. Sophia had no time to spare with this nonsense. If she hoped to ride to Fanny's house, she needed to walk into the stable and ask for her horse.

A large gloved hand covered her mouth, smothering Sophia's scream. Rough hands dragged her off the pebbled path and into the foliage. Sophia raised her walking stick and stabbed the sharp point into her attacker's foreleg.

"Bloodthirsty wench!" Reign growled in her ear. "And here I thought you needed rescuing."

CHAPTER TWELVE

Sophia would have fallen to her knees if Reign had not caught her up into his arms. Her head lolled back against his arm as she stared at him with wonderment.

"Reign, I cannot believe it is you!"

He savored the caress of her hand against his cheek.

"How did you find me? Did Lucy send you?"

"Who the devil is Lucy?"

Sophia frowned. "My maid. If you did not—Reign, why are you here?"

"I already told you. I came to rescue you." He grinned down at her stunned expression. "Though I'm beginning to regret it now that you've put a hole in my leg with your walking stick."

"I-I thought you were Stephan."

Reign suddenly had the urge to hit something. Ravenshaw would do. "Where is he?"

"I do not know. Lucy said that he left the house. I assume to meet with Lord Mackney. Henry is inside, supposedly watching my bedchamber door."

His eyebrows rose in an inquiring fashion. "Supposedly?"

Sophia shrugged. "Henry was rather neglectful in his duties. Lucy was able to unlock the door so I could slip out of the house." Now that she had recovered from her fright, she was able to stand without his support.

The bastard had locked Sophia in her room.

Reign was tempted to stroll into the house and seek out young Henry. Northam was not Ravenshaw, but he clearly had been unwilling to stand against his older brother.

"Where were you heading?"

Sophia peeked around the large bush to make certain that they had not been overheard. "The stables. Lucy told me that one of the grooms had readied a horse. I was going to Fanny's from there."

Reign gave her a look of disbelief. The notion of Sophia riding a horse down the streets of London was terrifying. "Are you mad? How were you going to manage that?"

Her lower lip protruded slightly as his insult struck its mark. "I will have you know that I am capable of riding a horse."

"In the country, perhaps, when you only have to worry about trees and grazing sheep," Reign said, letting himself get momentarily distracted by Sophia's harebrained plan. "The London streets are no place for an inexperienced, half-blind lady on horseback. You would have likely broken your foolish neck, and I want to throttle you myself for even contemplating such a reckless challenge."

Sophia's lip quivered. "I was desperate," she said simply, her beautiful blue-green eyes filling with tears.

Hell. Reign felt like a brute for lecturing her after everything she had been through. Without waiting for an invitation, he gathered her into his arms and hugged her. "I know." His only excuse was everything he had set into motion since Frost had told him about Ravenshaw's plan to marry Sophia off to Lord Mackney.

After years of burying his feelings, Sophia had slipped under his skin and triggered all his protective instincts. If Ravenshaw had been unlucky enough to stumble upon them, Reign would have gladly murdered the man and not felt a twinge of regret. It was a sobering realization that he had more in common with his sire than he thought.

"I still do not understand," Sophia said, banishing his dark thoughts. She stepped out of his arms. "If Lucy did not send for you, then why are you here?"

Reign rubbed the back of his neck. He suspected that Sophia was going to be difficult when she heard his plan. "Is it not obvious? I have come to collect my bride."

Sophia was speechless.

Lord Rainecourt was proposing to marry her? Impossible.

From what she had learned about his first

marriage, it had been a disastrous affair of the heart that had ended with the countess's untimely death. Reign himself had told her that he had no desire to bind himself to another lady.

No, Sophia thought, she had misunderstood him.

What words rhyme with bride? *Pride . . . guide . . . died?*

Reign took advantage of her silence and led her away from the stables toward the street. With his arm gallantly hooked through hers, they strolled down the street to the awaiting coach. At their approach, the coachman scrambled down from his perch. He opened the door and tipped his hat.

"A lovely day, is it not, milady?"

Sophia mutely stared in horror at the coachman as if he had sprouted horns from his forehead.

Reign placed his hand on the small of her back as he helped her ascend the steps of his private coach. Behind her, he addressed the servant. "We have tarried here long enough. Let us be off."

"Very good, milord."

She waited until the earl settled in next to her. "Reign, I must have misunderstood. Did you say that you were collecting your, uh, *bride*?"

A small cynical smile curled the corners of his mouth. "There is nothing wrong with your hearing, Sophia."

"Me?" Her voice squeaked, forcing her to clear

her throat. "I do not understand any of this, my lord. How did you learn of Lord Mackney's offer of marriage? Were you at the club?"

Reign patted her hand in a soothing manner. Sophia glanced down at their entangled fingers, unaware that she had reached for his hand. "I was not at the Golden Stag, but several of my friends were."

Dismayed, Sophia's shoulders slumped. "So everyone knows? Then you might as well return me to the town house. I cannot defy Stephan so publicly."

"Giving up so easily?" he taunted softly.

Sophia straightened and glared at him as Reign had hoped that she would. "No! Can you not see that I have no choice? I had hoped my brother's exchange with Lord Mackney was a private one. I should have known Stephan would have insisted on witnesses so Lord Mackney could not withdraw the offer without fearing reproach. With so many people privy to the earl's offer and my brother's consent, I see no other choice but to yield to Stephan's wishes."

Reign shook his head. "No. I doubt that Mackney's conversation with your brother is common knowledge, and I will make certain it remains that way. Frost just has a unique skill of collecting elusive information."

"Frost . . . You are referring to Lord Chillingsworth?"

Reign seemed to sense her unspoken question, and he gave her hand a friendly squeeze. "Do not fret about Frost. He will hold his tongue, or deal with me."

Sophia blinked at the controlled violence in Reign's promise. She suspected very few people dared to risk his ire. "It is not as simple as soothing Lord Mackney's injured feelings and my brother's temper. Stephan needs—"

"Ravenshaw will have to figure out another way to recover from his bad investments, Sophia," Reign said, sounding like he did not give a farthing about her brother's fate. "If he is set on marriage, then he can hunt for an heiress."

She shifted in her seat so her knees brushed against his as the coach wobbled down the street. "You think a betrothal will stop my brother?"

Sophia scowled, wishing the interior of the coach were not so dim. Reign's face was cast in shadows that seemed to blend with the ones she carried with her.

"A betrothal? Not at all. Ravenshaw would merely reclaim you," Reign said, presenting her with his profile. "What I am offering is marriage. I had to call in many favors, some that were not even mine to claim, and I have secured a special license from the Archbishop of Canterbury. With your consent, we shall be married this afternoon."

Sophia brought her hand to her breast, overwhelmed by Reign's generous offer. "You told me that you would never marry again."

A particularly bone-shaking jostle of the coach's compartment sent her colliding against Reign as the wheels dropped into a worn rut in the road.

Sophia clutched at his dark blue frock coat that matched his eyes, and stared up into his handsome face. She felt his arms encircle her as his mouth hovered inches from her.

"You need a husband, Sophia . . . but not a bounder like Mackney," he amended. Reign teased her lips with his as he huskily whispered, "Allow me to protect you."

"And my brothers?"

Reign snorted in derision. "You are one-and-twenty, Sophia, and of legal age. Ravenshaw cannot have our marriage annulled, and I would welcome the challenge if he tried."

Sophia inhaled, taking the lovely masculine scent of him into her lungs. She would be lying if she denied that she was tempted. Reign had intrigued her almost from the beginning. Their first kiss on Lord and Lady Harper's garden terrace was something she had often dwelled upon in quiet moments.

He obviously felt the same connection, though she suspected that Lord Mackney's offer of marriage had spurred Reign to propose instead of the noble, loftier sentiment of love. "I would be selfish to agree."

"You would be foolish to deny me!"

Now she had angered him or pricked his pride. "Reign," she said, the muscles in her throat constricting with emotion. "This marriage . . . what would you get out of it?"

"This." Reign lowered his head and crushed his mouth over hers. The kiss was not of a tender suitor intent on wooing his love. Reign's kiss was born of frustration, and a longing Sophia could not comprehend. She allowed her left palm the luxury of sliding up Reign's chest to his shoulder. The coach bounced, and she clung to him, yielding to his drugging caresses and the hard lines of his body.

If Sophia consented, Reign would be her husband. A man like Reign would not be satisfied with kisses. He would lay claim to her body, over and over, a lifetime of living a loving born of his generous sacrifice.

Would it be enough?

Yes, her heart whispered.

Reign felt the subtle change in Sophia as her body accepted his claim even if her mind was still conflicted. His lips parted, and he softened the kiss, drinking her in. Suddenly her corset seemed too tight and she pulled away from his mouth, gasping to catch her breath.

"Sophia?"

With a hooded glance, she asked, "Tell me, Reign, what do you expect in a wife?"

"Faithfulness and respect," he said without hesitation. "A wife who will willingly share my bed and bear my children."

Sophia nodded. She had already concluded that she would be giving Reign what Stephan thought he could take. "And love?"

Reign placed his large hands over hers. He gently moved her hands from his chest and placed them on her lap. "Poetic drivel. A frivolous sentiment. I learned from my first marriage that love creates false expectations in those it infects. I loved my first wife, and both Beatrice and I were unhappy for my weakness. No, Sophia, I will not demand your love, nor offer you it in return. I will give you my protection, faithfulness, friendship, and loyalty. I swear, I will dedicate my life to ensuring that you are content in our marriage."

His words were not the sort a young miss yearned for from her ardent suitor. Nevertheless, Lord Mackney was her brother's choice while Reign was hers.

Despite her tender smile, she wiped away a wistful tear from her cheek. "You honor me, my lord. However, I cannot allow you to sacrifice yourself on the marriage altar for my sake."

Sophia visibly braced for Reign's temper, but he surprised her by laughing.

"Very well, I see desperate measures are required."

"Desperate measures?" Sophia echoed, wary of Reign's amusement. "What do you intend to do?"

"Live up to my reputation," Reign said, lightly pressing a kiss to her cold lips. "Sophia, my dear lady, I fully intend to ruin you."

CHAPTER THIRTEEN

Perhaps, Reign silently mused, it had been too much to hope that his outrageous announcement would have left Sophia speechless so that he could have a few moments to contemplate his remaining hours as an unmarried man.

Sophia was unwilling to appreciate the humor of their situation.

The future Countess of Rainecourt had no intention of following him meekly to the marriage altar. Reign took Sophia's hand and helped her descend from their coach. He gave her an equal measure of flattery and threats to convince her to walk through Lord and Lady Bramsbury's front door. Reign was afraid that if he released Sophia's hand, she might be foolish enough to flee into the street.

"You cannot be serious," Sophia hissed under her breath after they had paid their respects to their host and hostess, and had moved out of earshot. "Are you aware that I *slept* in my dress last evening because Stephan refused to allow Lucy to attend me?"

Reign bit his inner cheek to keep from grinning. Poor Sophia sounded as if she were committing a grievous sin by wearing a slightly wrinkled dress.

"You look delightfully rumpled, my dear." He nodded to people that he knew, pointedly ignoring any attempts to engage him in conversation as he escorted Sophia through the drawing room and library and outdoors.

"Where are you taking me?" she demanded, not softening her annoyance.

Reign brought Sophia's hand up to his lips and kissed it. He deliberately lingered over the task, knowing they were being observed by the other guests.

"Reign?" Sophia pleaded huskily, unaware that her anxiety and exhaustion made her sound restless for her lover's touch.

Only Reign knew the truth.

"Where—?"

Reign placed his hand on Sophia's back as he guided her toward the steps. "Where all young lovers prefer to tarry . . . the lower terrace."

Sophia could not resist glancing back at Lord and Lady Bramsbury's lovely house. Her vision swirled as she turned her head so she gave up and concentrated on the ground in front of her.

"You are aware that it is afternoon."

"The sun has not escaped my notice." Reign

pointed at something in the distance. "That spot over there should suit us nicely."

The crunch of gravel gave way to the soft padding of cut grass.

"Everyone is probably watching us," Sophia grumbled, clearly not appreciating the simplicity of her ruination. "You were barely civil to our host and hostess."

"No one expects the Devil of Rainecourt to be civil."

Reign tugged her toward the two shrubs that had caught his eye.

Sophia rolled her eyes heavenward. "I suspect you and your friends relish your notoriety too much to surrender it willingly."

"And spoil our fun?" he asked in feigned outrage. "Perish the thought, my lady!"

Reign nudged Sophia until he was satisfied that their discreet audience could still see them even though they were standing in front of the waist-high shrubs.

"Take a step closer."

For the first time since he caught her as she headed toward Ravenshaw's stables, Reign noted a hint of a smile forming on Sophia's full lips. "Hmm . . . you seem to be quite the expert when it comes to ruining a lady's reputation."

Matching her lightening mood, he said, "Some tasks are more pleasurable than others."

Her blue-green eyes blazed like gems in the sunlight. "Have we dallied on the lower terrace long enough? Will Lord Mackney view me as a wanton lady with a rather unsavory acquaintance with one particular Lord of Vice?"

Sophia allowed him to guide her hands until he had positioned them on the sides of his waist.

"Soon," he promised as he lowered his head to her parted lips. "By the time we bid farewell to our host and hostess, the gossips will guarantee that Mackney will be unable to forgive your wicked nature, my lady."

Reign was certain their audience above saw exactly what he had staged for their benefit: two lovers so caught up in each other that they had forgotten to be discreet.

Sophia did not resist his kiss. Her lips softened beneath his as he kindled a passionate response from her. He felt her fingers dig into his waist. Reign willed himself not to respond to the siren call of her body.

While he had brought Sophia to Lord and Lady Bramsbury's house for the purpose of despoiling her under the speculative gaze of the *ton*, Reign had no intention of making love to Sophia under the shrubbery.

Appearances would suffice.

Reign coaxed Sophia to rotate 180 degrees before he circled her waist and lowered them down on the grass so they disappeared from view. He pulled back and admired her well-kissed mouth.

Sophia scowled up at him. "Good heavens, Reign, get off me! How ever will I explain the grass stains on my skirt?"

"Trust me, my dear lady, no explanation will be necessary." She was adorable when she was vexed with him. He leaned closer and kissed the tip of her nose. "The bits of grass on our clothes will seal our fate."

"Reign must be addled to contemplate getting leg-shackled to Ravenshaw's sister."

Alexius Braverton, Marquess of Sinclair, watched from one of Reign's library windows as his wife was conversing with Lady Frances. At Reign's request, he and his wife had called on Lady Sophia's dear friend and brought her to the house for the wedding. His friend had hoped to put his future bride at ease by including one of her friends.

Juliana laughed at something the dark-haired woman had said, and once again Alexius was enthralled by his wife's beauty. A breeze caught the strands of golden-blond hair that had slipped from its confines. The ends floated like dandelion puffs. Juliana absently captured the errant strands and tucked them behind her ear.

As if sensing his perusal, his wife glanced up at the window and grinned. Her smile, artless and full of love, warmed him even at a distance. Alexius waved. Juliana blew him a kiss before she and Lady Frances continued their stroll through Reign's gardens.

"Did you even hear what I said, Sin?" Frost inquired snottily, annoyed that he was being ignored. "Stop flirting with your wife and pay attention. Reign tends to heed your advice more than mine."

Frost's expression was one of puzzlement, as if he could not fathom why anyone would prefer Sin's advice to his. Alexius took no offense. If one ignored Frost's arrogance and sarcastic wit, he could be a tolerable companion.

"You were the one who told Reign about Ravenshaw," Dare said from his reclining position on the sofa. Thanks to Frost's mischief, none of the Lords of Vice had gotten much sleep.

Frost glared at Dare, but the gent had his eyes closed. "Reign was supposed to knock Ravenshaw on his arse, break a few ribs, and bloody the puppy's nose. If Lady Sophia was feeling generous, she might have invited our surly friend into her bed. No one, least of all *me*, expected him to rush off to the Doctor's Commons for a bloody special license!"

Dare raised his head and adjusted the small pillow he had tucked under it. "Then you have not been very observant. Reign wants Lady Sophia. For weeks, he has been trying to figure out the how and why of it, and you and Ravenshaw just gave it to him. Congratulations!"

"Utter twaddle!" Frost scoffed, his hair falling rakishly over his left eye as he admired his boots on Reign's desk. "Over the years, all of us have had the pleasure of observing Reign's interaction with females. When he puts his hands on them, the gent certainly knows what to do with them."

"Lady Sophia is apparently different," Alexius interjected.

"Not that different," Frost said dourly. "Beatrice married Reign because she needed a proper sire for the bastard she carried in her belly."

Dare opened one eye to glare at Frost. "Have some respect, Frost. The lady and her child have been dead for the past eight years."

Frost's response to Dare was a dismissive wave. "Lady Sophia needs something from Reign, too."

Dare shot Frost an incredulous look. "And Reign wants to give it to her. Leave it alone."

"I don't trust her," Frost grumbled. "Reign's old man went mad lusting after Lady Sophia's mother, and shot his face off in the end. Maybe we should bury Reign's pistols before he returns to the house."

Alexius abandoned his post at the window and walked over to the desk where Frost was sitting. "Stay out of Reign's affairs," he advised, intimately familiar with his friend's meddling. "If you interfere, he is likely to do more than break a few ribs and bloody your lip."

Stephan seized his brother by his dark brown frock coat and slammed his back against one of the walls of the front hall.

"Tell me, Henry, how is it that our sister has vanished from her room?" he silkily inquired, inches away from his brother's face, which was bathed in sweat.

"I-I swear, I do not know," Henry, the whining weasel, stuttered.

Stephan lightly cuffed his younger brother on the side of the head. "My orders were simple for even you to follow. Keep the servants away from Sophia, and guard her door."

"I did!" Henry's face darkened to a red hue. He cringed as he felt the sting of Stephan's knuckles against his temple. "I swear it on our mother's grave! The servants were too terrified to interfere. You made certain of it."

Someone had to have assisted Sophia in her escape. His sister was not cowardly, unlike sniveling Henry, but she did have her limitations. Stephan's lip curled in disgust as he scowled at his brother. How their father had sired such a culver-headed dandy was unfathomable to him.

"And what of Lucy?" The sharp-eyed chit would have cheerfully laid down her life for Sophia.

"Sitting in her quarters like you told her to. She has been demanding to see Sophia all day."

Stephan bared his teeth in frustration. He reached into his brother's waistcoat pocket, retrieved his handkerchief, and tossed it at him. "Mop up the snot on your lip." He whirled away, pressing his fingers to his brow. "How did Sophia do it? Was she clever enough to pick the lock?"

Henry sagged against the wall. "Maybe she climbed out the window? She could have fashioned a decent rope with the bedding?"

Stephan paused, turning his head to glare at

his brother. "And did you find evidence that our clever Sophia created such a rope?"

Henry floundered and glanced at his boots. "Well, no . . ."

"Why do I bother? You are a simpleton."

Stephan's anger was directed not only at Henry, but also at himself. She had run off because he had lost his temper with her. Now she was wandering the streets of London alone. He was surprised to discover that some of the fear churning in his gut was for his vulnerable sister.

With a decisive stride, Stephan moved to the center front hall and shouted for the butler.

"What are you going to do?"

Henry flinched when Stephan clapped his hand on his brother's shoulder.

"We, my dear brother, are going to search every street, and pay calls to our sister's friends. Sophia will be seeking an ally, and I would wager Lady Frances is high on her list."

They had actually done it.

She was now Sophia Housely, Countess of Rainecourt.

For the hundredth time, Sophia studied the band Reign had slid onto her left hand. The gold glinted under the candlelight. She felt the weight of both the ring and her decision as she tilted her head to the side, admiring it.

"I can imagine how you must feel," Lady Sinclair—no, Juliana, as she insisted on being called—said, sensing the new bride was quietly reflecting on the commitment that she had made to her husband.

After a lavish wedding dinner that included courses of venison, joints of veal, and mutton served with celery and cream, artichoke pie, and lastly, chocolate and almond puffs, not to mention several fruit pies, the ladies had retired upstairs to the drawing room while the gentlemen adjourned to the library.

Reign and his friends, however, had not lingered downstairs with their port and brandy. One of his friends, perhaps it had been His Grace, the Duke of Huntsley, had teased that Reign could not be parted from his new wife so the gentlemen had decided to join the ladies.

Her new husband had endured his friends' teasing with an easy grin and a bawdy retort. He had even walked over to the sofa where Sophia was seated and kissed her cheek. The chaste kiss seemed to vastly amuse his friends, in particular Lord Chillingsworth, though she could not fathom why.

Sophia cast a shy glance at Reign, who was standing on the other side of the rectangular drawing room, debating politics with Lord Sainthill and Lord Hugh while the other gentlemen listened. Occasionally, one of the other gentlemen interjected an opinion into the often heated exchange.

She gave Juliana a slight smile. "I must confess that all of this is overwhelming. Legal or not, my brothers will not accept this marriage."

Fanny put down her teacup hard enough to make the cup rattle against the saucer. "Ravenshaw and Henry will have no choice."

Juliana looked back at the seven gentlemen. They seemed too large, too uncivil for the gilded grandeur surrounding them. Her husband murmured something to Reign, causing the earl to toss his head back and laugh. "I have learned never to underestimate the members of the Lords of Vice. Reign called in a great number of favors to ensure that you were under his protection by nightfall."

With her hands in her lap, Sophia entwined her fingers together in a nervous gesture. "So I have been told. Before Reign caught up to me at the stables, I had managed to do rather well on my own. I had planned to ride to Fanny's."

Fanny, sitting to Sophia's left, touched her on the arm to gain her attention. "Ravenshaw will be searching for you, Sophia. My family's town house will likely be one of his first stops. Rainecourt was clever to steal you away from your brothers. They never did appreciate you."

"Fanny, you do not seem particularly troubled by the drastic measures Reign has taken on my behalf this afternoon."

"You forget that I have been quietly observing your rather odd courtship with Lord Rainecourt."

"Courtship!" Sophia sputtered. "Oh, no, there was no courtship."

"Of course there was a courtship," Juliana

said, her green eyes alight with humor. "Although, knowing Reign, he was probably about as unaware of his intentions as you were."

As she noted Sophia's confusion, the young marchioness cast a hasty glance to ensure the gentlemen were not eavesdropping on the ladies' conversation before she leaned forward. "If you are under the impression that Reign married you out of some misguided notion of chivalry, I can assure you that you are wrong. Reign married you because it suited him."

Sophia thought back to Reign's response in the coach when she had asked him what he wanted in a wife.

"Faithfulness and respect. A wife who will willingly share my bed and bear my children."

Her husband had seemed to know exactly what he wanted in a wife, and that included what he did not want from her. "Perhaps, Juliana, you are right," Sophia conceded. "I confess, all of this feels strange to me."

"I am scarcely an expert on marital bliss, since I have hardly been married a year; however, let me offer you this piece of sage advice—be patient with Reign. His first marriage, well, no one likes to speak of it. Despite what the gossips say, I know he is a good man. Unfortunately, like most thickheaded males, he is set in his ways. With a little proper training and he should be a good husband."

Sophia raised her brow. "Truly? And how does your husband view this so-called training?"

Juliana brought her first finger to her lips and winked.

All three ladies laughed.

As the conversation casually switched from husbands to the recent fashions in *La Belle Assemblée*, Sophia let her thoughts drift while she stroked the gold band on her finger.

Their wedding ceremony had been brief, and if the clergyman Lord Sainthill escorted into the drawing room that afternoon had been curious about the couple's haste, the man had been well-schooled in the subtle art of discretion.

As she took in the opulence of the drawing room, Sophia had lamented about her dress. Though beautiful, if Reign had given her some warning about his plans, she would have attired herself in a dress that had possessed fewer flounces and less black brocade. Since Stephan had deprived her of Lucy's services, Sophia had been forced to slumber in what was to be her wedding dress. She was tired, bedraggled, and feared that she was less than sweet-smelling.

Her spirits plummeted further upon glimpsing Lady Sinclair and Fanny. Both were smartly attired, her dear friend Fanny in a white dress with a fancy purple embroidered border at the bottom of her skirt, while Lady Sinclair—or Juliana—was wearing a round dress of India muslin over a light peach satin slip.

Compared with the other ladies, she looked like a rook that had flown backward through a thunderstorm.

Sophia's distress had been apparent to both ladies. Before Reign could object, they had whisked her away from her self-appointed protector and taken her upstairs to one of the bedchambers. There she was stripped of her wrinkled dress, where it was given to a maid for pressing. Another maid brought her a basin of warm water, towels, and a ball of soap so she could wash her face and limbs. Once she had freshened up, Fanny took the pins out of Sophia's hair and brushed her long, blond tresses. An hour and a half later, Sophia entered the drawing room, wearing her neatly pressed dress and her hair arranged in a manner that did not remind her entirely of a rat's nest.

With approval gleaming in his dark blue eyes, Reign brought Sophia's gloved hand up to his lips and brushed a light kiss on it.

"Will you have me as your husband, Lady Sophia?" he had asked her, giving her one last chance to escape what seemed fated from their first meeting.

"I will, Lord Rainecourt," had been her reply.

They were married fifteen minutes later with the Lords of Vice, Juliana, and Fanny bearing witness to their vows.

Sophia started at the sound of clanking metal coming from the other side of the room. Fanny and Juliana had also grown silent as all three women turned their heads to find the source of the commotion.

Lord Vanewright and Lord Chillingsworth had apparently raided Reign's silver plate, for both men possessed serving trays the size of small shields and large silver spoons. The noise they made could have woken the dead.

"A toast, a bawdy boast, then take your lady to bed . . . to bed," the men chanted, and then Lord Sinclair, Lord Sainthill, Lord Hugh, and the duke of Huntsley were joining their friends.

Juliana sent Sophia an apologetic glance. "Clearly, we have left the gentlemen too long with their brandy."

Sophia's eyes widened as Reign climbed up on one of the chairs and raised his glass to her.

"A toast to my lady, gents!" He swayed slightly before finding his balance.

"To Lady Rainecourt!" Lord Hugh said, and the others echoed his words.

"Now a bawdy boast!" Lord Chillingsworth challenged, casting a sly look at Sophia.

"A boast," Reign muttered under his breath as he tried to think of something appropriate for the occasion. "My lady's lips taste as sweet as honeyed clover; be they high or low!"

He jumped down from the chair and emptied his glass.

"Ho-ho!"

"To your lady's sweet lips!" shouted all of them in turn.

The very lips her husband had just praised parted in surprise. Sophia stood as Reign and his friends approached, uncertain what she was supposed to do.

Reign delivered an exaggerated bow, and extended his hand. "To bed, my lady."

CHAPTER FOURTEEN

"My friends, my lady and I bid you a good night!"

With his friends goading him, Reign swept Sophia into his arms and tossed her over his shoulder.

"Reign!" she shrieked in protest.

"Five hours married, and already sounding like a shrew," Reign said mournfully, giving her bottom a playful smack. He strode out of the drawing room, across the hall, and toward the center staircase.

It was not surprising that the drunken merry-makers followed them into the hall. Sophia caught glimpses of white and peach, and assumed that Fanny and Juliana had joined the men.

"This is highly improper, my lord!" she said, burrowing her face into his back.

Reign realized her intentions when she nipped his skin with her teeth. The high ceilings echoed with his friends' cheers and his own laughter. His insides were warmed by the brandy he had imbibed, and the notion that the lady dangling over his shoulder belonged to him.

He affectionately rubbed her backside. "Behave yourself, Lady Rainecourt, or we will be spending our wedding night under the watchful eye of a surgeon because one of us is bound to crack our heads."

"Ho-ho. If you want an audience, Frost and I will volunteer!" Vane shouted as he raised his glass in their honor. "We are not squeamish."

A disagreeable noise rumbled in Frost's throat. "Speak for yourself. I, for one, have no desire to see Reign's hairy, bare arse!"

"The feeling is mutual, Frost," Reign called out over his shoulder.

"I say, another toast . . . to Lady Rainecourt's lovely ankles," Saint declared, beckoning everyone to raise their glasses.

"To Lady Rainecourt's ankles!" Dare seconded, and everyone, including the ladies, echoed the toast to his countess's perfect ankles.

"Good heavens, Reign," Sophia said, her embarrassment increasing with each toast. "First my lips, now my ankles . . . I am showing an indecent amount of leg if your friends are commenting on my ankles."

His sheltered bride was unused to the frank appreciation of his friends, and he found her innocence charming. "My friends mean no disrespect. And truthfully, you do have very lovely ankles, my dear."

"Oh, you are all impossible!" she said, or

something close to that remark. It was difficult to tell with her voice muffled by his frock coat.

Once Reign reached the top of the stairs, he strode down a passageway and nodded to the two maids leaving the bedchamber he had ordered the servants to prepare for his new bride.

"It appears that Lady Rainecourt will not require your assistance, after all," Reign said, giving both young maids a jaunty wink. "You both may retire for the evening."

"Aye, milord," they said in unison, curtsying as the couple walked by them. "Good tidings to both you and your new bride."

"Reign, you have had your fun. Set me down at once!"

He grinned at her surly tone. "Be patient, Sophia. I am yours to command."

His outrageous remark was overheard by the maids. He and Sophia could hear their giggles as they vanished around the corner.

His valet had anticipated Reign's arrival and opened the door. "Good evening, Lord Rainecourt . . . Lady Rainecourt."

Reign had originally planned to retire to his bedchamber to give his bride some time alone as she prepared for her wedding night. He had done the same for Beatrice, and it had been a miserable night for both of them. She had come to her marriage bed reluctantly, and had cried at what she had described as his awkward fumbling. He had left her bed bitter and unsatisfied.

He refused to make the same mistakes with Sophia.

"Fellows, you may retire for the evening." Reign slowly allowed Sophia to slide down the front length of his body until her feet touched the floor. He ignored the peevish look she shot him as she shook out her rumpled skirt. "Lady Rainecourt will see to my needs."

"Very well, milord," Fellows said cheerfully. "Good evening to you both."

Sophia whirled around and stabbed her finger into his chest. "Honestly, Reign, was that truly necessary?"

Reign gave her an unrepentant grin. "I thought every young lady dreams of being swept off her feet by a gallant gentleman?"

Sophia crossed her arms over her breasts. She was pretending to be vexed by his actions, but she could not conceal the spark of humor in her eyes. "You tossed me over your shoulder as if I were a sack of grain and provided the opportunity for your mischievous cohorts to ogle my ankles on our ascent. This is not the stuff of romance, you annoying man!"

Sophia swung her fist at him and missed. Reign spun her and tugged her slender back against his chest. "Admit it. You like my friends."

She leaned her head back against him. "Yes."

Reign kissed the top of her head. "And they like you."

None of his friends had approved of Beatrice.

He winced at the unbidden comparison. It seemed unfair to both women.

"Is it important?" Sophia asked, staring straight ahead as he rocked her slowly in his embrace.

"They are my family," he said simply.

Sophia nodded. "Then I shall think of them as brothers."

Her quiet acceptance humbled Reign. Her dire circumstances with her brother had forced her into a marriage that she had not wanted, and yet Sophia was not one to bemoan her fate. She was willing to accept Reign into her life and into her bed.

For the first time in his adult life, he stared at his bed with apprehension. How does one go about seducing one's wife? There had been other ladies in his life since his wife's death; a steady stream of mistresses to prove to himself that his failings with Beatrice could be blamed on youth and inexperience.

Sophia had taken a great risk in marrying him, and Reign did not want her to come to regret her hasty decision.

"Are you nervous?" he murmured, idly stroking his fingers down her right arm.

"Yes." Sophia turned in his embrace and concentrated on his face. His answer seemed important to her. "Are you?"

Sophia mentally cringed at her ridiculous question. Reign was a man of the world. He had been married once and had known loss. Why would he be anxious on his wedding night? After his wife's death, he had probably bedded dozens of mistresses. Hundreds. It had been a foolish thing to blurt—

"Yes."

Her eyes widened at his quiet admission.

"You seem surprised." His hand lightly caressed her cheek. "I do not have much experience with innocents. After . . . well, it just seemed best to avoid them. I want to please you."

Her heart skipped a beat, and then raced at his words. "Then you will," she said, smiling brilliantly up at him.

Sophia stepped out of Reign's embrace and offered her back to him. Although her knowledge of what transpired between lovers was sketchy at best, even she knew her dress would no longer be required.

She shyly glanced over her shoulder. "Since you dismissed the maids, you will have to assist me."

Reign teased the tiny curl at the nape of her neck with his finger. "Are you eager to sample the delights of our marriage bed?"

Sophia brought her hand to her throat as she considered the question. "I must admit that intellectually I am curious to separate truth from exaggeration. I have been told that there will be pain."

And blood, she thought with a delicate shiver.

Reign unfastened her necklace, and the heavy links slipped into her hand. Sophia could feel the weight of his stare as his gaze dropped to the buttons on her dress. "When a lady takes a lover for the first time, some discomfort is unavoidable. Nevertheless, I would rather leave you a virgin than to have you fear my touch."

Sophia suspected her new husband was grimly dwelling on the unwelcome specters of his past. She had learned enough from others that Reign's marriage to Beatrice was an unhappy affair, long before her unfortunate accident. Would the lady always stand between her and Reign?

"You have been nothing but kind to me," she said tenderly, suddenly understanding that he expected her to reject him now that she had secured his protection and was safe from her brother's influence. "I trust you, husband."

Reign buried his face into the hollow of her shoulder and inhaled the floral scent she had applied as she dressed for her wedding. "Then you are more innocent than I could have ever guessed."

Before Sophia could question Reign on his meaning, he had moved away from her and opened the door. "It was thoughtless of me to rush you into bed. I will send Sin's wife to you. She will know what needs to be said."

Reign was leaving her. Dread fluttered in her stomach as she took several careful steps toward the door. "My lord—Reign, have I offended you?

If so, please forgive me. It was not my intention."
Without her walking stick, she felt vulnerable in
the unfamiliar room.

"Wait for Juliana."

He shut the door, ending the discussion.

Sophia blinked, perplexed by what had driven
her husband out of the bedchamber. Reaching
out to steady her gait, she slowly walked to the
empty bed. She placed her palm on the dark green
velvet covering and sat down.

Perhaps Lady Sinclair could provide some insight on how she had ruined her wedding night.

CHAPTER FIFTEEN

Sophia raised her bowed head at the soft knock on the door.

"Sophia?" Juliana entreated from the other side. She paused for a response. "May I enter?"

Without waiting for a reply, Juliana opened the door and poked her head in. The marchioness sighed as she noted Sophia's miserable expression. "Husbands can be a trial," she said, her soothing voice laced with sympathy. "Most wait until they have had their pleasure. Leave it to Reign to be a most unusual husband."

Sophia burst into tears.

Juliana strode purposely to Sophia's side and embraced her.

Unsettled nerves and disappointments are often best settled with a good cry.

"Where is Lady Fanny?" Reign asked, filling his glass with a generous portion of brandy. From the corner of his eye, he noticed that Vane had succumbed to his overindulging. Facedown, he was sprawled out on one of the sofas. His raspy snores filled the awkward silence in the drawing room.

"Saint offered to escort her home shortly after you carried your bride upstairs," Dare said, his arms crossed and resting on his chest.

"Speaking of your bride," Sin said, pointedly raising his gaze heavenward. "Why are you here, and my wife upstairs?"

Frost snickered as he straddled a chair. "No steel in his velvet sword, I wager."

Reign choked on the brandy he had swallowed. He grimaced and wiped his mouth with the back of his hand. "Stifle it, Frost. I am in no mood for your vulgarity and insinuations."

Sensing that the two friends could come to blows, Dare and Hunter positioned themselves in front of Reign.

"Insinuations?" Frost said, sniffing at the word. "I thought I was being rather obvious. Perhaps your cock prefers poking whores instead of virtuous deeds."

"Frost," Sin said, his tone clearly a warning.

Oblivious to the danger, Frost folded his hands on the back of the chair and then used them to prop up his chin. "I mean no offense, Reign. Truly. Lady Sophia is a lovely prize for a gent set on marriage. While some poor-spirited gentleman might view her damaged eyes as a flaw—"

"Arse," Dare muttered, stepping away from Reign.

"Dimwit," Hunter concurred.

Both gentlemen parted, content to leave Frost in the dank hole he was digging for himself.

"I believe a lady who by her very nature can turn a blind eye to her husband's affairs is by far an asset, in my opinion," he added in his typically candid manner.

"Did your mother drop you on your head, Frost?" Dare asked, his brows raised. "It would explain your idiocy."

"More like a death wish," Sin said, shooting Frost a menacing look. "Enough."

Frost straightened his spine as his hands parted in exasperation. "What? For speaking the truth? Bollocks! Beatrice almost ruined our friend. Forgive me for expressing some concern when Reign loses his head and marries a chit to keep her brother from selling her to a scoundrel." He stood as his indignation increased. "What prompted such insanity? Did you think sacrificing your life would cleanse your soul for murdering that duplicitous bitch of a countess?"

Reign slammed his glass down on the sideboard. "You go too far," he said, shaking his head. "Beatrice has nothing to do with this."

"Christ," someone muttered.

His friends never spoke of Beatrice or their suspicions that he had killed her in a drunken rage. Frost had crossed the line by dragging his dead wife into the conversation.

Reign took a threatening step toward Frost. "Although it is no business of yours, I married

Sophia because it suited me to do so. I wanted her. Her brothers' stupidity dropped her neatly into my hands and I took advantage of the situation."

"You did not have to marry the chit to save her," Frost argued. "You could have bought her a little house and a maid to keep her from tripping over the bloody furniture. With some coaxing, even a penniless virgin would have learned her place, and parted her thighs for the Devil of Rainecourt! Hell, I would have fu—"

Reign rammed his clenched fist into Frost's jaw, ruthlessly ending the conversation.

"Feel better?"

Sophia smiled and nodded. "You have been very kind, Juliana. I feel like a fool for crying all over your beautiful dress."

Thankfully, Sophia's tears had been fierce, yet brief. After she had sobbed out her frustration with Reign, her new friend had acted as her personal maid. The marchioness had helped Sophia undress so that only her chemise remained to protect her modesty and had tucked her into Reign's bed as if she were a child. Together they had removed the pins from Sophia's hair.

"Nonsense. I am glad Reign asked me to join you while he was called away." Juliana retrieved small tortoiseshell comb from her reticule and returned to the bed. Settling in next to her, Juliana set about smoothing Sophia's tangled blond tresses.

Sophia gave Juliana a wry look. "Reign was not called away. He practically ran out of the room."

"I do not mean to pry—well, maybe I do," Juliana hastily amended. "Can you tell me what happened?"

A soft hiccup escaped Sophia's parted lips. "I confess, I am as bewildered as you. When we spoke of the discomfort of—of . . ." She trailed off, unable to speak of intimacy.

Fortunately, the very married Juliana understood. "Ah, yes. Well, that is a disconcerting subject for most gentlemen."

"No, that was not what upset him," Sophia said, closing her eyes. She found Juliana's gentle strokes with the comb soothing. "I told him that I trusted him, and he accused me of being too innocent." Her eyes snapped open. "Honestly, how can one be *too* innocent? One is either innocent or one is not."

Juliana paused midstroke. "Men are complicated beasts." She resumed her tender ministrations. "I highly doubt Reign would appreciate us gossiping about his past. Nevertheless, I am certain you have heard the rumors."

"I know the *ton* believes Reign murdered his wife," Sophia said cautiously. "I do not believe it."

"Neither do I," Juliana said staunchly, increasing Sophia's respect for the marchioness. "Still, others believe he had good reason to murder the lady, and there are those who keep the scandal alive."

Lord and Lady Burrard.

Satisfied with her efforts, Juliana gave Sophia's hair an affectionate stroke with her fingers and laid the comb in her lap. "According to Sin, this was not the first scandal Reign has endured."

"You speak of his father's death—and my parents'," Sophia said bluntly.

Even before she had met him at Lord and Lady Harper's ball, her life and Reign's had been entwined by murder and scandal.

"And his mother's suicide," Juliana reminded her. "Reign has lived in the shadow of speculation and scandal for so long, it is a part of him. He knows no other way to live."

"I have not asked him to change."

"Of course not. You possess too much intelligence to waste your time on a fool's endeavor," Juliana said, clasping Sophia's hand in a gesture to reassure her. "However, like my Sin, Reign has many admirable traits. Both of them are honorable gentlemen. I cannot speak for Reign, but I would not be surprised if he concluded that he is unworthy of you."

"What rubbish!" Sophia sputtered.

The bed bounced slightly as Juliana shrugged. "He has pulled an innocent into his dark world. An honorable gentleman might belatedly question his selfish decision."

"Reign was not selfish," Sophia protested. "I do not expect you to understand. He spared me from being sold off like the rest of my family's possessions."

Juliana's grip on Sophia's hand tightened. "I understand the horror of what your brothers put you through more than you know, but we will put that sad tale aside for another day."

Juliana was merely attempting to assuage Sophia's humiliation. Good grief, the lady was the Marchioness of Sinclair. She was beautiful, articulate, and she had married well. What could they possibly have in common?

"Sophia?"

She and Juliana had been so immersed in their conversation, they had not noticed that Reign had returned to the bedchamber. There were some notable changes in her husband's appearance. In his absence, he had discarded his coat and waistcoat. The tails of his linen shirt had been pulled out of his trousers, and the perfect folds of his cravat had been undone. Even his dark hair was in disarray as if he had been scrubbing his scalp with his fingers.

"I was concerned, my lord. Is all well with you?" Sophia inquired demurely.

"I am fine."

Juliana slipped off the bed and crossed the room to Reign. Sophia lifted the covering to join them, but quickly realized that all that she wore was a chemise.

"And my husband; is he fine as well?" Juliana asked, stuffing her comb into her reticule.

Reign casually braced his arm against the open door. "Sin is in good health. He and the others are helping Frost into his coach."

From the bed, Sophia asked, "Is Lord Chillingsworth ill?"

"Do not fret, my lady," her husband said, seemingly unconcerned about his friend. "Frost is merely paying for his numerous sins."

Juliana nodded, her gaze meeting Reign's as she completed her task. "Alexius has often told me that Frost has an unfortunate habit of speaking before good sense has a chance to catch up with his tongue. It is often a painful lesson to learn."

"I did my best," Reign said, showing plenty of teeth.

Juliana's eyes crinkled in merriment. "I would imagine so." She walked back to the bed and impulsively gave Sophia a quick hug. "When you have settled, I hope you will think of calling on our household. If it is possible, I will introduce you to my sisters."

Sophia smiled at the marchioness's generous offer. "Thank you. I would enjoy such a visit."

"Your friend Fanny is welcome, too." She waved farewell as she walked to the door.

Reign stepped aside and widened the opening for the marchioness. "You also have my gratitude, Juliana," he said, clasping her hand and bowing. "Thank you for staying with Sophia."

Juliana brushed her fingers against his cheek in a loving gesture. "My pleasure. You did well for yourself, Reign. Take care of her."

"I will."

He shut the door and twisted the lock.

Sophia glanced pensively at her discarded dress,

her petticoat, and the corset that Juliana had laid over the back of one of the chairs. Reign walked over to the table and extinguished the lamp. Next, he crouched in front of the small hearth and tended the glowing coals.

The silence that stretched out between them as her husband went about the mundane tasks was straining her nerves. "My lord—Reign?"

"Yes, Sophia."

He seemed content to linger at the hearth. "Juliana insisted that I undress and rest during your, uh, absence," she said, in an attempt to explain why she had climbed into his bed without his permission. "The hour grows late. Would you mind terribly if I asked you to escort me to my bedchamber?"

Reign straightened and slowly turned to face her. "I would, actually." At her blank expression, he said, "Mind terribly, that is." He seized the ends of his shirt and pulled it over his head as he approached the bed.

Sophia's lips parted in amazement as her ruined eyesight gave her intriguing glimpses of Reign's bare chest. He carelessly tossed his shirt over her garments on the chair.

"You belong in my bed."

CHAPTER SIXTEEN

Reign was encouraged when his new bride did not begin shrieking at his brazen declaration. After he had rushed her into marriage, and then by all appearances had abandoned her on her wedding night, it was not unrealistic to assume that his bride had spent the past hour and a half contemplating the notion of having their marriage annulled.

"All of this must be awkward for you," Sophia said, clutching the edges of the sheet that covered her bare legs.

What the devil had Juliana and Sophia discussed in his absence?

Reign gave her a wary glance before he sat down on the edge of the bed. Leaning forward, he concentrated on the task of removing his boots. "No more or less than it is for you, I would wager," he said, dropping, in turn, each boot onto the floor.

Her eyes cast downward, Sophia smoothed

the edges of the sheet in a nervous gesture. "The night I first met you, someone explained the origin of your nickname. He—I was told that it had something to do with a vow you had once made."

Reign's jaw tightened with annoyance. Of course she had heard the rumors. "Since my nickname is simply a variation on my title, the conversation must have been short and rather boring."

With unexpected stubbornness, she persisted, "You once boasted to a crowded ballroom that you would rather reign in the lowest bowels of hell than bind yourself to another lady."

Reign's hand curled into an impotent fist on his thigh. He had been bitter about his marriage to Beatrice, and more than a little drunk the night he had silenced the ballroom with his derisive statement. At the time, he had embraced the declaration as a vow.

"That was many years ago. Besides, my friends were calling me Reign long before my marriage to Beatrice."

Sophia tucked an errant strand of hair from her cheek. "I forced you to break your vow, did I not?" She gave him an anguished glance. "And now you regret it. Am I responsible for you having to put Lord Chillingsworth in his coach, too?"

The soft breathy catch in her voice spurred Reign into action. He refused to endure another wedding night in which he helplessly watched his bride sob out her regrets in their marriage bed. Sophia gasped as he crawled across the mattress and pulled her from the warm confines of the bedding.

"My lord—Reign," she began.

"Pay attention," Reign said, giving her a slight shake. Her startled blue-green eyes locked onto his face. He held her close, savoring how the gentle swell of her breasts flattened against his bare chest. "I made that drunken boast long ago. It is no secret that my first marriage was not a happy pairing. The entire affair left me embittered, and I was determined not to embrace such a blunder again."

"I understand."

"Not likely," he muttered under his breath. "If a vow was broken, it was mine to break."

"And Lord Chillingsworth?"

Reign was not going to reveal Frost's true feelings about the couple's marriage. Sophia was already skittish and likely seeking reasons to refuse him. "The man bedevils everyone. I usually ignore him, until it is impossible to do so."

Still skeptical, Sophia raised one delicate eyebrow. "This evening was one such night?"

"Exactly."

Reign lightly stroked her long blond hair. Sophia grew still in his arms, but did not cringe away from him. It was the first time he had ever seen her glossy tresses unbound, and he took a moment to appreciate its beauty. Her hair was longer than he had guessed, the ends curling teasingly at the lady's elbows. He cupped one of the curls in his hand and marveled that such a magnificent bounty was as light as a plume. The texture reminded him of the finest silk.

"My God, you are beautiful," Reign murmured, his hand reverently brushing her silken hair aside until it settled down her back.

Sophia shivered as his fingertips delicately scraped the bared flesh at her shoulder. "You are generous in your praise, my lord."

She was lovely and guileless, and unlike the ladies he usually consorted with when he ventured from his lands. "I cannot decide if it was carelessness on your brothers' part or a bloody miracle that some gent did not carry you off to a vicar during your first season in London."

"The first year my brothers deemed me old enough, a chill settled into my chest on the journey to London," she confessed, hesitating when Reign slid the chemise lower and exposed more of her shoulder. "I-I had to endure a month in bed. By then, Henry was responsible for some unfortunate incident and the entire family was obliged to return to the country."

"And the following year?"

Sophia sighed.

Reign's temper flared to life on her behalf. Her brothers were not only reckless, they were cruel. Stephan, in particular, sparked Reign's ire. In some ways, young Ravenshaw reminded Reign of his callous sire.

"Carelessness, then," he said, nuzzling her temple with his chin.

The gesture was intended to be soothing, a balm for the ills wrought by her brothers. Nevertheless, Reign felt the muscles in his abdomen tense as the desire to claim his bride could no longer be ignored.

"Stephan and Henry—" she began.

"Will be dealt with, I promise you," Reign said flatly. "However, I do not wish to bring your brothers into our bed."

Sophia blushed. "Oh. You are quite right."

"I can think of more pressing issues," Reign said, circling her left nipple with his finger. The sensitive nubbin puckered in response.

"Such as?"

"Kissing my bride."

Reign lowered his head, brushing his lips against hers.

After Reign's scuffle with Frost downstairs, Sophia was bemused by the gentleness of Reign's kiss. His tenderness seemed at odds with his size and temperament, and it added an intriguing facet to her husband's character. With her eyes closed, Sophia concentrated on the tantalizing contact of his firm lips moving leisurely over hers. The sensation was almost unbearable. No man had ever kissed her in such a manner!

The ground was spinning beneath her. Sophia swayed in his embrace and grabbed his upper arms to keep from falling. The warm, bare masculine flesh reminded her that he had removed his shirt.

Startled, she hastily released Reign, but he slid his left hand to the small of her back to anchor her.

"You can touch me, wife," Reign said, sounding amused. "I like being petted."

With his right hand, he took her left hand and brought it up to his lips. She felt the tingling effects of that kiss all the way to her toes. He brought her hand up until her fingers curved around his neck.

"Now place the other on my chest," he instructed.

Sophia tentatively complied. Beneath her fingers and palm, she savored the differences between them. He was well formed and muscular, she mused, as her fingers danced lightly over the thatch of crisp hairs that bisected his chest.

"You are marvelously warm, my lord," she said, pausing in her exploration to let his internal heat sink into her palm. "Is it the brandy?"

"No, it is you." He brought Sophia's hand to his cheek. "You make me burn, my lady. Forgive me, but I cannot wait."

Reign's hands moved brazenly to her thighs. Before she could guess his intentions, he grasped the hem of her chemise and pulled the thin linen garment over her head.

"Reign!" she gasped, crossing her arms over her breasts.

He inched forward on his knees, not allowing her to retreat. "Seems only fair since you are fondling my chest."

Sophia sputtered a wordless denial. "I was

not fondling your chest." *Exactly*. "You were the one who placed my hand there!"

His rich laughter filled the room, warming her almost as thoroughly as his body had. "My outraged little innocent. How can I resist you?"

Reign lifted her into his arms as if she weighed no more than her discarded chemise and kissed her. Using his mouth, he silently coaxed her to respond. Sophia did not want to disappoint her new husband. Regardless, all of this was too new. Her brothers would have quietly murdered her if she had dared to allow a gentleman such liberties.

But Reign had earned the right to touch her so boldly. It seemed shameful to admit it, even to herself, but she was not a reluctant participant in his lovemaking. The Earl of Rainecourt fascinated her, and had from their first meeting. She was drawn to the low, soothing cadence of his voice, his intelligence, and the manner in which he treated her. Some people treated her like a child because of the limitations placed upon her by her fractured eyesight. Reign saw only the woman.

Sophia wanted to be worthy of his esteem and sacrifice.

She was breathless when Reign ended the kiss. "Should I not be doing . . . something?" she asked, making a small approving sound as her husband's lips trailed down to the side of her neck.

Reign cupped her breast and rubbed her nipple with his thumb. The small nubbin of flesh puckered and swelled at his caress. "You are.

Your body is so exquisitely responsive." His hand slid lower, following the natural curve of her waist to her hips. "So perfect."

Sophia inhaled sharply at a wet, decisive flick of Reign's tongue over her nipple. Instinctively, she tried to rise up from her prone position, but his hand on her shoulder held her in place. She reached for him, threading her fingers into his hair as he suckled at one breast and then the other. Pleasure shot through her like shooting stars.

"You liked that, did you not?" he said, very pleased with himself.

"It seems awfully wicked."

Reign raised his head, and she glimpsed a knowing gleam in his dark blue eyes before the shifting shadows obscured his masculine beauty. "Oh, my sweet innocent, I have yet to demonstrate the full measure of my wickedness."

To demonstrate, Reign slid down her body and settled between her thighs. Without giving her any warning of his intentions, he parted the intimate folds of her femininity and kissed her in the most carnal fashion.

"Good heavens!" she exclaimed, her hands splayed out on the mattress for support. "You cannot . . . you should not . . . oh!"

Speechless, Sophia fell back against the pillow. Reign was correct. His wickedness exceeded her limited experience and vast imagination. The man skillfully found every sensitive spot on her body and exploited it. With his hands gripping her hips, he suckled and licked the tender flesh between the fleshy folds until she was gasping.

"I like the taste of you, Sophia," Reign said, nibbling her inner thigh. She expected him to resume his delightful torment, but he surprised her. Instead, he sat up on his knees, and his hands went to his waist. It was then that Sophia realized that he was preparing to remove his trousers.

She rolled onto her side as Reign undressed. He quickly stripped out of his trousers and linen drawers. Offering his profile, she admired his muscular buttock as he leaned over to untie the garters to his stockings. He straightened, and even his profile could not conceal his arousal.

"Like what you see?"

Sophia gave him an owlish blink when Reign faced her and moved closer to the edge of the mattress. The man was entirely comfortable with his nakedness and her scrutiny.

"Yes." Sophia reached out and captured his thick manhood. The heat and velvet smoothness was a revelation. The size of him gave her a moment of concern. She nibbled on her lower lip. "Do you think you will fit?"

Her husband groaned in response, and moved against her hand. "Ah, Sophia, you sorely test a man's restraint. Do not fret, sweet, I will fit."

Reign gently disengaged her hand and crawled onto the bed until he had caged her with his body. He kissed her reverently as if to soothe her for what was to come next, as the blunt head of his manhood pushed restlessly against the nest of curls between her legs. Bracing his weight with one hand, Reign circled his fingers around his arousal and guided the rigid length to the dewy depths of her womanly folds.

Sophia gasped as she felt his thick arousal press against her.

"Am I hurting you?" Reign asked grimly, his face an expressionless mask.

"No," she replied, uncertain if she was telling him the truth.

Reign moved against her, using the wetness to ease himself deeper. Sophia gripped his forearms as she squirmed against his persistent onslaught. He was murmuring soft words of encouragement, but she barely heard them. Sophia was wholly focused on the tightness building within her. Her body was warming and opening for him, and the ebb and flow of Reign's short thrusts were stretching her to the point of discomfort.

"Reign?"

Her husband knew her body better than she did. With clenched teeth, he suddenly surged upward and breached her maidenhead with a single thrust. Buried deep inside her womanly sheath, Reign held himself still.

He kissed the damp tracks left by her tears. "You have survived the worst, my dear Sophia. Only pleasure from this moment onward."

Sophia was not feeling as optimistic. His initial intrusion was almost unbearable. It was simple to deduce that the poets had lied about the beauty of lovemaking. As the minutes ticked by, her body seemed to relax and accept her husband's intimate invasion. So much so, Sophia was prepared to reevaluate her opinion on the matter.

"Pleasure, you say?"

Reign chuckled softly and kissed her on the forehead. He moved his hips against her, proving that her body would accept him. Sophia gasped at the ease with which his manhood slid in and out of her sheath. She brought her left knee up in a restless gesture.

"Is there more?"

He shook his head in disbelief. "Are you trying to kill me, woman?"

Sophia giggled in the face of his mock outrage. "Is that even possible?"

Reign bit her earlobe. "Hmm . . . dying from pleasure? It sounds like a tempting challenge. God knows, I have risked my life for less worthy causes."

Before Sophia could question Reign on specific details, he quickened his thrusts and her questions scattered from her thoughts as a tingling heat steadily began to build within her. She shut her eyes, letting her skin, nose, and ears make up for her flawed vision.

Reign had the innate ability to engage her on all levels. Oh, she was wholly aware of his thick manhood as he pummeled into her, branding her as his alone. His dogged determination to claim her could not be ignored. Still, as she arched her pelvis, meeting his exquisite thrusts, her body slowly awakened to his sensual onslaught.

The earthy scents of their lovemaking filled her nostrils. She buried her nose into the hollow of his shoulder, savoring the masculine fragrance that she identified as Reign. Their joining had mingled their unique essences, and the results were intoxicating as a full-bodied wine. Sophia arched her spine in sheer delight and Reign growled his approval.

He captured one of her breasts in his hand and squeezed the curvy, pliant flesh. There were calluses on his palms and fingers, something Sophia had not expected from a gentleman. There was more to Reign than the reckless rake facade that he presented to polite society, she silently mused, but it was swiftly forgotten as he brought her breast to his mouth.

Reign's tongue laved her swollen nipple several times. Sophia moaned in response and twisted in his arms.

"You taste divine, sweet wife."

His greedy lips covered over her nipple as his clever tongue undulated against the tender flesh. The pleasure of his suckling was as acute as it was devastating in its carnal assault to her senses. Reign switched to her other breast, ruthlessly determined to inflame every part of her body. His hands seemed to be everywhere at once, touching her face, the curve of her shoulders, her buttocks, and then pressing against the nest of hair between her legs.

Something was happening to her. Reign seemed to sense the peculiar tension constricting every muscle in her body because his breathing had changed. His hot breath reminded Sophia of a stallion pushed beyond its limits.

"Do not fight it!" Reign growled in her ear.

What does he think I am fighting? Sophia thought mindlessly. She was not fighting anything or anyone. Pinned to the mattress with the weight of Reign's body, she trembled and tried to meet each thunderous thrust as his manhood renewed its claim again and again.

Then suddenly . . .

Every feeling that seemed to be spinning out of control reversed its outward spiral and collapsed upon itself like an imploding sun.

"Reign!"

Sophia slammed the back of her head against the pillow and cried out as the darkness beneath her eyelids went white, reminding her of a flash of lightning on the horizon. The sensitive flesh between her thighs rippled with each of Reign's frantic thrusts.

Perhaps a person could die from pleasure!

Reign groped for her buttocks and pulled her tightly against him. Sophia's eyes fluttered open at his clumsy roughness. His eyes were shut and his teeth were clenched as if he was anticipating a wave of unbearable agony. The breath Reign was holding burst from his lungs, and the skillful strokes he had used to evoke passion within her disintegrated into blind lust. Reign gave a hoarse shout, and collapsed against Sophia as his strength abandoned him. Deep within her sheath, she felt

Reign's manhood bump and thicken against her womb as his hot seed pumped into her.

Sophia quietly held Reign while his breathing returned to normal. She grinned as a thought occurred to her. Whereas Reign had laid claim to her by taking her innocence, his loss of control at the end had unequivocally made him hers.

CHAPTER SEVENTEEN

It was with some reluctance that Reign stirred, peeled his damp cheek from Sophia's shoulder. Replete from their lovemaking, he could have happily slumbered where he lay, but he doubted his new wife was as comfortable.

Sophia made a faint protesting sound as Reign eased his softening cock from her snug channel. A twinge of guilt jabbed him in the gut as he realized that he had hurt Sophia. The pain had been unavoidable, he silently rationalized, but he did not want his new wife to think of him as a brutish savage.

After the debacle with Beatrice, he had avoided virgins for precisely this reason. A lady's innocence carried too many complications. What he had sought out after Beatrice's death were ladies of experience. Skilled lovers who understood the need for mutual satisfaction and required nothing more from him than an entertaining evening and perhaps a trinket or two as a gesture of his appreciation.

"Are you leaving me?"

Reign frowned at the fear infused into her question. He stood, not bothering to hide his nudity from her. "The room is too cold. I thought to add some coal to the dying embers." He had another reason for climbing out of his warm bed, but he saw no reason to panic his lady.

Sophia drew the sheet over her breasts as she sat up. She had a rather odd forthright manner of staring at him that was unexpected from a lady. Reign attributed it to her poor eyesight, but there were times when it was damn unsettling. A superstitious gent might have thought that Sophia possessed the uncanny ability to see beyond a man's flesh, muscle, and bone. It was as if she were attempting to peer into his soul.

If he had one, Reign mused, he was certain it had been tarnished long ago by past sins.

An awkward silence filled the room while he went about the task of tending the coals in the small fireplace. It was cold enough to shrivel a man's cock, but glancing discreetly downward, he discovered that his own was immune to the chill. It was a revelation that he was still semi-erect even after satisfying himself so thoroughly within Sophia's slick, tight channel.

Reign set side the small shovel, idly wondering if Sophia would think him a beast for demanding his husbandly rights twice in one evening.

"There," he said, standing. "In time, the room should be warmer."

"With you beside me, I had not noticed the chill, my lord," she said shyly.

He walked over to the opposite wall to a small table. "Reign," he said absently as he picked up a Staffordshire jug and poured water into its matching shallow basin.

"I beg your pardon?"

Reign shot her an irritated look, but he was too far away for her to notice. He plunged his hands into the water and scrubbed the coal dust from his hands. "I have spent the good part of an hour pumping myself between your luscious thighs, Sophia. Marriage and intimacy gives you the right to call me by my given name." He plucked a small towel from the table and wiped the moisture from his hands.

Sophia hugged her knees to her chest. The shadowed interior of the bedchamber made it impossible for him to see if his frank language had caused her to blush. "Yes, of course, my lord. Forgive me. Uh, I—Reign."

He tossed aside the small towel and selected another. "An apology is unnecessary, my dear," he said, feeling indulgent. He stuffed the towel into the jug and paused. "This marriage is foreign to both of us, and allowances must be made."

"Of course, Reign," she said meekly.

Reign snorted. Sophia, he was discovering, was anything but the meek creature she was pretending to be. He retrieved the towel and squeezed the excess water into the basin. With the wet towel dangling from his fingers, he returned to the bed.

Sophia slipped lower under the bedding. "Is that for me?" she asked, preferring to stare at his hand rather than his misbehaving cock.

"Yes."

She wrinkled her nose. "I am not weak-spirited, Reign, or prone to a fit of vapors. I do not need a damp cloth for my head to recover from our lovemaking."

"Indeed?" His mouth quirked in amusement. Perhaps his bride was as eager as he was to sample the carnal delights of their marriage bed again. "The towel, however, is not for your head."

Her brow puckered in bewilderment. "Is it for you?"

Reign laughed at the absurd notion. "No." He ignored her squeak of surprise as he pulled the sheet from her grasp and exposed her naked body. "The towel is to ease your soreness."

Sophia's face turned pink. "There is no need, my lord . . ."

"Oh, I insist, my lady," he said, thoroughly enjoying himself.

Reign sat on the edge of the mattress beside her. His cock twitched and lengthened against his thigh. There was little he could do about his arousal. Being in Sophia's presence tended to bring out the beast in him. "Be a good girl and part your legs for me."

"This seems outrageous." In a petulant manner, she straightened her legs and parted them as he had requested.

His jaw clenched. "I hurt you, Sophia," Reign said, his humor fading when he noticed the smear of blood on her upper thigh. "Let me take care of you."

Reign pressed the towel against her womanly cleft. Sophia sucked in her breath as the cool wetness caressed the sensitive flesh. "Does that hurt?"

"No," she denied, shaking her head. "Reign, you did not hurt me."

She was being too generous.

"There is blood on your thigh, Sophia."

Reign removed the evidence with a swipe of the towel. "I have little experience with virgins," he said in a rush of unexpected frustration.

Sophia covered his hand to still his gentle caressing strokes. "And I have little experience with husbands. Nevertheless, we both survived."

Reign gave her a suspicious glance. "Are you mocking me, wife?"

Her half smile confirmed it. "A little, perhaps. Is that terribly wicked of me?"

"Yes." Reign dropped the small towel, and lunged forward, caging her with his lean body. They were both acutely aware that the side of his rigid cock was resting against the nest of curls between her thighs. He bowed his head, letting their foreheads meet. "Teasing me has consequences, Sophia. Are you prepared to pay the price?"

Reign shifted his position so the head of his cock nestled in the opening of her sheath. Her body responded, coating his head and shaft, which deepened the penetration. All he wanted to do was thrust until she cried out his name again in pleasure.

Still, he waited.

Sophia wiggled as she pondered his question. The small movement brought him one inch closer to madness.

"Hmm . . ."

"Sophia?"

His wife was determined to torment him with her newly found power over him. If he was wise, Reign mused, he would nip this outrageous behavior before Sophia deduced that she could keep him out of her bed.

Sophia tilted her chin upwardly in a smug fashion and smiled at him. "Yes, my lord, I believe I am willing to pay the price." She wrapped her hands around the nape of his neck and pulled his mouth to hers.

Reign did not need any further encouragement. Such outrageous behavior should be rewarded.

CHAPTER EIGHTEEN

Sophia awoke at the sound of the maid opening the curtains. She winced at the sunlight streaming in and turned her face away. There was a soreness between her legs that was not unexpected, considering how many times her husband had reached for her throughout the night. She lifted her head and glanced at the other side of the bed. It was empty.

Reign had left her.

"Good morning, Lady Rainecourt," the servant said cheerfully.

"Good morning," Sophia echoed, unable to conceal her uncertainty. She sat up, and then quickly fumbled for the sheet when she recalled that she was naked.

"My name is Hannah, milady," the maid said, moving about the room with the enthusiasm of two people. "Lord Rainecourt sent me to you. He said that you would be needing a personal maid, since you were unable to bring your own, and thought I would do in a pinch. That is, with your approval, milady."

"Where—" Sophia cleared her throat. "Where is my husband?"

Reign must have warned Hannah about his new wife's ruined vision. The maid approached Sophia and stopped directly in front of her.

"His lordship is in the study, milady, attending to business."

She rubbed her eyes and peered at the servant. Hannah was young. Sixteen would be Sophia's guess. The girl barely had enough meat on her bones to be considered thin, but she was tidy and eager. Sophia prayed the maid was patient, too.

Sophia placed her hand over her grumbling stomach. "Has Lord Rainecourt had his breakfast?"

"Aye. It is almost midday."

"Midday?" Sophia exclaimed, aghast. "I had no idea . . ."

"His lordship gave the staff strict orders not to disturb your slumber, milady," Hannah said, oblivious to her mistress's distress. "Would you prefer to have a tray brought to you or do you feel up to sitting in the breakfast room?"

Sophia struggled with indecision. She was now Lady Rainecourt and she did not know the first thing about being Reign's countess. There was more to being a wife than what had transpired during the long hours after midnight. Sophia began to fidget, belatedly realizing that she was sitting in the middle of Reign's bed. Had Hannah and the rest of the staff speculated on how Lord Rainecourt had exhausted his new bride?

"My walking stick?" Sophia blurted out in a panic. "Have you seen my walking stick?"

It had been forgotten when Reign had swept her gallantly into his arms and carried her upstairs, she realized. She was unfamiliar with the layout of the town house. How could she go downstairs to the breakfast room without her walking stick? And what of Lucy? Stephan was cruel to deny Sophia her personal maid. Lucy had been her friend and faithful companion for years. How was Sophia supposed to go about her day without Lucy's calm support?

Hannah searched the chair where Sophia's dress and undergarments had been discarded. "It isn't here, milady. But never you fret, I will have one of the footmen search the house for it."

"I just need—" Sophia's throat tightened, preventing further explanation.

The maid murmured a wordless sound that was meant to soothe as she clasped Sophia's hands into her own. "There, there, my lady. Say no more. It has been an eventful day and a half, and I expect most brides suffer a bout of nerves when they find themselves in a strange house and a new husband to manage."

Sophia smiled, her eyes bright with unshed tears. "You are too young to be so wise."

"My mum had five daughters and six sons,"

Hannah explained. "Seven of my elder siblings have married, so you are not the first bride I have seen sniffle into her handkerchief after the deed had been celebrated."

Hannah gave Sophia's hand an affectionate pat as she straightened. "I know just the thing." The maid walked across the room and opened a wardrobe. "Aye, this will suit our needs."

It was not until Hannah had returned to Sophia's side that she noticed the dark green banyan in the girl's hands. "His lordship won't mind you borrowing this so we can get you settled in your bedchamber. Now give me your arm, milady."

Sophia dutifully extended her arm. She glanced down at the sheet that she had clasped to her breasts and frowned. Lucy had always been the one to dress her. Of late, it seemed as if she was always undressing in front of strangers.

"Oh, there is no call for modesty between a maid and her mistress," Hannah said, taking the decision out of her hands. The maid skillfully plucked the sheet from Sophia's grasp, nudged her off the bed, and had Sophia's naked body covered in Reign's banyan before a single protest was uttered.

Hannah nodded, pleased with her efforts. "That particular shade of green flatters your complexion, milady," she said, gathering up Sophia's dress and undergarments. She squatted and peered under the chair to retrieve Sophia's slippers. "If I may be bold—"

Sophia bit back a smile. "Your restraint until now has been remarkable."

Unrepentant, Hannah chuckled. "My mum is to blame. More stubborn than seven mules, my da is fond of saying." She shifted the bundle of clothes to her left arm and took hold of Sophia's arm. "Once I have you settled in your bedchamber, I'll have Cook send up a tray. The breakfast room can wait another day. Several trunks arrived this morning and it would be best if you were there to supervise the unpacking."

Hannah was indeed a marvel. The awkwardness and panic Sophia had felt when she had awakened in Reign's bed had been soothed away by the maid's cheeriness and efficient manner.

"Hannah?" Sophia asked as they paused at threshold.

"Aye, milady."

"My husband was correct when he said that you would do in a pinch. However, I will need someone at my side while I learn this house and my duties as countess of Rainecourt. My eyesight is appallingly dreadful, and I confess that I will probably be more demanding than most mistresses," Sophia warned. "Do you want the position?"

Hannah squeezed Sophia's upper arm as her head bobbed vigorously. "Aye, Lady Rainecourt. I was hoping that I was making a good impression."

"I doubt anyone with your enthusiasm could make any other kind."

* * *

At the tentative knock, Reign's attention shifted from the ledger in front of him to the door of the study. "Enter."

To his great pleasure, it was Sophia's face that peeked from behind the partially opened door. He had not seen her since he had slipped from the bed early in the morning. It had taken all his restraint to leave her to her well-deserved slumber.

"Good afternoon, my lord. May I join you?" Sophia's expression revealed her uncertainty over her welcome into his private sanctuary.

Reign rose from his chair and beckoned his new bride to join him. "Please." He mentally chastised himself as he recalled Sophia's poor eyesight. She managed well enough on her own, and he admired her independent nature. However, the house and his servants were unfamiliar to her and he did not want her to be injured because he had been careless. Sophia was his, and he intended to look after her properly.

Reign crossed the expanse between them, allowing his bare hands to slide down her upper arms in a soothing and intimate gesture. He smiled as she lowered her lashes in a shy manner he found endearing.

"Did you sleep well, Lady Rainecourt?" he queried huskily.

Sophia's eyelashes fluttered open at the reminder that she was a married lady. "Y-yes, my lord," she stammered, her gaze fixed on his left shoulder. "And you?"

"How could I not after being so thoroughly exhausted by your enthusiasm for our marriage bed."

Sophia's soft, inviting lips parted in surprise. "Oh."

He had no desire to torment Sophia, so he led her over to the small sofa. "I slept well, knowing that you were safe and at my side."

Reign blinked, taken aback that he had spoken the truth. He usually preferred to sleep alone. Beatrice's pregnancy and unwelcoming temperament had kept him from his wife's bed. After her death, he had taken numerous lovers, but his interest in each lady waned when his lust had been sated. He had not lingered in their beds unless he hoped to prolong their lovemaking, and he never allowed himself to sleep with a lady.

Until Sophia, he had not permitted himself to be that vulnerable to a lady.

"Come, my dear. Please be seated," he said, sitting beside her. "It was not until this morning that I realized our marriage has deprived you of your personal maid. I hope Hannah will suffice?"

His wife nodded, though the corners of her mouth pulled downward. "Hannah was wonderfully kind and efficient, my lord. However, I miss Lucy. She has been by my side for years, and I do not know what I shall do without her."

"Then I will bring her into our household," Reign said, wanting to make her smile again.

"It is very kind of you to offer. However, Stephan knows how much Lucy means to me," she said, looking defeated. "He will refuse to give her up, just to spite me for what I have done."

Because I defied my brother and am now beyond his control.

Reign was not about to feel regret over stealing Sophia away from Ravenshaw. He and Henry were unworthy guardians. The realization that Ravenshaw would be furious by the news of Reign and Sophia's marriage made his victory sweeter.

"Do not fret, my dear Sophia," he said, removing the tear trailing down her cheek with a light kiss. "I will figure out a way for you to have your Lucy back."

"Thank you, my lord." Sophia gave him a tentative smile. "You have been so generous with me. I do not know how to pay—"

Reign put his finger to her lips. "Enough. You are my wife now. I am content with our arrangement. Let us not speak further of debts and obligations."

He expected her to debate him. Her forehead wrinkled in silent frustration as Sophia fidgeted beside him. Reign braced himself for whatever argument she might put forth, but she surprised him by saying, "Very well, Reign."

"Gabriel."

Her blond curls tipped to the right as she tilted her head inquiringly. "My lord?"

Reign suddenly felt defensive as she peered intently at him. "Now that we are married, Sophia, it would not be unseemly for you to call me by my given name," he said stiffly.

"I see." She bit her lower lip as she quietly contemplated his command. "I must confess that when I awoke from my slumber, I realized that I did not know how to go about my day as your wife."

"Despite my first marriage, I am woefully ignorant on how to be a husband," Reign confessed, sensing the fear in her quiet confession. "There is no doubt that we both will make mistakes. Nevertheless, we can make this a good marriage, Sophia. I swear it."

"Then we will figure this business out together." Sophia took a deep breath. "If I may, I do have a question that has been on my mind for some time."

"Ask it."

"Does a husband expect his wife to kiss him in the morning?" Sophia asked, her eyes crinkling with amusement and mischief.

Reign responded with a wolfish grin. Sophia laughed as he pulled her into his arms and proceeded to demonstrate how much he approved of them kissing in the morning.

CHAPTER NINETEEN

"So the rumors were true."

Sophia whirled around at the sound of Mr. Enright's voice. Although it took her longer than most people to take in her surroundings because of her damaged eyesight, even she could deduce that the gentleman was unhappy. Much to her surprise, she realized that the last time she had spoken to Mr. Enright was the night of Lord and Lady Harper's ball. After Reign had run the gentleman off, Sophia had initially hoped that Mr. Enright might approach her again so she could apologize for their abrupt parting.

Between the nasty dealings with her brother and her meetings with Reign, Sophia had almost forgotten about the gentleman.

Sophia curtsied. "Mr. Enright, it is so good to see you again." She tried not to visibly wince as his firm grip squeezed the blood from her fingers.

"That remains to be seen," Mr. Enright said enigmatically. "I have heard the most dreadful gossip, my lady, and I pray it is not true."

Sophia's throat tightened in response to the distress that she heard in Mr. Enright's voice. "What have you heard?"

Had Mr. Enright heard tales of her outlandish behavior at Lord and Lady Bramsbury's garden party? Reign had promised to ruin her so Lord Mackney would abandon his quiet ambition to marry Sophia, and Stephan was spared the humiliation of breaking his oath. Since Reign promptly married her after their dalliance in the Bramsburys' lower terrace garden, even in the eyes of the *ton,* her sinful nature had been cleansed by the sanctity of marriage. Had Stephan stirred up mischief with Mr. Enright in an attempt to provoke her husband?

Stephan could be cruel but, if true, his actions bordered on lunacy. Reign would retaliate, and the hostility between the Rainecourt and Ravenshaw families would only escalate.

"Pray tell, Mr. Enright, of what rumors do you speak?"

The gentleman's nose twitched as his lips thinned with disdain. "Is it true that four days ago, you and Lord Rainecourt were married by special license?"

Relief coursed through Sophia's body. Her hand tightened on the handle of her walking stick as she offered Mr. Enright an apologetic smile. "Yes, it is true."

"I was afraid of this."

Before Sophia could respond, Mr. Enright took

her by the arm in an attempt to distance them from the other guests in the drawing room. "Mr. Enright, what are—"

Mr. Enright cast a wary glance at the other guests. No one seemed to be paying attention to them. "I realize that I ceded all rights to speak as your friend when I abandoned you to Rainecourt's tender mercies the night of the Harpers' ball. Even knowing the truth of what that man was capable of, I would have never guessed that he would have beguiled and bound another innocent to him."

"Mr. Enright, you do not understand. Lord Rainecourt was attempting to—" Reluctant to mention her awkward predicament with Lord Mackney, Sophia did the sensible thing and closed her mouth.

"Attempting to do what? Marry you?" Her companion sniffed. "Rainecourt apparently succeeded. What amazes me is that Lord Ravenshaw permitted such an alliance, considering the dark history of your families."

"And what exactly do you know of my family, Mr. Enright?"

The gentleman seemed to sense that he had made a grave error in mentioning her dead parents. "Not much," he conceded. "I only know that your parents were once dear friends of Lord Rainecourt."

"Reign's father," she reminded him.

"Yes. The father," he said, his expression taking

on an intensity that burned through the murky shadows of her vision. "Then you know that their friendship with Rainecourt cost your parents their lives."

Sophia was in no mood to be lectured. "I know my family history, Mr. Enright."

"Perhaps you should pay attention to your husband's family history, Lady Rainecourt. The son is more like his sire than most people know."

"I have heard enough."

"He killed her, you know."

Sophia froze at the solemn admission. She did not pretend to misunderstand. "You speak of Reign's first countess. Beatrice. I heard that her death was an accident."

A soft despairing sound came from Mr. Enright. "Is that what Rainecourt told you?"

Sophia was not going to discuss Reign's private business with a gentleman whom her husband clearly disliked. "I have no interest in discussing this further."

She tried to pull away.

"You must listen to me," he said, his voice laced with desperation. "Your husband murdered his first wife."

"Rubbish."

"The Rainecourt name spared your husband from the gallows," Mr. Enright said, his words rushing together as fear drove him to make his case. "Everyone knows that Beatrice was unhappy with her marriage. She would have returned to her family if Rainecourt had not murdered her."

"Please stop saying that my husband murdered his wife," Sophia said crossly. "No wonder Reign loathes you. I would be annoyed with you, too, if you were spreading lies about me."

"Forgive me, my lady," Mr. Enright said, bowing his head. "I did not mean to upset you. You are just so much like her."

"Her?"

"Beatrice. So beautiful, so full of life and laughter . . . the Rainecourt men are drawn to beauty, but they are careless with their possessions."

"I am *not* Rainecourt's possession."

Mr. Enright gave her a pitying glance. "Defy Rainecourt and you will learn that I speak the truth about your husband."

"Exactly what truth are you discussing with my wife, Enright?"

Reign did not trust himself to speak to Sophia as they sat across from each other in the compartment of the coach on the journey to the town house. If it had not been for his friend Dare, Reign might not have known that Enright had brazenly cornered Sophia in the drawing room.

How dare he? Reign thought with a silent outburst of raw fury.

He should have called Enright out for approaching Sophia. The man deserved a bullet for touching her and filling her head with lies.

Reign regretted that he had not dealt with Enright years ago.

He wanted to confront the man this evening.

Instead he had calmly escorted Sophia away from Enright after she had asked Reign to take her home.

"I think you should know that I do not believe him."

Reign's gaze rose from his clenched fist to his wife's pale face.

"What did he tell you?"

Sophia seemed to hesitate as if she had reconsidered the wisdom of repeating her conversation with Enright. "He had heard of our marriage, and was concerned."

Was he, indeed?

Reign brooded, as he could well imagine what Enright had told Sophia. "I suppose he mentioned Beatrice."

"Yes."

The single word told Reign everything he needed to know. "And you did not believe him."

It was not a question.

Sophia sighed. "I have heard the rumors about your first wife, Reign. And no, I do not believe that you murdered her. If you had arrived earlier, you would have overhead me defending you to Mr. Enright."

Reign glowered at her. "I do not need your defense, madam."

"Well, you have it just the same, Reign," she snapped back at him.

Sophia gasped as Reign lunged for her and

pulled her into his lap. Her walking stick fell to the floor and rolled out of reach.

Nose-to-nose, the knot in Reign's gut eased as he noted annoyance rather than fear in his wife's eyes. "Did you already forget my name, wife?"

Sophia raised her eyes upward as if asking for divine intervention. "No, Gabriel, I have not. Are all husbands so irksome?"

"Is that what I am?" he asked, liking the way her body molded against his. "Irksome?"

"Among other things," she said, feeling clearly provoked by his amusement.

Reign let his fingers dance down the side of Sophia's face. He sobered as his thoughts shifted to Enright. "Stay away from Enright, Sophia. Like the Burrards, he believes that I got away with murder, and nothing will dissuade him."

Sophia's gaze clouded with concern. "Why is he so convinced that you murdered your first wife?"

Reign glanced away. "Enright knows that Beatrice did not love me."

"But how—?"

He silenced her question with a kiss. When he pulled away, he said, "Enough talk about Enright. I will deal with him if he tries to interfere again."

Reign deliberately slid his hand over Sophia's left breast to distract her. "Have you ever been ravished in a coach, wife?"

Sophia pursed her lips together. She tilted her

head, intrigued by the notion. "No, I do not believe I have."

Reign spent the next twenty minutes thoroughly and pleasurably dispelling Enright's mischief from Sophia's head.

CHAPTER TWENTY

Sophia awoke to the sounds of two males arguing. Still half asleep, she wondered what had provoked the fight between Stephan and Henry.

Then she remembered where she was.

She sat up and reached out for Reign. The sheets were cool to the touch. When they had arrived home from the ball, Reign had carried her upstairs to her bedchamber to finish what he had started in the shadowed interior of the coach.

Sophia's hand idly caressed her right nipple, as she recalled how it had felt to have Reign's mouth suckling at her breasts. Her toes curled beneath the sheets.

Her husband was an exceedingly skilled lover.

Sophia glanced down at her bare breasts, irritated that she had been so exhausted by Reign's lovemaking that she had forgotten to put on her nightgown. He claimed that he preferred her naked, but he was not the one who had to face the servants in the morning.

She slid her hand over the bedding until her fingers brushed against her wrinkled nightgown. "Damn it, I want to see her!"

Sophia frowned and swiftly pulled the nightgown over her head. Was that Stephan? She had no idea what the hour was, except that it was before dawn. Sophia started to head for the door, and then realized that the male voices that she heard were not coming from downstairs in the front hall. The argument was outside the house.

Wary, Sophia moved slowly toward the open window. She was certain that the window had been shut when she had fallen asleep.

Had Reign opened the window?

Sophia pulled the curtain aside and peered, concentrating on the lamp that seemed to float just above the ground. It was too dark to see much, and her eyesight was barely adequate in daylight.

"Go home, Ravenshaw," Reign said, sounding bored and unsympathetic. "You can pay your respects to my wife when you have sobered up."

Sophia's eyes narrowed at the way Reign emphasized the words *my wife*. Mr. Enright's comment that she was Reign's possession intruded on her thoughts.

"Smug bastard," Stephan jeered. "How did you learn of Mackney's offer so quickly?"

"You were not as discreet as you thought," Reign taunted.

"Neither were you with that business in the Bramsburys' lower gardens," Stephan yelled back.

Sophia heard a shuffling noise and a grunt.

Oh, this was frustrating! Sophia wished that she could see Reign and her brother. Were they fighting or just circling around each other like moths around the lamp?

Stephan was breathing heavily. "Perhaps you had been plotting to steal Sophia away. Who helped you? Did you bribe my bloody servants?"

"How Sophia came to be in my custody is irrelevant, Ravenshaw."

Sophia could hear the pleasure resonating in her husband's voice. He was savoring his victory.

"What should concern you is that Sophia is now a Rainecourt. She is no longer in a position to help you, and after you locked her up and tried to hand her over to Mackney, there is a good chance that she no longer cares about your fate."

"Liar," Stephan spat. "Sophia loves me and Henry. She would never put a Rainecourt above her real family."

Sophia squinted as she heard more scuffling sounds and Stephan cursed.

"My wife understands where her loyalties lie, Ravenshaw," Reign said calmly. "If you are short of funds, I would suggest that you spend your days and evening searching for an heiress to wed instead of drinking yourself blind each night, and gambling away what's left of your fortune."

"I do not need any lectures from a murderous Rainecourt!" Stephan roared. "I just want to see my sister, you bastard."

"Why?" Reign sounded genuinely curious. "She cannot save you."

"Maybe I've come to save her from you," Stephan shouted at Reign, his voice full of importance and belligerence. "Sophia and her stubborn ways can drive a saint to commit violence. Lord knows, I have wanted to throttle her a dozen times. With one wife moldering in the ground, and the tainted blood of your sire flowing in your veins, I suspect that it will be only a matter of time before our sweet, gentle Sophia meets a similar fate."

Sophia inhaled sharply at the sickening thumps of fists striking flesh.

"Sophia!"

She instinctively took a step away from the window. She had not realized that she had revealed herself to her brother and Reign.

"No, no—wait!" Stephan shouted up at her. "Sophia, I never meant to hurt you. Forget my interest in your dowry; Mackney would have been a good husband to you. I just went about it wrong that night because I was drunk—"

"You *are* drunk, Ravenshaw," Reign drawled. "What's next? Groveling?"

"I am not groveling, damn it!" Stephan lashed out at Reign. "This is between me and my sister." He moved toward the window. "Sophia, come home. The marriage was probably not even valid."

Her husband chuckled. "Oh, the marriage was very real. As was the wedding night."

Sophia brought her hand up to her face and

despaired. Reign was not helping the situation by provoking her brother into a mindless rage.

"Damn you, Sophia!" His next words were almost inaudible. "You did not have to whore yourself to this murderous devil. Mackney was honorable . . . I swear it!"

Stephan believed she had betrayed her family's honor. Did Henry feel the same way?

With her brother's words ringing in her ears, Sophia staggered away from the window, returning to the bed. She crawled to the center, and then pulled the bedding up until she was fully covered.

Minutes later, Reign entered the room.

Sophia stared blankly at the wall, waiting for her husband to get into bed. Reign remained near the door.

"Do you regret marrying me?"

His question surprised Sophia. "No," she said huskily. Stephan did not consider her marriage to Reign as valid. It stung to know that if she had been foolish enough to go with her brother, Stephan would have ignored her protests and tried to marry her off to Mackney.

"Good." He did not venture closer. "Tomorrow we will leave for Addison Park."

Sophia tossed aside the bedding she had used to cocoon herself and sat up. She did not need Reign to explain that he thought she would be safer if they put some distance between her and Stephan. "Do you truly believe this is necessary? I know that Stephan is very angry at both of us. However, my brother would never hurt me."

"Sophia," Reign said wearily. "Look in the mirror. Your brother has already hurt you."

Her nose suddenly burned with the tears she had been fighting. Reign was telling the truth. Sophia nodded. Stephan had betrayed her, and she had not quite recovered from it.

"You always seem to be protecting me."

Reign gave her a long unreadable look. "In this instance, I am protecting your brother."

Sophia blinked. "How so?"

"Leaving for Addison Park will stop me from putting a bullet into the damn man." He ignored Sophia's startled expression, and elaborated, "Your brother is feeling desperate, and desperate men are unpredictable. If Ravenshaw was foolish enough to kidnap you, I would be obliged to hurt him." Reign gave her a lopsided grin. "And that would have made you unhappy. Do not look so surprised. Just because your brother has been behaving like a horse's arse does not mean you have stopped loving him."

Sophia brought her hand up to her forehead. She had been prepared to despise Stephan, but her feelings for both of her brothers were more complicated than that.

"So we are journeying to your country estate so you will not have to shoot my brother?"

"Exactly."

Sophia groaned and slid down into the bedding.

Reign walked over and pulled the blankets over her. He kissed her on the temple. "Get some sleep, Sophia. We have a long journey ahead of us."

She listened to her husband's footfalls as he walked through the doorway and softly shut the door.

Addison Park.

Sophia had been so distracted by her problems with Stephan that she had not considered that Reign would expect her to reside there. Addison Park was part of her past. It was the source of her nightmares. The last time she had been there, she had almost died. It was where his father had murdered her parents.

And Reign was taking her back there.

Sophia rolled onto her back and waited for the dawn.

CHAPTER TWENTY-ONE

"Does this week's menu meet your approval?"

Sophia lowered the piece of paper in her hand, and gave the housekeeper a gentle smile. Two weeks had passed since Reign had whisked her off to Addison Park, and she still felt more like a guest than its mistress. "As usual, you have outdone yourself on the menu, Mrs. Ivey. I would not change a single dish." Sophia handed the paper to the servant.

Mrs. Ivey accepted the paper with a curt nod. "Very good, milady. I will tell the cook immediately that we have your approval." The housekeeper curtsied and hurried toward the door. She paused at the threshold. "Before I go about my other duties, would you care for some tea? It will put a spot of color on your face, if you do not mind me saying so."

"It is kind of you to offer, Mrs. Ivey. Perhaps I will ring for some tea after I have taken a stroll in the gardens."

The housekeeper's forehead furrowed at her

mistress's announcement. Reign had departed at dawn to attend to some business with several of his tenants. He must have ordered Mrs. Ivey to look after his new countess. The housekeeper's hesitation was slight but noticeable. She clearly was not pleased that Sophia was planning to leave the house. "Very well, milady. Shall I fetch one of the lads to walk with you?"

"That will not be necessary," Sophia said, retrieving her bonnet and gloves from the table. "I shall not be straying far from the house."

In the five minutes that it took Sophia to escape the house, the butler, two footmen, and a maid had delayed her with their offers of assistance.

By the time Sophia had reached the white gravel path that outlined the elegant gardens at the back of the house, she had worked herself into a fine temper. She stabbed the sharp end of her walking stick into the ground with brisk enthusiasm as she increased her distance from the house.

The staff was treating her as if she were a sickly child who fainted at her own shadow. The situation was intolerable!

And she only had herself to blame, she thought uncharitably, recalling her initial reaction as she entered the front hall of Addison Park. While Sophia glanced up at the impressive staircase, silently admiring the opulent interior, she had been overwhelmed suddenly by lightheadedness. As the walls began to spin, she saw buried glimpses of the past: Her childish hands gripping the balustrades, shadows of violence from within the drawing room, and an unexpected explosion of white blinding pain.

Sophia absently touched the back of her head where she had received what should have been a killing blow. If Reign had not caught her, Sophia might have disgraced herself in front of the entire staff by fainting dead away at their feet. Shouting orders, Reign had carried her to the nearest chair. He had blamed himself for not feeding her properly in his haste to leave London. Sophia did not bother correcting her husband's erroneous assumption. It was kinder than telling him that his ancestral estate was riddled with ghosts.

Sophia abandoned the gravel path and its herbaceous border that outlined the garden, and headed toward the heart of the garden. At its center, the trimmed hedge walls soared above her head, and provided a small haven from prying eyes. Hidden within the green alcove, a painted wooden garden seat was raised on a rectangular stone step to keep the dampness at bay.

She halted when she heard a soft shuffling noise.

"Is anyone there?"

There was no reply to her inquiry. Sophia chuckled at her own foolishness. It was probably a few birds searching for twigs and leaves for a nest.

Grateful to be alone, Sophia climbed the three shallow steps to the garden seat and sat down.

Feeling very much like a queen sitting on her throne, she inhaled deeply and allowed the mingled scents and beauty of the garden to calm her.

It came as a surprise, but Sophia longed to return to London. The discord between her and her brothers felt like an iron chain around her heart. She also missed Fanny. Oh, if only she had her dear friend's kind ear this afternoon. Reign would think her daft if Sophia confessed that there was something about the house that unsettled her. Nor could she quite shake the odd sensation that she was being watched, even though she knew in those moments that she was alone.

Several pebbles scattered as Reign crossed the gravel path in search of Sophia. When he had inquired after his wife's whereabouts, Winkler had directed him to the back gardens. Sophia seemed to prefer the outdoors when he was obliged to leave her alone. Not that he blamed her. It had taken him years before he could enter the drawing room without dwelling on the murders. Reign had intended to give Sophia more time to accept that Addison Park was now her home, but Ravenshaw's midnight visit to the town house had forced Reign to change his plans.

Until her brothers accepted her marriage to Reign, Sophia was safer in the country. He just had to convince his wife of that fact.

Reign found her in the center alcove of the garden. He stepped over several low hedges to reach his countess. "Good afternoon, lady wife."

"Reign!"

Her welcoming smile warmed his heart.

Sophia abandoned the garden seat and met him at the bottom of the three steps. Reign opened his arms in silent invitation. His wife did not hesitate. She walked up to him and slipped her arms around his neck.

"So you missed me?" he teased.

"Dreadfully." She pulled away, and clasped his hand. Together, they returned to the garden seat. "What about you? Did you think of me?"

For a man who thought he would never marry again, it was frightening how many minutes of the day his thoughts were dedicated to her. "Once or twice"—Reign tugged Sophia onto his lap and caressed her cheek—"Or thrice," he murmured against her lips before he deepened the kiss.

Sophia kissed him back with an innocent abandonment that he had come to treasure. What she lacked in experience, she more than made up in enthusiasm. She was breathless and her cheeks were rosy when Reign pulled away.

"Are you enjoying the gardens, wife?"

Sophia glanced pointedly at his right hand that had slipped beneath the bodice of her gown and corset. "Very much so, husband."

Reign deliberately brushed her nipple before he withdrew his hand. As much as he was tempted to seduce Sophia in the garden alcove, it was not the reason why he had sought her out.

"I pray this means you are not vexed with me

for abandoning you," he said, pressing a kiss to the side of her neck.

Sophia glanced back over her shoulder to see if he was teasing. He wasn't. She shrugged and said, "It will be an unhappy marriage for both of us if I am vexed at you for attending to your business affairs."

Reign rubbed the sudden ache in his brow. "Are you unhappy, Sophia? Be truthful. There was little honesty between Beatrice and me, and we both suffered for it. Winkler tells me that there have been several incidents during my absences that have upset you."

Sophia frowned. "Have you ordered the servants to spy on me?"

"Do not be a goose," Reign said, nipping her earlobe lightly with his teeth. "Winkler was merely concerned, especially when you fell the other day. Why did you not tell me?"

His wife's expression grew mutinous. "Tell you what, precisely? That I am as graceful as a doe running across a frozen pond? I believe you are aware of my faults. I distinctly recall that you accused me of being clumsy the first evening we met," she said, her blue-green eyes hot with temper.

"I thought we both agreed that I was an arse that evening." His fingers trailed down Sophia's arm in what he hoped was a soothing gesture. Reign did not have much experience when it came to calming a lady's ruffled feathers. He had never cared enough to bother. Nevertheless, it had not been his intention to upset Sophia. "And what of the locked door this morning?" Reign pressed. "The housekeeper said that you were convinced that someone locked you in the informal parlor."

Sophia's lower lip trembled. "I was mistaken, though I swear I heard—" A soft sound of distress vibrated in her throat as she shook her head. "It is truly nothing, my lord. I would have mentioned the incidents myself. However, later, it all seemed ridiculous. The house is old. One expects doors to stick and floorboards to creak."

She gave him a lopsided smile.

"You have not entered the drawing room."

Sophia's smile faded. She attempted to slip from his embrace, but he wrapped his arm around her waist. Reign had a sudden irrational fear that if he let Sophia go, he would lose her. Perhaps it had been a mistake to bring Sophia to Addison Park. His ancestral home had witnessed the demise of more than one Lady Rainecourt. His mother had known such despair that she had taken her own life, and many years later, Beatrice had died in her frantic attempt to escape him.

"I am aware that I am asking much of you, Sophia," Reign said, his lips against her ear. "All I am asking is for you to trust me. We cannot scrub away the tragic past of Addison Park, but we can soften the sadness by adding happier days."

Sophia turned so that their lips almost touched. "Something about this house frightens me."

Reign rubbed his nose against hers. "It is just a house, Sophia. Nothing will hurt you here. You are safe with me. I promise."

With her blue-green eyes glistening as the sunlight touched her face, she said, "I know."

Reign cuddled her and savored how well his countess filled his arms. He did not want to spoil the tender moment with his admission that he would have to leave her again this evening. Word had reached him that Ravenshaw had been seen at the village tavern. If Sophia's brother had some crazy notion of kidnapping his sister, then Reign intended to impress upon the gent the folly of his course.

Reign was prepared to pound the lesson into Ravenshaw's thick skull with his bare fists if the occasion warranted it.

After her husband's tender vows of protecting her, Reign had abandoned her.

Again.

With only the enigmatic assurance that his departure was a matter of life and death, he kissed her fully on the mouth in front of the butler and hurried out of the house.

Oh, there was no doubt that Sophia was positively vexed.

As the hours passed, Sophia filled the silence by writing letters to Fanny and Juliana. She also dallied over a letter to her brothers, but she set the unfinished letter aside. Sophia was not about to apologize for her marriage to Reign. Stephan and Henry would eventually come around once they realized that her husband was not the devil his reputation purported him to be.

The sound of a door closing downstairs brought Sophia to her feet. Reign had returned. She reached out for her walking stick and moved to the chimneypiece in her bedchamber to glance at the clock. The servants had retired several hours earlier so there was no one awake to attend to her husband.

Regretting her chilly farewell, Sophia crossed the room to the door with the intention of giving Reign a warmer greeting now that he had returned to her.

It was not his fault that the house unsettled her.

"Reign?" she called out softly as she descended the stairs.

Her greeting was met with silence.

Fortunately the butler had left several oil lamps burning for his lordship's return. Sophia frowned as she reached the second landing. She peered over the railing, but the front hall was empty.

Where was Reign?

As she realized where she was standing, Sophia gave the shut door to her left a wary side-glance. Beyond the door was the drawing room. Reign was right. She had yet to enter the room. This was not, however, the hour to test her courage. With the notion of returning to her bedchamber, Sophia turned away from the drawing-room door.

Out from the shadows, the blow to the side of her head was swift and brutally efficient. Sophia was knocked to the floor before she had the chance to draw air into her lungs for a scream. There was nothing she could do but let the darkness claim her.

Sophia awoke with pain buzzing in her skull like angry bees. It took her several minutes to comprehend that she was in the drawing room. How had she gotten there? Where was Reign? She tossed back her head to remove the strands of hair from her face. Her hair had come undone at some point. Had she tripped? While she had been unconscious, someone had placed her upright in a chair. This had not been done out of kindness. It had just made the task of binding Sophia's arms behind her back easier, she thought, her struggles weak and useless. She tried to move her feet, but each leg had been tied to the chair with rope.

"You are not supposed to be here."

The woman had been so quiet, Sophia had thought that she was alone in the drawing room. Oddly dressed in a billowy chemise and men's breeches, the woman stood in front of the large mirror that was across the room, and calmly coiled her long, dark hair that was streaked with silver. She secured her tresses with the pins she had stolen from Sophia's hair.

"Who are you?" Sophia demanded, silently cursing as the shadows swirled and muted the clarity of her vision.

"**I have** no time for games, my dear. Reign will return soon, and I have much to accomplish," the woman said, giving her hair a final pat before she glanced at her prisoner. "You know who I am."

Perplexed, Sophia shook her head. She immediately regretted the action as sharp pain sliced through flesh and bone. "My apologies, madam, but I do not recall meeting you. Who are you?"

"Silly goose," the woman chided softly. It was not until she approached that Sophia noticed the pistol in her captor's hand. "Did I hit you too hard? You are addressing the Countess of Rainecourt."

A look of horror washed over Sophia's face. Suddenly the pain in her chest was fiercer than the one in her head. "B-Beatrice?" she stuttered, suddenly afraid that Reign's dark secrets were far worse than she had ever guessed.

The woman frowned in annoyance. Her expression and the way she tilted her head to the side seemed vaguely familiar to Sophia. Her own muddled brain was working out the solution when the woman said, "Beatrice is dead. She died a long time ago. No, I am Lady Colette, Reign's mother."

Sophia licked her dry lips and grimaced at the sting. She also tasted blood. "No, that cannot be. Reign's mother died when I was a child. I was told that she took her own life."

The woman who claimed to be her mother-in-law smiled, her eyes humorless and empty. It was like staring into the void of madness. "Oh, I tried, but my husband found me bleeding and barely conscious. Rainecourt tended my wounds, and then locked me away in one of the abandoned tenant cottages. He hired a few servants to care for me, and paid them well for their silence. I learned only later that my husband had told everyone, including my beautiful son, that I had died."

Reign had once told her that the servants believed the ghost of his mother haunted the Rainecourt lands. Little did he know that it was more or less the truth. Whether it was right or wrong, Reign's father had locked away his troubled wife, and then pretended that she had taken her own life. Had the guilt eaten away at the edges of Reign's father's sanity? So much so that years later, he would murder her parents before he ended his life with a single bullet?

She flinched as Lady Colette's fingers brushed back strands of blond hair from Sophia's face. Her hair was matted behind her left ear. Sophia assumed it was blood.

"It was wrong of your husband to do that to you. Reign mourned you, my lady."

The dowager countess pulled back and brought her fist to her head. "I know . . . I know . . . !" she said, digging her fingers into her bound hair. A section of dark hair was pulled from its confines. "It took me a long time to find my way back home." Her gaze was moist with torment and a poignant plea. "You must believe me. I had to be clever. Oh, so clever."

How many years had Reign's mother been

locked away? Sixteen? Seventeen? The isolation must have plunged the already fragile mind of the forgotten woman into madness. Sophia winced as she tilted her head, studying the woman before her. The fact that she was talking to a dead woman proved Lady Colette to be a very clever ghost. "I wager that your husband never realized there were times when you escaped your keepers?"

Lady Colette straightened, and the distress in her expression faded away. She smiled indulgently at Sophia. "Oh, Rainecourt figured it out . . . eventually."

"I know your secret. I know he hurt you."

Sophia did not bother hiding her confusion. "Who? Stephan? He was not thinking clearly when he locked me in my bedchamber." Her fingers curled into impotent fists to ease the growing numbness. The rope around her wrists was unyielding. She was at the complete mercy of this creature.

"I speak of Rainecourt," she said sadly. "He told me all of his secrets when he thought he was safe."

Was it possible that Lady Colette had been there the night Rainecourt and her parents had died? Had the countess seen Rainecourt strike down the six-year-old Sophia, who had awakened to the sounds of angry voices?

"You say Rainecourt hurt me," Sophia said, striving to keep calm. "Did you see him hit me?"

"Hit?" Lady Colette pondered the word. "Most ladies enjoyed Rainecourt's attentions. Or so he often bragged. Oh, there were times when he was rough. Too rough. Did you fight him when he pushed you onto the bed and tried to lift your skirts, too?"

Good heavens! Her eyes widened as she realized in sickening dread that Lady Colette was speaking of Sophia's mother. "No, you are wrong. Confused. Rainecourt was my father's good friend. He would never have touched my mother," Sophia said, too appalled by the notion to consider that Reign's father might have attacked her mother.

I do not believe it.

What if she was wrong? No, Sophia immediately discarded the thought. She refused to believe the ravings of a madwoman. For a betrayal this vile, her father would have murdered Rainecourt . . .

Murder.

Sophia straightened her spine. Everyone had assumed that Rainecourt had murdered her parents. What if her father had shot his wife and friend before turning the pistol on himself?

"You know the truth."

Sophia was feeling too addled by the blow to know anything for certain. "Lady Colette, do you know who I am? I am Sophia, Lady Ravenshaw's daughter," she said, hoping to break through the confusion that muddled the older woman's mind.

"Sophia." The countess returned to the chair and knelt at Sophia's bound feet. Her face lightened with affection. "I remember you. You were such a pretty child."

It was difficult, but Sophia did not flinch away when the countess caressed her cheek. "My wrists hurt. Could you untie my hands? I would very much like to talk to you about my mother. The staff has retired for the evening; however, I could make us some tea while we wait for your son's return."

"Tea?" Lady Colette slowly straightened her legs. "No—no, I do not think that would be wise. You might use trickery to make me sleep."

"No, I have not the skill for trickery," Sophia said hastily.

Where were Lady Colette's attendants? To ensure her obedience, they must have been drugging her food and drink for years.

Slyness crept into the countess's panicked expression. "Now you are being deceitful. Is that how you tricked my Reign into marriage?"

"No! Reign offered marriage to spare me—" Sophia could have bitten off her tongue for almost giving the woman another reason to keep her tied to the blasted chair. She took a deep breath. "Reign loves me. He will be quite upset if you hurt me."

"His grief will ease. I just cannot bear for him to suffer another faithless wife." Lady Colette whirled away, her head moving from side to side as if she was searching for something. The pistol in her hand connected with a tall rectangular vase, and the motion sent it crashing to the floor.

Both Sophia and Lady Colette shrieked at the noise.

"My lady, I love your son."

"Lies!" Slamming the pistol on the table, the countess picked up something from the floor. Sophia did not recognize the object until the pale razor-sharp shard of porcelain was pressed against her throat. "And what of the babe you carry?"

"W-what babe?" Sophia wailed as she craned her head away from the lethal edge of the shard in Lady Colette's hand. Was the countess confusing her with Reign's first wife? "Madam, I am *not* Beatrice. Remember? I am Sophia. There is no babe . . . no babe!"

Sophia inhaled loudly as the porcelain shard scraped lightly across her neck like death's sweet kiss. The side of her neck burned. She could not prevent the sob from bubbling up in her throat when Lady Colette staggered away and returned to the mirror that had originally captured her attention.

With pain came a shocking clarity. Sophia gasped. Beatrice had not been carrying Reign's child.

"Did Gabriel know the babe was not his?"

The shard clattered as it hit the floor. Sophia blinked away the tears that threatened and squinted at her mother-in-law. Lady Colette touched the smooth glass of the silvered mirror.

"My son knew," the countess said hollowly. She peered deeply into the mirror and traced the line of her jaw with her fingertips. "I overheard them fighting one night. Gabriel was drunk and belligerent, sounding very much like his father. Beatrice had been packing, you see. With her parents' encouragement, she had married my son for his title. The silly chit had already given herself to another man, but her lover lacked the position and wealth that the Burrards craved."

"Beatrice knew she was breeding when she accepted Gabriel's offer of marriage?" Sophia asked.

Unhappy with her reflection, Lady Colette slapped her hand over the mirror. "Beatrice seduced my son. Fooled him into thinking that she came to his bed a virgin. When he learned that she was carrying a child, he had no reason to doubt that it was his."

Any sympathy that Sophia felt for Beatrice being bullied into a loveless marriage faded when she thought of Reign. He had loved the girl. It had been cruel of Beatrice and her parents to take advantage of his tender feelings.

She moistened her lips, turning the countess's revelations and Reign's quiet admissions around in her head as if each was a piece in a puzzle that Sophia was close to solving. "You claim that you saw Gabriel and Beatrice fight that final night. How did you observe them without their knowledge?"

Lady Colette crossed the drawing room. "This

house has many secrets. A fire more than a century ago destroyed a section of it."

Much to Sophia's dismay, the countess retrieved the pistol from the table.

"During the reconstruction, Gabriel's great-great-grandfather had passageways built into some of the walls. He told his wife that it was a measure to protect their family. However, the truth was, like all the men who have claimed the Rainecourt title, the earl was serving his own selfish interests. The passageways prevented his wife from learning of his numerous trysts with houseguests and servants."

No doubt, the countess's husband had taken advantage of these same passageways. And what of Reign? Had he known about the hidden halls? It seemed unlikely. The secret had probably died with his father. "All this time, you have been watching over your son, have you not?"

It was a bit unsettling to realize that the countess had been observing her and Reign since their arrival. How often had the woman moved silently through the passageways, more ghost than alive, as the living went about their day? How many intimate moments had she intruded upon? Had she been there behind the walls of the bedchamber, watching the love play between Sophia and Reign?

"Yes."

She started at the countess's reply, but quickly realized that the older woman was responding to Sophia's question. Or was she? Sophia's eyes narrowed as Lady Colette paced in front of the chair. "You know what really happened the night that Beatrice fell and died?"

The countess brought her fist to her temple. "I cannot discuss—no, it is entirely inappropriate. Secrets must be kept!"

Sophia's mouth thinned in frustration. "Gabriel was too deep in his cups to recall what happened after he threatened Beatrice and told her she could not leave the house. A part of him fears that he might have killed his wife, and this possibility, as well as the guilt Gabriel feels over Beatrice's death, has kept him from defending his good name to the Burrards or anyone else who has called him a murderer behind his back. You claim that you have watched over your son, but where were you when he needed you? How could you stand in the shadows and allow him to suffer? You could have eased your son's pain, if you had revealed yourself and told him the truth!"

Lady Colette whirled and lunged toward the chair. Sophia yelped as the countess snarled and braced her hands one on each armrest, the madness in the woman's eyes piercing the shadowy veil of Sophia's vision. She warily glanced down. Though her finger wasn't on the trigger, the barrel of the pistol in Lady Colette's right hand was aimed at Sophia's stomach.

"My son would not find comfort in the truth. Neither will you, my sweet girl."

CHAPTER TWENTY-TWO

Sophia's mouth quivered, her lips fighting to form the words for the unthinkable. "You will never convince me that Gabriel murdered Beatrice."

Sophia refused to believe it. Oh, she was not so naive as to assume that her husband was incapable of violence. She had witnessed his unleashed temper when Stephan had come upon them kissing in the Harpers' garden terrace. However, punishing a quarrelsome future brother-in-law was different from coldly murdering a wife.

"I have no reason to debate you, my dear. Gabriel did not murder his wife." Lady Colette paused as Sophia sagged in soundless relief. "I did."

Staring into Lady Colette's fathomless dark eyes, it was not difficult to imagine that the lady was capable of murder.

"Gabriel returned to Beatrice that night," the countess said, releasing her grip on the armrests and circling the chair. "He had returned to reason with her . . . to issue more threats. If he had been content to stay away and drown his regrets with brandy, Beatrice might have left the house with her little secret."

The babe.

Understanding sharpened Sophia's gaze as she turned her head to address the countess. "That was when Beatrice revealed to Gabriel that he had no claim on the babe she was carrying."

"You know better than to underestimate a Rainecourt," Lady Colette said lightly, drawing a frown from Sophia. "You have felt his strength, have you not? The pain as he held you down. You cried out when he thrust into you and left evidence of the violence he had wrought."

"My lady?" Sophia was uncertain how to proceed without angering the woman. Was she implying that Reign had attacked his wife in anger? Or was the lady confusing old violence with recent passion? Had Lady Colette silently observed her son as he made love to Sophia?

Both thoughts were rather unsettling. Reign's mother was very ill and confused. Sophia's gaze dropped to the pistol in the lady's hand.

And extremely capable of violence.

The fact that the older woman had struck Sophia and bound her to a chair quelled any sympathy that she could muster on the older woman's behalf.

Lady Colette snapped her chin up. "I beg your pardon?" she asked, unaware that she had ceased speaking.

"My hands, my lady," Sophia said, lifting her shoulder as she slanted her eyes to the right in the hope that the countess might free her.

"Oh, of course, my dear."

To her surprise, Lady Colette circled to the back of the chair. Sophia held her breath as she felt the brush of the older woman's fingers against her wrist.

Then nothing.

"Mayhap later," the countess said, straightening and continuing past the chair.

Sophia wanted to scream at the woman. Fortunately, common sense caught hold before she did anything rash. Where was Reign? Should he not have returned home by now?

Unless . . .

A sudden lump crowded her throat at the horrible thought that Lady Colette had done something to Reign. Sophia swallowed, fighting back the urge to cry. It was ridiculous to succumb to unfounded fears. Her husband was safe. For reasons unbeknownst to her, the man had chosen the wrong night to be late!

"What happened to Beatrice?"

Sophia really did not want to know the grisly details. However, the longer Lady Colette stared blankly into the empty drawing room, the more Sophia's anxiety increased. The countess appeared to be working herself into a state. Sophia prayed the lady was not quietly convincing herself that she had to do away with another of her son's wives.

"Divorce was unthinkable," Lady Colette said after a few minutes. "No Rainecourt had ever been scandalized by a divorce."

No, only with murder, Sophia thought but wisely held her tongue.

"As one might expect, Gabriel struck out blindly when Beatrice told him that the babe was sired by another man. She fell against the mattress and laughed . . . laughed," Lady Colette said, shaking her head as if she still could not fathom Beatrice's response. "She told my son that he was living up to the Rainecourt name—that his father would be proud."

Sophia stiffened her already cramped muscles as she studied the countess's back. She did not need to ask the countess how she felt about Beatrice's comparison of father and son.

Lady Colette shuddered. "Gabriel asked Beatrice what she wanted, and she arrogantly told him that she already had his name and money. Now she wanted her freedom."

To be with her lover.

What a blow to Reign's pride it must have been to learn that the woman he loved had tricked him into marriage, only to discover that being countess of Rainecourt was unpalatable.

"Did Gabriel grant Beatrice her freedom?"

"She broke him," Lady Colette said forlornly. "Her lies, her hate . . . she had left him with nothing but bitterness. He told her that she could leave in the morning with his blessing. That the Rainecourt name had weathered far worse scandals than an adulterous wife."

It sounded like something Reign would have said. Sophia did not know what to believe. Had Lady Colette truly witnessed that last argument between Reign and his first wife, or was her unstable mind twisting details to justify her hatred of Beatrice?

One thing, however, was undeniable. After Beatrice's death, her husband had avoided entanglements. Innocents in particular. Sophia silently marveled that when Reign had offered her marriage to escape her brothers, he had risked committing himself to another loveless union.

But there was a difference.

Reign had loved Beatrice when he married her. He had not repeated his mistake with Sophia. He had offered her affection, friendship, and protection. Love had not been part of the bargain.

Sophia attempted to shy away from the unpleasant detail. While Reign had been more than willing to consummate their marriage and treat her with the respect and loyalty one might expect from one's spouse, he had withheld a part of himself. Even when she had slipped and confessed her love for him, Reign had resisted returning the words that she craved. It wasn't pride that had prevented him from speaking from his heart. Perhaps his mother was correct when she said that Beatrice had broken her son.

Reign was not in love with Sophia.

She choked and gasped as a sharp pain lanced her breast. If there was comfort to be found, it was in the fact that her husband had never lied to her. Reign had suffered betrayal and lies from his first wife. He would never submit Sophia to such a grim fate.

"Madam, I would never hurt your son."

Lady Colette turned and glanced in Sophia's direction. "I think man was born with cruelty bred into his bones. Kindness is something we must be taught."

Sophia sighed. "Is that what you were trying to do when you revealed yourself to Beatrice?"

The question startled the countess. "What did I have to gain? My son was done with her." Lady Colette's gaze grew moist, reminding Sophia of a lake just as twilight faded into night. "Beatrice wanted her freedom, but she intended for her unborn son to be the Rainecourt heir. Gabriel had unknowingly claimed another man's child as his own. Everyone believed that Beatrice was carrying the Rainecourt heir. Do you not see . . . I could not let that happen!"

"Gabriel told me that it was an accident. That Beatrice must have tripped and fallen."

Lady Colette shook her head. "She had dragged a table in front of the door after Gabriel staggered off. Needless to say, she was rather surprised to discover that she was not alone in the bedchamber. Frightened, Beatrice tried to run for the door and tripped as Gabriel and the magistrate had guessed. She lay on her back, dazed from the blow that she took when her head hit one of the bed-posts, her belly swollen with the evidence of her betrayal to my son and the family name. I—"

The countess's eyes narrowed as she peered down at the drawing room rug, apparently see-ing the helpless Beatrice struggling to climb to her feet as she stalked toward her. "I simply put my hands around her neck and held them there. Stifling her denials of innocence . . . making her choke on her lies. Oh, Beatrice tried to stop me, clawing at my arms and hands. However, over-indulgence and her lover's child had weakened her constitution. It was over rather quickly. In those last minutes, do you think Beatrice was longing for the husband she had cast aside?"

Sophia shut her eyes and did not bother reply-ing. The tears that she had held back slid down her cheeks—tears for Beatrice and her unborn child. What Beatrice had done to Reign had been cruel, but she had not deserved to die for her sins.

Reign's mother made a soft sound of distress as she returned to Sophia. "There, there . . . child." She used a portion of her chemise to wipe away Sophia's tears.

"Why have you revealed yourself to me, Lady Colette?" Sophia asked hoarsely, her throat tight with misery. "I am not Beatrice. I am not aban-doning your son, nor am I carrying another man's child. I will not hurt Gabriel."

"You already have!" Lady Colette shouted at Sophia. "Did you think that you could keep secrets in this house? I know you tricked my son into marriage."

"No!" Sophia said, the pitch of her voice climbing with her desperation. "It was Gabriel's suggestion that we marry. At first, I-I refused him, but he was so insistent and seemed to make sense when everything was such a damn muddle."

Sophia figured God would forgive her for cursing. It was not every day that someone pointed a pistol at her head.

"And were you going to tell him about the child?" Lady Colette said, the deadly calm inflection somehow more terrifying than if the woman were screaming at her.

Sophia's pulse leaped in her throat. This was not the first time the countess had mentioned the possibility of a child. Was Lady Colette rambling about the past again, or had she been watching her son's new wife closely? It was only recently that Sophia had begun to suspect that she might be carrying Reign's child. If true, the babe had likely been conceived on their wedding night.

"You do not understand," Sophia said hastily, rushing her words until it sounded like one nonsensical combination. "I am not keeping secrets! What can I say to make you believe me?"

Lady Colette moved in closer to guarantee that she would not miss when she pulled the trigger. "I promise that you will not suffer. Not like before. Just close your eyes."

Not like before? Before what exactly?

"Please!" Sophia sobbed, pulling frantically against her restraints.

"Get the hell away from my wife!"

From the corner of her eye, Sophia saw Reign and Stephan standing in the doorway. *What is my brother doing here?* she wondered, distracted momentarily by Stephan's unexpected appearance. Both men were poised for action.

Especially Reign. There was a mute fury radiating from him. Sophia had never been so grateful to see her husband.

"Dear God, Rainecourt," the older woman said, the shock whitening her already pale face. "How can this be?"

Reign stared impassively at the disheveled creature in his drawing room. Who was she? He had not seen a woman dressed in breeches since Vane and Frost had thought it would be amusing to escort two outrageously dressed doxies to the theater in men's garb. Was this some sort of jest? If so, then why the devil was the woman pointing a pistol at Sophia's head?

"Wife, you did not tell me that you had planned to entertain this evening."

Reign sensed the subtle tension coming from Ravenshaw. Sophia's hotheaded brother was unhappy with this unexpected turn, but this was not the time for recklessness. He restrained the man with a hand gesture.

Sophia's eyes shimmered with unshed tears.

Reign's heart clenched at the sight. "Husband, you were right about the ghosts."

"Ghosts? What nonsense is this?" Ravenshaw spat, revealing his impatience.

Reign glared at the older woman. "Who are you? If you know me, then you should understand that the pistol is unnecessary. No one will harm you."

Ravenshaw snorted. "Speak for yourself, Rainecourt."

Reign ignored his brother-in-law's outburst. "If you have come to steal silver or food, you can take your fill and leave in peace."

Just stop aiming that bloody pistol at my wife's head!

The color was returning to the woman's face. There was something vaguely familiar about her, though Reign could not place where he had met her. Initially, when he and Ravenshaw had entered the house, Reign had thought Sophia had retired early for the evening. He had been heading toward the stairs to wake her when both men heard Sophia scream.

The woman tilted her head in a regal fashion as her dark gaze narrowed. "Oh, I know you, Rainecourt. You as well, Ravenshaw. I also know that this pistol is necessary, gentlemen. You should not be here, but no matter. I shall put things right again."

"She is mad, Gabriel," Sophia said with such solemn conviction, he did not doubt it.

"Who is she?" Ravenshaw took a challenging step forward. "I will get a confession."

"No!"

Both ladies started shouting at Ravenshaw.

"Stay where you are!" Sophia yelled at her brother with such grim authority that it revealed just how precarious her situation was.

Fortunately, her brother halted, and Reign took the opportunity to grab Ravenshaw by the arm and drag him back. He gave the younger man an irritated glance. The gent was going to get his sister shot if he persisted.

"Leave us," the woman said, gesturing with the pistol. "This does not have to concern you."

"Wrong," Reign replied tersely. "You have my wife. Surrender her, and we will leave."

"Rainecourt—" Ravenshaw began, but Reign cut him off with a vicious glance. It was apparent that every time the Rainecourt name was evoked, it increased the woman's agitation.

"I give you my word, madam," he said, staring into the woman's eyes and feeling that odd connection again. "Step aside, and allow me to untie my wife. Consider it a trade. Her life for your freedom."

"Gabriel, you do not understand," Sophia said, cringing away from the barrel pressed against her temple. "She is your mother."

CHAPTER TWENTY-THREE

"My mother is dead."

Sophia did not blame Reign for the resounding denial. From what he had told her about his childhood, his father had been an uncompromising man who used his fists on his wife and young son. He had been aggressive, competitive, and channeled his power politically. What mother would abandon her defenseless son to such a man?

"It is true, Gabriel," Sophia said, hating that she could not go to him when he needed her. She did not know if Lady Colette intended to tell Reign the truth, nor did she care; the time for secrets had ended. "Your father kept her hidden away on Rainecourt lands with attendants as companions. He told everyone, including you, that she had died."

I am so sorry, she wordlessly mouthed to her husband.

Reign sucked in his cheeks, revealing the firm lines of his jaw. He shook his head, refusing or perhaps not wanting to believe that his father had executed such a cruel deception. "Sophia, I do not know who this woman is, but she is lying. I saw my mother's body. I saw . . . !"

"A dead woman with long dark hair," Lady Colette said, her eyes glistening. "Probably some poor creature from the village, I would guess."

Reign started to respond, but seemed to catch himself. The past could wait. It was the present that concerned him. He stabbed his finger at the countess. "Let us be clear, madam, I do not care if you are my mother or claim to be Demeter herself, searching for her long-lost daughter. What grievances you have should be directed at me, not my wife. Release her at once!"

"Oh, love, can you not see that she will never be yours?" Lady Colette said, moving behind the chair as she gently stroked Sophia's hair.

"What is she rambling on about?" her brother muttered.

Reign's burning gaze did not waver from his mother's face. "You are not helping, Ravenshaw."

Sophia closed her eyes and willed her brother to remain silent. Stephan did not seem to comprehend that Lady Colette's grasp of the present was tenuous at best. One misstep and the countess might fire the pistol.

"Madam," Reign said, holding out his hand. "You are among friends. Give me the pistol."

"You tried to take the pistol from me that night, too." Lady Colette's hand seized a handful of Sophia's blond hair and pulled when Reign tried to move forward. Sophia's cry of pain halted his slow advance. "And failed."

Reign parted his hands in surrender. "What night?"

Sophia drew in a shaky breath. The back of her head throbbed from the blow the countess had delivered earlier, and her stomach roiled in protest. "The night your father and my parents were murdered. Lady Colette was there, and I think—"

She craned her head to glance up at the older woman. "Good heavens, you were the one who hit me that night. When I came down the stairs to find my mother, I saw my mother and father from the doorway. I heard Lord Rainecourt's angry shouts." The memories from that night were elusive and insubstantial as smoke.

Still . . .

"Someone struck me from behind," Sophia said, wondering why no one had considered that there had been one more person in the house. "It was you."

"She was a baby, you crazy bitch!" Stephan yelled, his face reddening with suppressed fury. "You almost killed her!"

Sophia blinked, taken aback by her brother's outrage. Then again, perhaps it was not surprising. That horrible night had left its mark on all of them.

"Steady, Ravenshaw," Reign warned, though his underlying calm was a facade. "Think of Sophia."

"Yes, Ravenshaw," Lady Colette hissed. "Think of Sophia." The countess pressed the walnut stock of the pistol to her temple, and trembled.

Without hesitation, Stephan and Reign took advantage of Lady Colette's momentary lapse by edging closer to the two women. They froze when the countess's head snapped up, her eyes blazing with righteous fury. "How can you defend her, knowing that she betrayed you?"

Uncertain of his part in this drama, Stephan glanced warily at Reign and shrugged.

Sophia cast a furtive glance at Reign. The same enigmatic expression was on her husband's face.

"What? You have nothing to say?" Lady Colette taunted.

"Be careful, Gabriel," Sophia said softly when her husband shifted his stance. "Do you not see? All the players are present. Just like before. Rainecourt, Ravenshaw, and Lady Ravenshaw."

And Lady Colette.

It was happening again. The countess was reliving the horrifying night that had ended in death.

Someone was going to die.

Reign did not want to believe that woman standing over Sophia was his mother. After his mother's death, his father had removed his wife's portrait from the gallery. Reign had assumed that it had been a painful reminder of loss. Now he was not so certain. The portrait had been forgotten, leaving Reign with faded memories.

The woman before him did not remotely resemble the raven-haired beauty who used to visit him in his dreams. The dark tresses he recalled had silvered with age. Her mouth had thinned with bitterness, and lines marred the once smooth face that had seemed so full of vitality. It was the lady's eyes that troubled him the most—intense and steeped in shadows. He did not like how the woman stared at Sophia.

Reign was frightened for his wife. He had seen the miniature of Lady Ravenshaw that Sophia kept on her dressing table. The resemblance was startling, and Lady Colette seemed too eager to embrace the past.

He longed to assure Sophia that he understood what she was trying to convey. Unfortunately, her vision was too unpredictable, and Reign did not want to tip his hand to his mother. The scandalous tale of the Rainecourt-Ravenshaw murders that had tantalized the *ton* for so many years had been based on speculation. Everyone, including Reign, had assumed that his father had coveted Lord Ravenshaw's wife, and a fight had broken out between the two men that had ended in two murders and suicide.

No one had guessed that there had been another person in the room that night.

Or that the real killer had walked away after she had mercilessly murdered three people and left six-year-old Sophia barely clinging to life.

"You will not succeed this time, madam," Reign said, his gaze shifting from his wife to Stephan, willing the man to not lose his head for his sister's sake.

Lady Colette laughed. "You are free to collect the pistol from me, Rainecourt, if you dare." She brought the pistol up so it was level with Sophia's temple.

The worn, hollowed shell that had once been his mother was still being tormented by her husband. One way or another, Reign intended to end it.

"You only have one pistol, madam," Reign said, ignoring the soft whimper coming from Sophia. "You cannot shoot all of us."

Stephan cleared his throat, dividing the countess's attention. "Unlike the night you killed my parents." His grin did not have a trace of humor as he brazenly took a small step forward, practically daring the woman to shoot him.

Shrewdness crept into Lady Colette's narrow face. "I do not have to shoot you to hurt you, Ravenshaw. All I have to do is shoot *her*."

Reign's heart lurched in his chest. Denial clawed up his throat.

Before he could speak, Ravenshaw said, "Pull the trigger and you will forfeit your life, madam."

"Brave words, sir." Lady Colette cocked her head and studied him. "But hardly truthful. When I pressed the barrel of my pistol into your wife's spine and fired, you thought naught of revenge. You gathered your fallen wife and rocked her in your arms."

Sophia bit her lip and choked on her wordless denial.

As much as he longed to, Reign could not afford to comfort his wife. Not with her life in jeopardy. The key was to keep the countess talking until she made a mistake.

"You had more than one pistol that night, did you not?" Reign mused aloud. "What did you do, use the other to shoot Lord Ravenshaw?"

Lady Colette beamed at her son's astuteness. "The man was so beset with grief, he did not notice the other pistol in my hand. I simply aimed and fired. Ravenshaw was docile as a lamb before the bullet tore out his throat. He died choking on his own blood."

Sophia was openly sobbing now. Her soft hiccups made Reign's stomach cramp with impotent rage.

"And my father," Reign said tightly. "Rainecourt was not a docile lamb, madam. He would not have sat there quietly while you reloaded."

His father was intimate with violence. He would not have hesitated to kill a woman everyone thought was already dead.

Lady Colette did not bother confirming his suspicions. Instead she said, "Do you know why Ravenshaw and Rainecourt were fighting?"

"Was there a fight?" Stephan asked, startling the countess. While she was distracted, he had gained a few inches.

"Careful," Lady Colette chided. "Or you will be slipping in your lady's blood."

Sophia shook her head, silently begging her brother to remain where he was. "Y-you told my father that Rainecourt had betrayed him," she said, attempting to do her part even though she was grieving for her parents.

Reign marveled at his wife's fortitude. A weaker lady would have been hysterical and begging for her life by now. Sophia was a fighter. Pride and love swelled in his chest.

"Did you send him a note?"

With her unencumbered hand, Lady Colette brushed aside a strand of hair that was tickling her face. "A note could be discarded. Ignored. I did something Ravenshaw could not ignore." She laughed, amused by her own cleverness. "I came back from the dead. When he was alone, I approached him and told him about Rainecourt's wickedness. At first he did not believe me. Then the doubt began to creep into his heart. He knew his friend's weakness for women. His fondness for rough sport. He also knew his lady's sweet nature, and her desire to protect her husband."

Sophia cleared her throat. "Was it true about Rainecourt and—and my mother?"

Lady Colette frowned as she pondered Sophia's question. "The truth hardly matters. Your mother would deny it. So would Rainecourt. With my subtle encouragement, Ravenshaw came up with a brilliant plan. We would confront them together."

"But something went awry." Sophia shuddered and sniffed. "My father and Rainecourt were already arguing. I awoke because I heard them shouting."

Though Sophia could not see it, Lady Colette nodded. "Foolish man. Ravenshaw could not hold his temper. With his unsuspecting wife and young daughter in tow, he brought a pistol to the house with the intention of gaining a grand confession from Rainecourt."

Stephan slid his foot to the side and shifted his stance. "Your plan was already unraveling. Rainecourt was on guard, and Sophia wandered downstairs in search of our mother. You had not counted on having a witness, even if she was just a six-year-old child."

"Sophia . . . I remember her. Such a lovely little girl, and well mannered for one so young," Lady Colette said, forgetting that she was pointing a pistol at the adult Sophia. "I never understood why Lady Ravenshaw brought the girl."

The countess scowled.

Reign had been away at school when the murders had occurred. Over the years, he had often wondered whether his father would have killed him if he had been in the house that evening. He stared at the woman who had given birth to him and felt nothing. No kinship. No loyalty. Did she feel the same? If he lunged for the pistol, would she aim the barrel at his heart or would some lost part of her shy away from the notion of murdering her only son?

"Damn you, halt!" Panicked, Lady Colette

pointed the pistol at Ravenshaw. "I told you that—that I would shoot her!" Ravenshaw froze when the countess pressed the end of the barrel into Sophia's skull.

Keeping his gaze fixed on his mother, Reign shortened the distance between them.

Focused on the past, Sophia nodded. "There was no time to reload. Gabriel is correct, Rainecourt would have stopped you. You used my father's pistol to shoot your husband, did you not?"

"Rainecourt's arrogance was far more dangerous than any bullet, my dear," the countess confided to Sophia. "When I picked up Ravenshaw's pistol from the floor, can you believe that my husband laughed? It did not bother him that his best friend and the man's wife lay dying at his feet. He did not even seem particularly amazed that I had escaped my captors, and had been doing so for years."

"My father was confident that he could overpower you," Reign murmured.

"Rainecourt did not believe that I could pull the trigger," Lady Colette corrected. "He was still laughing when the pistol discharged and the impact from the bullet took off half his face."

"My-my apologies, but I think I am going to be sick," Sophia said faintly, a convulsive sound erupting from her throat.

Lady Colette glanced down at Sophia.

Both Reign and Ravenshaw charged the countess at the same time. Reign reached his mother first, seizing her by the wrist and wrenching her arm upward in a bone-cracking motion. Lady Colette still refused to relinquish the pistol.

"Curse you, Rainecourt." The countess seethed and strained. *"No!"*

Locked together in a fierce struggle, Ravenshaw tipped the odds in Reign's favor by tripping over one of the legs of Sophia's chair and slamming into them.

The pistol discharged at the impact.

Reign stiffened as a sharp, burning pain stole the air from his lungs. In the distance, he could hear Sophia screaming hysterically, but there was no time to reassure her as he, Ravenshaw, and the countess staggered backward in a tangle of limbs listing toward the floor.

Something hard grazed his cheek as Reign fell, and the world went black.

CHAPTER TWENTY-FOUR

"Gabriel! Stephan!" Sophia had screamed their names so many times, her voice was becoming hoarse. She strained against her rope bindings, moving the chair in small uncontrolled increments that took great amounts of energy but did not bring her closer to the fallen men.

After the pistol had discharged, Sophia had seen her husband's body jerk before her brother had collided into Reign and Lady Colette as the trio fell to the floor.

No one stirred for several minutes.

Stephan was the first to recover. Sophia cried out his name, relieved to see his fingers flex against the leg of his trouser. Dazed, her brother sat up and touched his head. There was a trickle of blood coming from a small cut above his left eyebrow.

"Sophia," Stephan croaked as he shook off Lady Colette's arm. "Are you hurt?"

She shook her head, grateful that her brother had merely been stunned by the fall. "Stephan, is

Gabriel—? I cannot tell . . . is he wounded? The pistol . . ."

Sophia bit her lower lip as she squinted through the dark haze of shadows and tears, fearing for her husband. Every part of her body ached, and in particular, her arms. She felt pulled and stretched beyond the limits of her body, as if Lady Colette had tied her to a medieval torture rack.

Stephan crawled over to Reign's still form and gently turned him over. Sophia tilted her head from side to side, but her brother's broad back blocked her view.

"Is he . . . ?"

"Sophia, I am fine," Reign said, brushing aside her brother's attempt to help him stand.

"He took a nasty blow to the face," Stephan said grimly.

Sophia tensed, reacting to her brother's tone.

"Probably from your damn fist when you came charging to my rescue and tripped over your clumsy feet," Reign said, his voice laced his disgust as he gingerly fingered the swelling on his cheek. "My friends will never let me live down the fact that Ravenshaw knocked me out."

"Stephan can keep a secret," Sophia said quickly.

"The hell I can," her brother countered gruffly. "Every gent will want to pat me on the back for trouncing the Devil of Rainecourt."

"Bloody hell."

Sophia leaned forward as far as her bound arms would permit her. "Gabriel, is something amiss?

Is it Lady Colette?" She had been so concerned about Reign and her brother that she had been thoughtless not to ask about the countess's welfare. The woman was so still and quiet. Had she been knocked unconscious from the fall as Reign had been?

"Ravenshaw, untie your sister."

The fact that Reign was not rushing to her side, insisting that *he* see to the task, concerned her. "What is wrong?" When her husband did not respond, she pounced on the most logical conclusion. "Oh, no, *you* were shot! Do not bother denying it. You gasped in pain seconds after the pistol discharged. Tell me the truth, Gabriel. How badly are you hurt?"

Reign grunted. "Are you planning to nag me like this for the rest of our lives?"

"It depends on how much time we have, my lord," Sophia replied, her eyes filling with tears again.

Her husband cursed softly when he realized that his teasing had made her cry. "Aw, Sophia . . . no tears," he said helplessly. "I do not want you to fuss. The wound is not serious. The bullet sliced through the meat of my upper arm. It is messy, but hardly serious."

Sophia's brow furrowed in puzzlement. "If the bullet sliced through your arm, then where did it go?"

Reign started to shrug out of his coat. "Mayhap the floor." He did not sound as if he cared about the bullet's final resting place.

Stephan stood and staggered toward Sophia. He stiffened as he reached her. "Rainecourt, I believe I have found the bullet."

Something in her brother's cool inflection caused her to glance down at her bodice. Inches above her left breast, Sophia saw the bright red blotch of blood blooming and expanding as she stared in numb horror. "Dear heavens, I have been shot!" she exclaimed, and then she did the most sensible thing a lady in her situation could do.

Sophia fainted.

Sophia's eyes flew open the second Reign pressed the brandy-soaked cloth over the wound. Sucking in her breath, she tried to sit up, but he pushed her back down onto the cushions of the chaise longue.

"A vinaigrette under my nose would have sufficed," she snapped waspishly, which only made him smile. "Leave it to a man to rouse a lady from a faint by sticking her with hot pokers and needles."

"She's delirious," Stephan declared, earning him a glare.

"No, just furious!" Sophia replied. Her lashes fluttered open as she recalled what had happened. "Good grief, I have been shot."

Sophia clutched Reign's wounded arm, causing him to wince. She immediately released his arm and murmured a hasty apology. Ravenshaw had done a decent effort bandaging his arm while

Reign had torn open his wife's bodice and inspected the damage done by the bullet.

His wife's lower lip quivered. "I hurt. Am I dying?"

Reign had asked himself the same question as he had gathered Sophia into his arms and carried her across the room to the chaise longue. He had left the task of rousing the servants from their beds to Ravenshaw. No one was going to tend to his wife but him.

"More than a scrape to a knee," he said, brushing an errant tear on Sophia's cheek away with the pad of his thumb. "Less than the hole I wanted to put in your brother's head when I realized he had left you bound to that damn chair while he checked my wounds."

"It really was not his fault, Gabriel. I ordered him to check you first," Sophia said, recalling those frightful minutes when no one had responded to her shouts. "I could not bear to think that—that—"

Reign leaned forward and kissed her roughly on the mouth. "Do not dwell on it. I will heal. So will you, wife. You were damn fortunate the bullet tore through my flesh first."

"Pardon me if I do not see you getting shot as something that I should count my blessings over," she said crossly.

Reign grinned. Sophia was delightful when she was vexed. He favored the tiny indentation that formed between her brows whenever she was on the verge of scolding him. Reign placed a small chaste kiss on the dent. "It slowed the bullet down," he explained as he picked up the ragged edge of her chemise and corset. "The boning in your corset protected you further."

Reign began to lift the cloth to show her that most of the bleeding had stopped, but decided against it. Sophia had seen enough blood. "Trust me when I say that you will be back on your feet in a day or so."

Then he and Sophia would return to London. Reign longed to put some distance between the house and the memory of Sophia tied to a chair with a madwoman aiming a pistol at her head.

His mother.

Christ. It was going to take some time for Reign to think of that troubled woman as his mother.

Lady Colette had had every intention of killing Sophia, and she might have succeeded if his wife had not distracted the countess long enough for Reign to lunge for the pistol.

Reign looked up and met Ravenshaw's solemn eyes. The two men had come to a tentative truce for Sophia's sake. He did not particularly like Ravenshaw. The brash young lord had often reminded Reign of his father in temperament, so he had despised the man on principle. It had been one of the reasons why Reign had gone out of his way to provoke the man.

"Gabriel," Sophia said, attempting to sit up, only to be forestalled by her husband's hand. "You might think you have distracted me, but I will not be dissuaded. What of Lady Colette? Was she hurt in the struggle?"

Only Sophia would care about the fate of a murderess. Reign's throat hurt as he stared down at his wife's beautiful face. He idly wondered if he could pour enough brandy into her that she would sleep.

"Lady Colette is dead."

CHAPTER TWENTY-FIVE

"Dead."

The word had been echoing in Sophia's brain since Reign had dispassionately explained that Lady Colette had broken her neck. Her husband had not been forthcoming with the details, and Sophia could not help but think Reign might have used his bare hands to end his mother's suffering.

Reign pulled the white nightgown over Sophia's head. After he had told her about Lady Colette, he had carried her up to her bedchamber, insisting that she needed to rest. "There is no point in dwelling on it."

"It is not a matter of dwelling . . . ," she said, scowling in frustration as Reign swept her exposed legs under the bedding. He was treating her like a child, and she resented it. "We need to talk about this."

"Do we?" Reign gently pushed her back into the pillows, and pulled the sheet high above her breasts. "I would rather not." He turned away as if searching for something. He found what he desired on her dressing table.

"Here, drink this."

Sophia grimaced as the brandy burned her throat. "Ugh, no more," she said after a few swallows. "Horrid stuff."

"It will help you sleep."

"I do not want to sleep!" Sophia shouted at him, surprising both of them with her outburst. "Gabriel, I am not a child. Stop treating me like one!"

Reign plucked the glass of brandy from her hands and emptied it. "My apologies, madam. I thought I was being considerate." With a guttural cry, he pulled his arm back and smashed the glass against the opposing wall.

Sophia flinched, but she preferred her husband's temper to the detached automaton. "Please, we have to talk about what happened."

"Do we?" Reign sneered. "What precisely do you want to talk about, wife? Shall I tell you how helpless I felt when I saw you tied to that bloody chair while a madwoman stuck the muzzle of a pistol in your ear? Or do you want to talk about our family histories?"

"Gabriel," she said sadly.

"Let's talk about how my father might have attacked your mother."

Reign thought to shock her with his ugly revelation. Sophia bowed her head. "I think your mother was a very jealous and confused woman."

"You may be correct," he said, unimpressed

with her calm demeanor. "My father once told me that he had fancied himself a little in love with Lady Ravenshaw, but the truth is, my father was incapable of loving anything but himself."

Sophia shuddered. "Your mother was very ill, Gabriel."

"Yes," Reign said, staring at her with an inscrutable expression.

Sophia sighed and sought to change the subject. "You left this evening to confront my brother, did you not?"

Reign's face darkened. "I do not want to talk about Stephan."

"Then what do you wish to discuss?"

"What do I wish to discuss?" Reign echoed, his voice vibrating with anger. "Well, let me ponder this a moment since there are so many fascinating choices. Oh, I have a grand notion! Why do we not talk about my mother, Lady Colette . . . who has risen from the dead like some modern-day Lazarus!"

"Hardly dead, Gabriel," Sophia retorted. "She may have been walking the Rainecourt lands as a ghost, but her deadly deeds were quite real."

She peeled back the sheet covering her and sat up. How could she talk to her husband when she was cowering in the bed like an invalid?

"Damn you, stay in bed!" Reign roughly seized her by her elbows and gave her a hard shake. Sophia squeaked in protest, and it was enough for him to recall her injury.

Instead of releasing her, he pulled her closer

and hugged her. "Forgive me. I keep hurting you . . ."

"No . . . no," she murmured, her face buried against Reign's chest. "None of this is your fault."

The wound above her breast burned and throbbed at the contact, but Sophia ignored it. She relished the feel of Reign's strong arms around her. For the first time since she had awakened and found herself bound to that blasted chair, she felt safe.

Sophia tipped her head back and tenderly touched her husband's cheek. The pain in his eyes cut through the mist and shadows that obscured her vision. "I am not fragile, Gabriel."

The corner of his mouth curved almost into a smile. "So you keep telling me."

"And I will continue to nag you until you believe it!"

Reign leaned closer, pressing his lips against her temple. "By God, it sounds like an impossible task."

"I expect it will take years and years, my lord," Sophia said, her eyes twinkling with mischief. "Fortunately, I am steadfast when the endeavor is worthy."

Reign lifted his head as his fingers dug into the soft flesh of her upper arms. Awareness and heat flared to life in his dark blue eyes. "Oh, Sophia, I need—" he murmured achingly before slanting his mouth over hers.

Sophia parted her lips, and Reign deepened the

kiss. His tongue tangled with hers, claiming and demanding more of her. She grabbed the front of his shirt and held on, opening herself up to his ravenous sensual onslaught.

Reign instinctively rocked his hips against her as he blindly reached for the hem of her nightgown, and missed. Sophia knew what her husband needed. He wanted to cover her, claim her, and lose himself in the soft sweet depths of her body. After everything they had endured, Reign craved a physical declaration that Sophia still belonged to him.

"Yes," she said breathlessly.

He had discarded his coat and cravat hours earlier when Stephan had helped to bandage his upper arm. There was a bold spot of blood on the left sleeve of her husband's shirt, reminding her that the bullet could easily have struck his heart or some other vital organ. However, Sophia refused to drive herself as mad as Lady Colette dwelling on things that had not come to pass.

Reign was fine, and so was she.

Sophia tugged at Reign's shirt to get his attention. Choking on laughter, he released her long enough to pull the unbuttoned shirt over his head. Her gaze lingered on the bloodied bandage on his left upper arm before it dropped to the front of her nightgown. Since it was only fair, Sophia mirrored his efforts and discarded her nightgown.

"My God, wife, are you trying to kill me?"

Sophia laughed as she watched her husband hastily unfasten and strip out of his trousers, stockings, and drawstring drawers until there were no more barriers between them. The man could move fast, and the long, rigid staff rising from the thick patch of hair between his legs left no doubt in her mind that Reign was properly motivated.

It was only when his brooding, dark gaze drifted to the strip of bandages he had fashioned above her breasts that Reign hesitated. Sophia brazenly circled her fingers around his swollen manhood and said, "Little more than a scratch . . . remember?"

Reign shuddered as she stroked him from his testicles to the tip of the hard, commanding length. "I remember," he said huskily.

Effortlessly, he lifted her up, and Sophia wrapped her legs around his waist. Her mouth sought his, and Reign responded by crushing his lips to hers. With his manhood prodding her bottom, he carried her toward the bed. Reign placed his knee on the mattress, and in one fluid motion she felt the mattress cushion her back as his manhood filled her.

"Forgive me, love," Reign said, grasping her hips and deepening the penetration until she arched her back to ease the stretching fullness of his claim. "I am rushing you. But I need—I need."

No explanation or apology was required.

"Yes," Sophia said, scraping her fingernails across Reign's lower back. She was rewarded with a low growl.

Their coupling was rough and frenzied. It was unlike anything Sophia had ever experienced in her husband's embrace, and she reveled in it. She was discovering that she liked this side of Reign's nature. He was wild, enthusiastic, and it thrilled her all the way down to her toes that she had caused him to abandon the reins on the admirable control and patience he seemed to exude on her behalf.

Pleased with herself, she craned her neck forward and bit Reign on the chest. Hard. His response was swift and full of delicious retribution. Reign pulled out of her, and before she could protest, he flipped her over onto her knees, shoved her onto all fours, and mounted her from behind.

This was the scandalous gentleman the *ton* called Reign. One of the decadent Lords of Vice who indulged all of his appetites, and was drawn to the forbidden.

Uncertain of her part, Sophia clutched a fistful of the bedding as Reign pounded his manhood into her welcoming heat. He spoke low, guttural words of approval and carnal promises. He cupped her uninjured breast and squeezed. Her breasts, much like the womanly folds between her legs, were swollen and ached to be touched.

Sensing her need, his hand slid down her flat belly until his fingers found the sensitive nubbin within the drenched folds. Sophia bit her lip as he lightly pinched and rolled the hidden flesh. Her nipples hurt and she longed to rub away the dull pain.

"Gabriel . . . please!"

Reign's thrusts pummeled her backside. The musky scent of their lovemaking filled Sophia's nose as she listened to the energetic slap of flesh against flesh. She tightened her grip on the sheets and leaned into each thrust, needing to feel the full measure of him.

And, oh, how Reign filled her! Well-endowed and thick, his manhood stretched her while her slick arousal beckoned him to bury himself to the hilt.

"You know what I want," Reign growled. "Give it to me."

Sophia felt his manhood expand inside her, the telltale sign that Reign's release was upon him, and the awareness triggered her own. Pressing her face into the bedding, she cried out as her womanly sheath convulsed with wave after violent wave of sensation. She barely heard Reign's low keening response as his rhythmic thrusts disintegrated and his grace and strength left him. He seized her hips in a bruising grip and shuddered, surrendering his seed and passion.

Sophia smiled as she savored Reign's weight on her back. "If this is your reaction, I will have to bite you more often."

Her cheeky comment earned her a hoarse chuckle from her husband.

"I intend to hold you to that promise, wife."

Reign could not leave her.

He had not planned on remaining in Sophia's

bed. His wife needed rest and patience while she recovered from her ordeal. Instead, Reign had torn off his clothes and mounted her like a mindless brute. He might have summoned some disgust over his behavior if Sophia had not matched his lust.

With Sophia curled up against him sound asleep, her head using his chest as a pillow, Reign rubbed the mark she had left with her teeth and grinned. His back stung from the scratches she had made with her fingernails, and the mild discomfort made him long to wake her so they could continue their love play. The tireless flesh between his legs seemed to agree. His cock twitched just contemplating the thought of plunging into Sophia's snug channel.

"You should be sleeping," Sophia murmured and placed a kiss against his bare chest.

Reign tried to quell the rising excitement that Sophia might crave him again. "I thought I had done a fine job tiring you."

"An impressive effort, Lord Rainecourt." She yawned. "I confess, one of your best." Sophia stretched her arms and sat up. "However, when I close my eyes, I keep seeing Lady Colette. I was dreaming of her."

Leave it to Sophia to mention the one person who could shrivel his cock and his lust with one stroke.

"Do not think of it."

Even before the words were out of his mouth, Reign knew he was demanding the impossible.

His dead mother had managed to leave an impression on both of them. Fortunately, it would be her last.

While Reign had been tending to Sophia, her brother had summoned the magistrate. Eight years earlier, the man had been summoned to the house to rule Beatrice's death an accident. This evening, he declared a woman the world had believed long buried, officially dead. After listening to everyone's statements, the magistrate pulled Reign aside and quietly told him that he had no interest in stirring up old scandals. His parents and Sophia's parents were dead. The fact that Lady Colette had died twice did not alter the fact that justice had been served, albeit late. Tomorrow his mother would be buried, and hopefully the past with her.

"The magistrate was correct. What happened between your parents and mine, happened a long time ago. We know the truth now, and that is all that matters."

Reign rubbed Sophia's back and frowned at the tension he felt beneath his fingertips. "Sophia?" He sat up when she sniffed into her hand. "What is it?"

She swiped furiously at her cheeks to get rid of her tears. "Oh, Reign, when the magistrate asked for my statement, I told him something . . . something I have not had a chance to tell you about your mother."

Reign moved closer so he was positioned be-

hind her. He slid each leg to fit her backside between his legs. Sophia was dressed in her thin
nightgown again. She insisted on putting the
garment on because she loathed being caught by
the servants without her clothes on. Her explanation amused him since he was the one responsible for her shameful behavior, and he had no
intention of behaving himself.

Sophia leaned against his chest as he wrapped
his arms around her waist.

"Tell me."

"Lady Colette knew Beatrice was leaving you
for—" Sophia took a deep breath, reluctant to
utter the name of the gentleman who had sired
the child Reign had believed was his.

"Enright," he succinctly supplied.

Reign despised Enright, and his tenderhearted
wife knew it. The only thing that had prevented
him from putting a bullet into Enright was that
he, too, had been betrayed by Lord and Lady
Burrard. If the couple had considered the man
worthy enough to marry their daughter, Beatrice
would not have been forced to whore herself to
a man she would never love.

"I told you before the magistrate's arrival
that Lady Colette used the hidden passageways
to come and go as she pleased without notice."

Sophia shifted in his arms so she could see his
face. Reign lifted her up and positioned her so
that she sat on his thigh.

"For all of these years, your mother has

watched over you like a benevolent ghost. In her own way, she loved you."

"Love?" Reign sneered. "No loving mother would abandon her son to her husband's tyrannical and often abusive whims. And let us not gloss over the fact that my mother was a cold-blooded and calculating murderer. Lady Colette almost killed you when she discovered that you were going to ruin her plans. She murdered your mother, who was nothing more than a passing fancy of my father's lust. Your father was killed because he was an inconvenient witness to her crime, and, lastly, my father died for his arrogance. He thought he could lock away a woman that he no longer desired, and never considered that one day she would claim her revenge."

Sophia bowed her head. "I know. I cannot explain the workings of her mind but somewhere, twisted in that web of madness, was love. Love for her only son. She watched over you when you came home. She was there when you took up residence with Beatrice at your side."

Reign stilled, chilling at the thought that his unstable mother had quietly observed his disastrous marriage from afar. How many times had Lady Colette listened to Beatrice and him fighting? Or the nights when he had tossed aside his pride and begged Beatrice to love him again as she had before their marriage? How many suppers had ended with Beatrice sobbing in her locked bedchamber while Reign had drowned his rage with brandy in the library?

"My mother was there that last night when I told Beatrice she could not leave the house," he said tonelessly.

Sophia caressed his bare chest as if to soothe him. "When your mother learned that Beatrice carried another man's child, she saw it as a betrayal, not only to you but to the Rainecourt name. I am so sorry, Gabriel. While you were downstairs, your mother confronted Beatrice and murdered her."

"For eight years, I have lived with the weight of accusations and private doubt about the odd circumstances surrounding Beatrice's death." Reign stared down at his hands. "The morning I was told that my wife had had an accident, I noticed the bruises marring her neck and I said nothing. I let the magistrate rule Beatrice's death an accident, and I tried to get on with my life."

"You were entitled, Gabriel."

He chuckled softly. "Was I? The truth is, I barely recall much about that night after I told Beatrice that she was to remain at Addison Park until she delivered my child." He pulled Sophia closer, needing her warmth and proximity. "Beatrice tried to tell me that the babe was not mine, but I was convinced that she would have said anything to free herself from me. It was later, when my head was clear, that I realized she had been telling me the truth. At the funeral, a nasty confrontation with Lord Burrard gave me more insight into the lady I had married, and the fool Beatrice, her parents, and even Enright had made of me."

Sophia laid the side of her face against his shoulder. "All these years, Beatrice's family and Mr. Enright have encouraged the rumors within polite society that you had murdered your wife. The magistrate seemed to be willing to allow Lady Colette the peace in death that she was denied in life out of respect for your family. Nevertheless, if you let the truth be told about your mother and—"

"No."

His wife straightened at his curt dismissal. "But Gabriel—"

Reign kissed Sophia's pouting lips. "Listen, our families have been entangled longer than I care to remember. I do not give a damn if the *ton* continues to believe the Burrards' claims that I murdered their daughter. I have learned to live with the whispered accusations and disapproval. However, I will not allow you to be fodder for the gossips."

"You are being unreasonable," Sophia argued, her forehead furrowing with her increasing agitation. "When I married you, I became a part of it."

Her argument was valid, though he loathed admitting it. He should have stayed away from her, and had every intention of doing so until

Ravenshaw had foolishly provided Reign with the opportunity of claiming Sophia for his own.

"Do you honestly believe the truth will make a difference to Lord and Lady Burrard?" Reign cupped Sophia's face and nudged her to meet his gaze. "They have hated me for eight years, and I doubt the fact that my mother murdered Beatrice will wash the blood from my hands. The Burrards will always hold me responsible since their daughter was in my care."

The delicate arch of her right eyebrow lifted inquiringly. "I cannot change your mind?"

"No." Reign kissed her forehead. "No more arguments." He lifted the sheet, ignoring his nudity. "Come now, into bed, Sophia."

His wife dutifully crawled off his lap and slid under the bedding. Reign aligned his body against hers and covered them both with the sheet. With the top of her head tucked under his chin, his hand curved around Sophia's waist.

Silence descended in the room, leaving Reign with his dark thoughts. His brain was a jumble of images of Sophia, Ravenshaw, Lady Colette, and the very deadly pistol that she had held to his wife's head. "Sophia?"

"Hmm?"

"Before you fancy that I am being noble, I want to be clear. If anything had happened to you, if my mother had managed to—" He coughed to conceal the tightness in his throat. "—I would not be feeling so generous. I love you, Sophia."

Reign tensed, bracing himself for her reaction. The faint snore coming from Sophia indicated that he would have to declare himself again when his wife was not so exhausted.

CHAPTER TWENTY-SIX

Two weeks later . . .

The evening was ruined!

Sophia clutched her stomach as she hovered over the chamber pot for this latest bout of nausea to pass. She was blaming the rich food the cook had prepared for her miserable predicament.

Reign had warned her that their return to London did not warrant a celebration, but she had wanted to do something special for her husband. Since that fateful night when she had been at Lady Colette's mercy, Reign had seemed reluctant to leave her side during the evenings. He had only visited his club twice, and both occasions had been at her insistence.

A supper seemed an inspired solution.

Nothing too large or fancy, she had promised her husband. Just an intimate gathering of his friends and hers. When she had proposed the idea to Fanny and Juliana, both ladies insisted on helping, and Sophia had been grateful. She even had a special dress made for the occasion.

Sophia stared down at the splatters of fish and juices decorating the front of her dress and despaired.

"She seemed fine earlier," a feminine voice whispered just beyond the door of her bedchamber.

The voice belonged to Lord Sinclair's wife, Juliana.

Humiliated, Sophia braced her hands on either side of the commode and prayed the woman would go away.

"No, no . . . I should be the one to check on her," Fanny said anxiously. "Sophia gets sensitive about these delicate matters. She does not like it when people fuss about her."

Fanny was right. Sophia did not want to see anyone after her appalling behavior at the dining table.

She listened to the sounds of the door opening and closing. Perhaps if she just ignored the two ladies, they would take the hint and go away. Sophia started when Reign's strong and familiar arms encircled her waist.

"Your friends tried to stop me from coming in," her husband murmured against her ear. "They were worried about your delicate sensibilities."

Sophia made a sound in her throat that was part groan, part laughter. "Oh, Gabriel, I ruined everything." She turned in his arms and gestured at her dress. "Just look at my beautiful dress!"

Reign retrieved a handkerchief from the inner pocket of his coat and offered it to her. "If the dress is ruined, I will buy you a dozen to replace it. Come now, love, there is no need to cry. No harm has been done, and Frost will forgive you. Eventually," he added with a wry smile.

Lord Chillingsworth.

Sophia cringed. The man was going to be hard-pressed to forgive her for her insult. "I was so nervous this evening. Your friends mean so much to you, and I wanted to impress them."

She tried to pull away from Reign when he started to laugh.

"Forgive me for laughing, love, but you did make an impression no one at the table will forget. Least of all, Frost."

Sophia delicately blew her nose. "How can you laugh? Good grief, Gabriel, I knocked a platter of stuffed trout onto floor, and then threw up on one of your dearest friends."

Up until that moment, the evening had been lovely. It was only when the footman had placed the large silver platter of fish under her nose and she gazed down at the open mouth and lifeless eye that her stomach had lurched. The awful scent was her undoing. Blindly, she had shoved the platter away and leaped to her feet in a futile attempt to distance herself from the offensive dish. The startled footman had dropped the platter, and chaos ensued as everyone tried to assist her. Lord Chillingsworth had the misfortune to have been seated to her right. He had grabbed her arm to steady her, and she had rewarded his chivalrous gesture by throwing up into his lap.

Sophia wondered if anyone had ever perished from shame.

"Would it help if I told you that the Lords of Vice merely tolerate Frost? Or that Vane and Saint would make you a wealthy woman if you would come back downstairs and do it again?"

"Your friends are insane."

Sophia bit back a smile as Reign led her over to one of the chairs near the fireplace. He sat down and pulled her onto her lap.

"Do not think you can charm me into returning to the dining room, Lord Rainecourt," she said, trying to sound stern.

"I would not think of it," Reign replied, cuddling her closer. "This way I get to keep you all for myself."

"I am never leaving this room."

Reign raised his eyebrows at her declaration. "Come now, you are made of sterner stuff, Sophia. Frost will survive, and you have provided our friends with an entertaining tale that Vane and the others will likely regale the *ton* with for months just to annoy Frost." He sobered. "What is it? Are you still ill?"

Sophia wrinkled her nose and shook her head. "No, my stomach started to settle after—well, you know."

"Frost will be pleased that his sacrifice was not in vain," Reign said, not bothering to hide his amusement. His hand slid from her arm to rest possessively against her stomach. "When were you planning to tell me that you are carrying our child?"

Her lips parted in surprise. "I was just beginning to suspect. Your mother—"

"My mother! What does Lady Colette have to do with this?" he demanded.

"It was something she said that night," Sophia said, mentally sorting through the countess's muddled ramblings. "She mentioned a babe, and I thought she had confused me with Beatrice."

"Impossible," Reign said flatly. "You resemble her neither in looks nor temperament."

Although she had been told that Beatrice had been quite beautiful, Sophia assumed her husband had been paying her a compliment. "Perhaps she was referring to my mother. There were moments when she called me Lady Ravenshaw. Or . . ."

"Or?"

Sophia sighed. She should have kept her own counsel when it came to the subject of Lady Colette. Reign seemed unwilling to discuss what had happened at Addison Park or speak his mother's name. With the exception that he and Stephan had declared a truce, she suspected even his friends were unaware of the awful truths they had learned from his mad mother.

"Or?" Reign nuzzled her ear, which resulted in tingles that she felt all the way to her fingertips. "Tell me."

She glanced away and shrugged. "Despite Lady

Colette's tenuous hold on her sanity, she was very observant. I think she had her suspicions that I was carrying your babe. This is merely speculation on my part, but I would wager the news upset her. It might have been the reason why she decided to reveal herself to me. In her confused state, I became Beatrice, the deceitful wife who was determined to leave you, or I was my mother, a rival for your father's affection."

"Good God!" Reign said, his arms tightening around her.

Neither one of them spoke for several minutes. Both were aware that it did not matter which incarnation of Sophia had driven Lady Colette to act. Whether it was Beatrice, Lady Ravenshaw, or Sophia herself, who had married Reign to escape her brother's dictates, his mother had planned to murder her in a misguided attempt to spare her son from the pain of another false-hearted lady.

Sophia sensed the sadness pouring off Reign. Knowing him well, she suspected that he was still blaming himself for Lady Colette's treachery. Her finger idly twirled the ends of his hair, which was tightly bound into a queue at the nape of his neck. In an effort to distract him, she gave his hair a playful tug. "You are not to blame, husband."

"I do not know if I agree."

"Absolutely not," she said with resounding conviction. "You were a child when your father decided to fake Lady Colette's death and lock her **away**. If anyone is to blame, it is your father, and he paid dearly for his sins."

He thought about her words, and wearily nodded. "I suppose you are right."

Sophia planted a kiss on the side of his jaw as a reward for not arguing with her. "Besides, I prefer to discuss more pressing matters. Tell me, how long have you known about the babe?"

Reign gave her a suspicious glance, suggesting that he knew exactly what she was doing. He shrugged. "Since we departed Addison Park. If you recall, you were ill for most of the trip. I was worried that I had pushed you too hard about London, and that you were still too weak to travel. Then I recalled that you told me that you were not fragile, a weak creature who needed coddling."

"Good of you to notice," Sophia said wryly.

"It was later that I noticed other changes," Reign said, cupping one of her breasts.

His dark blue eyes heated at Sophia's soft gasp. The tenderness in her breasts had increased in the passing weeks, and her nipples reacted to the lightest touch.

"The most important clue was the fact that you have not had your monthly courses."

Sophia blushed. "Gabriel! To talk about such things!"

"I would wager our babe was conceived on our wedding night," he said huskily.

"You do not mind?" she asked, suddenly worried. Their marriage had been precipitated from necessity rather than love. Sophia had never doubted that children would be part of their lives when she accepted his offer of marriage. Nevertheless, she never expected to be carrying his child so soon.

His hand lovingly caressed her belly. The stomach muscles beneath his hand fluttered in response, as if the thick corset and layers of fabric were not barring his access to her sensitive flesh.

"Mind? Why would I?" he replied, kissing her tenderly on the mouth. "After all, I did nothing to prevent such a delightful outcome."

"Did nothing—" Sophia's eyes narrowed as he grinned unrepentantly at her. "Do you mean there are ways to—to—and yet you did *nothing*?" She slipped out of his grasp and stood so she could glare at him for his typical high-handed behavior.

Although she was thrilled to be carrying his child, Reign should have been more forthcoming. In the near future, she was going to have to have a private chat with Juliana, since Sophia's education was woefully lacking in these personal matters.

Sensing her peevish mood, Reign stood and approached her with a wariness that soothed her pride. "Sophia, I told you that I wanted children from this marriage, and you agreed. Are you unhappy with our bargain?"

Sophia did not resist when Reign pulled her into his arms. The uncertainty she heard in his voice tore at her heart. While Sophia was irked by the unflattering comparison, she knew her husband was worried that, like Beatrice, she would come to resent their marriage.

His vulnerability was her undoing.

"Of course not! I already love this child," she said passionately. "Almost as much as I love—" Sophia bit down on her lip, vowing not to burden Reign with her confession.

He had told her that he required a faithful wife, and that he wanted children. He had not asked for her love. It was a fickle emotion that he had learned not to trust.

Reign stalked her as Sophia edged away from him. "Love . . . what do you love, or rather, should I ask, who do you love?"

Trapped by her own words, she blurted out, "You. I love you, my lord."

Sophia shrieked when Reign all of a sudden swept her up into his arms so that they were nose-to-nose.

"Tell me again."

She squinted at him, wondering if he was teasing her. "I-I love you, Gabriel."

Her husband issued a celebratory shout and spun her around. Sophia's head and stomach both whirled. "Again."

"I love you. I have for some time," she confessed, relieved that she could express what she had tried to hide even from herself. "But I thought that you did not want—"

Reign smothered her words with a kiss. "I lied. To you and to myself. The first time I kissed you in Lord and Lady Harper's garden, I longed to carry you off into the night and claim you for my own."

"What stopped you?"

He shifted his stance, rocking her gently. "Ravenshaw. Your connection to him troubled me for some time."

Sophia could not blame him. She had been equally alarmed when she learned that he was Lord Rainecourt. "Then Stephan was suddenly agreeable to marrying me off to Lord Mackney because he viewed the match and my dowry as a means to settle his own considerable debts."

"You needed the devil on your side," he said, pivoting on his heel before he carried her toward the bed. "And I was happy to oblige since Ravenshaw's stupidity gave me the one thing that I craved."

Sophia bounced a little as she landed on the bed. "What?"

Reign crawled on top of her. "You. I love you, Sophia Housely," he said, his dark blue eyes glittering like sapphires.

Sophia tilted her head back as his questing mouth covered hers. His kiss was one of joy and reverence, hunger and promise. Her pulse quickened with the knowledge that Reign was wholly hers. She claimed his heart and soul, just as he had hers.

"What are you doing?" she asked when he seized the edge of one of the sleeves of her dress and tugged, exposing her bare shoulder. "Have you forgotten about our guests downstairs?"

He gave her a sullen look. It was apparent that he had, indeed, forgotten about the friends who were awaiting their return. "I suppose you are going to insist on being practical."

"Naturally!"

The corners of his mouth curved into a wicked grin. Sophia sensed she had once again fallen for his trickery before the trap shut with a decisive snap.

"Then I will have to get you out of this dress, madam. You do not want to return with the smell of fish clinging to your skirts," Reign said, his eyes twinkling with humor as he silently dared her to refuse him.

Sophia gazed up into the handsome face of the man she loved, already knowing that there was little she could deny him. Nor would she want to, because she would miss out on some new adventure that only he could give her.

"Well, it would be the most practical thing to do," Sophia said, surrendering herself to Reign's very capable hands.

Turn the page for a sneak peek at the next
book by Alexandra Hawkins

AFTER DARK WITH
A SCOUNDREL

Coming soon from St. Martin's Paperbacks

"Is Lord Chillingsworth pleased that you will be able to join him in London this season?"

Regan blinked, distracted by the innocent question. All she wanted to do was rend the paper in her hand into dozens of illegible pieces and scream. Instead, she carefully folded Frost's letter and smiled demurely at her friends' expectant expressions.

"Of course." Her fingers tapped the paper lightly. "While it has only been four months since I last saw Frost, I have not had the pleasure of visiting London in almost five years."

And if Frost has his way, another five years will pass before he grants me his consent.

"Our first social season in Town!" Nina sighed. Miss Tyne was nineteen, and possessed an overly optimistic view on life. The daughter of a baron, Nina was expected to make a good match for her family, and there was no doubt that her friend would succeed.

Or perhaps some of Nina's optimism had rubbed off on Regan while they were in school.

"Well, I say it is high time Lord Chillingsworth does his duty by you, and gives you a proper season, Regan. I will have you know that Mama agrees as well."

She did not have the heart to remind Thea that her mother was the person responsible for Regan's banishment from London in the first place. Frost would never have thought to send her away to school if it had not been for Lady Karmack's meddling. He had been too busy pursuing his own amusements to be bothered with giving his sister a proper education and polish befitting an earl's daughter.

Lady Karmack, on the other hand, had taken one look at Regan and feared that under the care of her notorious brother she would be destined to become a famous courtesan, or worse, the wife of one of the Lords of Vice. As a distant cousin, the older woman felt it was her Christian duty to remove Regan from her brother's ghastly influence.

It still hurt that Frost had not fought harder to keep her.

In the beginning, Regan had not appreciated Lady Karmack's keen interest in her welfare. She had been disrespectful, outrageous, and oftentimes deliberately obtuse when it came to her lessons. The first year away from Frost and the men she considered her family had been the worst, and Regan had not been shy about displaying her anger toward the people who sincerely believed that they were saving her from a life of depravity. It was at Miss Swann's Academy for Ladies that she gradually became friends with Thea and Nina.

Instead of looking down their noses at Regan's outlandish behavior like many of the other girls had, the two young women had been in awe. No one dared to challenge Miss Swann or speak their mind, and Regan often did both. The trio had banded together by the end of their first year and had been nearly inseparable. When Regan had not been sequestered at school, she had often spent her summers visiting her friends. If Frost was in residence at the family's country seat, she joined him. However, their weeks together were usually strained, and, in hindsight, Regan acknowledged that she was often to blame.

In those early years of what she had come to view as her banishment, she had written her brother dozens of letters, begging him to relent and come for her. She missed her old life. She missed Nox and the Lords of Vice. She had often wondered if Dare might kiss her again if she returned to London.

Frost never gave her a chance to satisfy her curiosity.

He always denied her requests. Not one for sentimentality, the only time her brother wrote to her was to tell her that she could not return to London until Miss Swann had transformed the hoyden into a lady. His casual rejections had taken a toll on their relationship, and Regan could not quite forgive Frost for sending her away.

However, she was willing to let bygones be bygones if her brother was willing to be reasonable.

She intended to spend the entire season in London with or without his blessing.

With Lady Karmack on her side this time, Frost was going to find it difficult to dismiss her polite request.

"Will you be remaining at our house or will you join Frost at his town house?" Thea asked.

"My brother undoubtedly will want me to reside with him," Regan brazenly lied. "However, it might be prudent to remain here until I have had a chance to speak to him."

Nina shut the book that she had been reading, and placed it on her lap. "Good heavens!"

Regan tried to appear innocent. "I beg your pardon?"

Her friend rolled her eyes heavenward. "I cannot believe your audacity. Now tell us the truth, is your brother aware that you are in Town?"

Thea gasped. "But you told Mama—"

Regan gave her friends an exasperated look. "Be sensible. Our recent travels have added to the delays in my correspondence with my brother. While Frost is looking forward to seeing me"— she crossed her fingers behind her back and prayed that her words were true—"he most likely has not received my last letter."

There was no reason to tell Thea and Nina

that Frost was expecting to see her in August when he returned to the family's country estate.

Her arrogant brother had not mentioned London at all.

Thea thought Regan's explanation was sound. "Should we send a messenger to his town house?"

Unconvinced, Nina glanced at Thea and then Regan. She nodded, silently agreeing to whatever plan Regan had concocted. "Or that club he frequents. Oh, what is it called?"

"Nox," Regan absently replied, rising from her chair. With Frost's letter in her hand, she gracefully strolled over to the small fireplace. "I do not believe that will be necessary, ladies. Some messages are best delivered in person."

Regan bent down and dropped Frost's letter onto the burning coal embers. The folded paper quickly caught fire, the flames greedily destroying the letter.

Her banishment was finally over.

Dare smoothed his hair back before he pulled the crimson drapery aside and entered the private theater box that Hunter had rented for the season. His late arrival would likely provoke a few comments from his friends.

Frost did not disappoint him.

With his chair positioned at an angle to accommodate his long legs, the earl grinned up at him. "Why, a good evening to you, Lord Hugh!"

Dare stepped over his friend's legs and nodded to Hunter and Saint, who had yet to take their seats. "Keep your nasty wit to yourself, Frost. I know that I am late. It could not be helped."

Frost pivoted, pulling his legs in as he faced Dare. "How kind of you to join us this evening. I must confess when I espied Lady Pashley sitting alone in her box, I feared that your honorable nature might rear its ugly head and put an irreparable blight on our promising evening."

"If true, Dare's honor might not be the only head rising this evening," Saint muttered to Hunter as he nudged the duke.

Dare acknowledged his friend's ribald comment with a low chuckle. He peered out into the sea of private boxes in search of his brother's marchioness. He spotted her one tier down. Another couple had joined Allegra, and with luck, they would remain at her side for the evening.

"Unlike you, Frost, manners and duty may dictate me to stop by Lady Pashley's private box to pay my respects. Nevertheless, I have no inclination to tarry."

Frost snorted, making his disbelief apparent.

"While you may find this difficult to believe, another lady has engaged my attentions this evening." Dare was in too good of a mood to be annoyed with Frost. "Mrs. Randall has invited me to call on her after Lord and Lady Quinton's ball."

Frost's eyebrows slid upward as he nodded with begrudging approval. Hunter and Saint offered their congratulations. The lovely twenty-eight-year-old widow had come out of mourning last season. She had rejected all suitors, and as far as anyone knew, all potential lovers. The young widow had even been impervious to Frost's charms.

"I assume you expect us to join you at Lord and Lady Quinton's ball?" Frost said, casting a sly glance in Lady Pashley's direction.

Dare braced his palm against the back of his friend's chair and stared directly into Frost's turquoise eyes. "Mrs. Randall never mentioned me joining her at the ball. Nor would she approve of me bringing the likes of you along to her town house."

"Widows are daring creatures. She might be agreeable with the proper enticement," Frost said, bringing his gloved hand up to the apex of his trousers to make his vulgar point.

All four men laughed, earning them several curious looks from the nearby boxes. Dare sat down beside Frost. He was looking for another subject to distract his friend when Saint came to the rescue.

"Has anyone heard from Reign or Sin this evening?"

Hunter slid into the seat in front of Dare. "Sin will join us later. His wife decided to sit with her mother and sisters this evening."

A noncommittal noise rumbled in Frost's throat. He did not exactly approve of Lady Sinclair, and the lady did not hide the fact that she was merely tolerant of Frost for her husband's sake.

Hunter gave their friend a bemused glance. "Show some respect, Frost. Lady Sinclair is expected to deliver the Sinclair heir sometime in September. Sin is just protective of his lady."

"And Reign?" Dare prompted.

"Worse than Sin, now that he is a father." Saint crossed his arms across his chest and braced his stance by bending his left knee. "He left London five days ago to collect his wife and infant daughter. Reign did not want them travelling alone."

Dare could not blame Reign. He had never seen a gentleman so besotted. Last season, when Reign had encountered Lady Sophia Northam at a ball, he had fallen hard for the demure blonde. Reign had had the lady wedded, bedded, and with child before the season had ended.

"Another good man . . ." Frost mumbled, the rest of his sentence unintelligible but his meaning clear to his friends.

Frost enjoyed ladies as well as any other gent. He just did not view them as anything permanent in a man's life. As far as the earl was concerned, marriage had ruined Sin and Reign.

To some degree, Dare silently agreed with Frost. His older brother's marriage to Allegra was a miserable union, and Reign's first marriage to Miss Roberts had been an unmitigated disaster. Still, both Reign and Sin seemed happy in their recent marriages. Dare did not begrudge his friends their newfound bliss.

While Saint regaled them with Vane's latest

mischief, Dare let his gaze wander from private box to private box. He immediately spotted Lady Sinclair. Seated beside Lady Harper, the marchioness was engrossed in a discussion with one of her sisters. Sin was nowhere in sight.

Dare moved on to another private box, recognizing some of the patrons as his gaze glided from box to box until he found her. It meant nothing if his gaze lingered on Allegra. After all, she was a beautiful woman. If his heart ached, it was his own damn business. Before his older brother had stolen her from him, Allegra had been his.

Frost often teased him about Allegra, but his friend did not understand Dare's inner conflict. While a part of him would always love the lady, he also hated her. His familial obligations kept him tethered, and he seemed doomed to never be quite free from her.

And his brother enjoyed Dare's torment.

Before he could dwell further on his dark thoughts, a glint of amber caught Dare's eye, distracting him from Allegra's private box. One tier up and two boxes to the right, a dark-haired lady in an amber evening dress presented her elegant profile to him. Captivated, he watched as the silken fabric of her dress gleamed like the sun as the candlelight from the chandeliers played across the angles of her puffed sleeves and skirt. Her dark tresses had been pulled high, and only a few curls near her hairline escaped. The lady's pale creamy skin was untouched by the sun, and yet, even in the dim interior of the theater, her skin glowed with health and vitality.

Dare watched as she extended her gloved hand to a gentleman who had slipped into their private box to pay the woman and her female companions his respects. Slightly envious that the gent had discovered the lady in amber before he had, Dare leaned forward as he watched the silent courtship play out for his eyes. The young woman smiled and gestured as she formally introduced her friends. The gentleman bowed, his eyes remaining on his amber prize.

Arrogant bastard.

He did not seem worthy of such a lady. The gentleman was older, and possessed a weak chin. Possibly two. A lady of wealth and beauty could do better. The three gentlemen entering the crowded box must have thought the same thing.

Dare stood when the young woman brought her hand to her heart, and then practically threw herself into the arms of one of her would-be suitors. His gaze narrowed as recognition flooded his envious heart.

"What the devil—is that *Vane*?" Dare said, his voice infused with such fury that Frost, Hunter, and Saint ceased speaking and stared at him with varying degrees of amazement.

He could not blame them for their curiosity. Dare did not understand his reaction himself. A small part of him was still half tempted to leap from box to box until he reached Vane so he could personally have the pleasure of tossing the rogue headfirst into the pit.

What spared him was that the woman in amber released Vane and stepped back. At Vane's urging, she looked across the interior of the theater. Dare inhaled sharply as his hungry gaze drank in her beauty. Familiarity tickled his senses, but it was elusive. Unexpectedly their gazes locked, and the dark-haired beauty seemed almost as startled as he was by the impact.

Recognition popped in his head like miniature fireworks.

The last time Dare had seen her endearing face, it had been sullied by soot and grime.

"Gents!" Sin said, bursting through the closed curtains at the back of their private box. He was grinning from ear to ear. "Why did no one tell me that our little Regan had come home?"